Amanda McCabe wrote her first romance at sixteen—a vast historical epic, starring all her friends as the characters, written secretly during algebra class! She's never since used algebra, but her books have been nominated for many awards, including the RITA® Award, Booksellers' Best Award, National Readers' Choice Award and the Holt Medallion. In her spare time she loves taking dance classes and collecting travel souvenirs. Amanda lives in New Mexico. Visit her at ammandamccabe.com.

THEIR CONVENIENT CHRISTMAS BETROTHAL

Amanda McCabe

MILLS & BOON

First published in Great Britain 2024
by Mills & Boon, an imprint of HarperCollins*Publishers* Ltd,
1 London Bridge Street, London, SE1 9GF

www.harpercollins.co.uk

HarperCollins*Publishers*, Macken House, 39/40 Mayor Street Upper,
Dublin 1, D01 C9W8, Ireland

ISBN: 978-0-263-32099-2

11/24

This book contains FSC™ certified paper
and other controlled sources to ensure responsible forest management.

For more information visit www.harpercollins.co.uk/green.

Printed and Bound in the UK using 100% Renewable Electricity
at CPI Group (UK) Ltd, Croydon, CR0 4YY

Prologue

Bath, England,
1817

Charles Campbell had no right to look so very handsome.

Mary St Aubin half hid behind the table of cake and sweets at her sister's garden wedding breakfast to stare without being seen as silly. She did *feel* rather silly—she was not known to be shy at all, with her love of parties and people, which had great advantages when making matches at the St Aubin and Briggs Confidential Agency. Yet ever since she'd met Charles Campbell at an assembly, each time he was near she turned into a blushing, tongue-tied miss.

But really, who could blame her? she thought as she looked up and up his long legs in buff breeches, then across his broad shoulders perfectly outlined in a dark blue coat. A strong jaw and dimpled chin above a simply tied, snowy cravat, pinned with an amethyst thistle. A blade of a nose, sharp cheekbones, sun-browned skin and vivid, bright green eyes. His dark hair, a bit too long for fashion, waved across his brow, carelessly swept aside. He was perfect.

He chatted with the bridegroom, their old friend and neighbour and now Ella's besotted husband, Frederick, Lord Fleetwood, and Fred's stepmother Penelope Oliver, laughing in the sunlight. The golden happiness of the day cast a glow over everyone, and Charles was no exception. She could have vowed that all the light was gathered only on him.

She hadn't been able to cease thinking about him for days. They saw each other often in Bath. At teas and garden parties, dances, cricket games, at the shops where he was accompanied by his young ward Adele Stewart. She had dared to try to get him to dance once, only to be turned away laughingly, but they often talked and walked together, and his scent of bergamot soap and sunshine made her dizzy with delight.

Ella sometimes mused on finding him a suitable wife through the agency. There were whispers of unhappiness in his past, a youthful marriage that somehow went awry. Sometimes she saw such shadows across his face when he thought no one was watching, and she longed to go to him, to make him laugh as the old Mary would. The Mary who went to parties and was careless of much else. But now Ella was leaving, and Mary was in charge of the agency and its future. She could not impulsively run to handsome gentlemen and hug them.

And they said he was returning to his estate in Scotland soon, leaving Bath. It made her so sad to think of never seeing him again, not having his presence to watch for at parties, not hearing his laughter.

She studied him carefully, as if she could memorise him for the greyer days ahead. The way he brushed his hair back, tilted his head as he listened to conversation, a small crease between his eyes.

He suddenly turned—and caught her staring, too late for her to run away. His smile widened, that dimple appearing in his chin, and she almost melted. To her shock, he excused himself from Pen and Fred and started across the garden, towards Mary, his steps lazy and long, his smile never fading.

'Miss St Aubin,' he said, his deep, chocolate velvet voice touched with a Scots brogue. 'What a splendid day for a wedding.'

Mary made herself smile carelessly in answer,

trying not to be nervous, not to blush and stammer. 'Indeed it is. Perfect, just as Ella deserves.'

She glanced at her sister and new brother-in-law, holding hands as they moved among their guests, smiling into each other's eyes as if they saw nothing else. Mary turned and strolled in the other direction towards a garden maze and was surprised and quite pleased when Charles went with her.

'They are a lovely couple,' Charles said. Mary thought he sounded wistful, his eyes unreadable as he studied the newlyweds. Did he think of his own lost wife? Her heart ached at the thought.

'Yes. They always have been, since we were young and ran through the woods together like a pack of wildings,' she said with a laugh, hoping to make him smile. 'Those were fun times! My father, being an ever so respectable vicar, was quite in despair of our manners. But he never needed to be so with Ella, she was always so perfect. So caring and unselfish.' Mary thought of all the times Ella had comforted her, reassured her, soothed her, laughed with her, and soon Ella would be gone.

Charles must have seen something of her thoughts. 'You will miss her,' he said simply.

Mary blinked up at him. He did always seem to *see* her every time they talked. Saw what she did not say. 'Yes, I shall. She has been like a mother to me for so long, as well as a friend. But I am over-joyed to see her so happy now. She above everyone deserves such love.'

'Doesn't everyone deserve love? That is what Penelope says your agency does—finds everyone their best match.'

'Yes, indeed,' she said, surprised he knew about the agency. 'Especially people who, for one rea-son or another, have—shall we say—extraordinary needs. Want a little something more, more under-standing, perhaps. We can give a bit of assistance in finding their other halves.'

'Very intriguing.' As he listened to her carefully, watched her unwaveringly, she felt her confidence grow. She forgot to feel flustered around him and just saw—well, saw *him*. 'You must meet such fas-cinating people.'

'Oh, yes! There was a botanist who wanted some-one to share his love of his hothouses, a historian who married a novelist who wrote medieval sto-ries, people who are shy or have too many cats or too large a house. Everyone has a tale to tell, hopes and fears and dreams.' She told him about a few more of their more interesting clients, revelling in his laughter, his attention, which never wavered.

She looked out over the wedding party, the guests, the cake and the ribbon streamers, heard the laughter. It was a wonderful day, one for friends and hope.

'Do you ever wish for such agency assistance for yourself?' he asked, his head tilted in interest.

'No, not at all,' Mary answered. And she did not. The work was what she loved, what she craved, and she couldn't bear the thought of losing it.

Mary often thought of those awful days when her mother was dying. How she was just a child but would sit beside Mama and bathe her brow and hold her hand, listening to her murmured words as Ella and the nurse hurried about looking for medicine and clean towels. As her father sat in his library, unable to cope with what was happening to his own family just above his head in the room that smelled of camphor and sweat. Mary thought if she held on to her mother tight enough, she couldn't leave.

But then her mother opened her eyes and whispered to Mary, 'My dear girl. My beauty. I see myself in your eyes now, your passion and longing for merriment, and your anger. At your father?'

Mary couldn't bear to nod, to tell her mother of her real anger towards her father for abandoning them at this moment. She blinked back the tears and tried not to show those terrible feelings. 'I shall curb my passion, Mama, I promise!'

Her mother shook her head. 'No, never do that!

It's what will make your life an adventure, my darling. But do not trust in men. Trust only in yourself. Your father—his work has always come first. I understood that when I married a clergyman. You must follow a different path. Promise me!'

Mary, frightened, shaken, had no idea what another path could be, yet she had agreed. What else could she do? And then her mother was gone.

Mary had only Ella after that, their father disappearing into his work more and more. Work and family did not seem to mix, Mary thought. Ella had sacrificed so much to be both mother and sister to Mary, to love and raise her. Then they had their own work, and Mary loved it. The agency gave them both what they needed…craved—security and control in a world where both were in such short supply. Just as their mother had said.

Mary had once cherished romantic dreams, it was true. She'd read poetry and fantasised about fair maidens and rescuing knights, about eternal love. Those faded away in the real world, and whenever her old self beckoned, she pushed her back. She couldn't feel that way again, couldn't take that risk.

But when she was near him, she was tempted indeed. 'I like to help others. We could certainly be of assistance to *you*, if you needed it.' She swallowed hard, wondering why she had said that. Helping him find a match was the last thing she wanted to do! Yet, she had told him the truth—she liked to help people find their happiness. If he needed that help…

He looked appalled. 'No, I am not good husband material, I fear. I must concentrate on my estate right now and on helping Adele.'

'Of course you are husband material!' Mary cried.

He was the most husbandly man she'd ever seen.

His dark brow quirked as he looked down at her. 'Do you think so?'

'Yes, of course. You are—are…' Handsome. Dreamy. Strong. 'You have every quality we look for in our clients. I promise you, ladies would clamour for your attentions.' Just as she did. 'You are as handsome as a medieval knight, kind and charming.'

He reached for her hand, holding it lightly on his palm as if it were a precious jewel. He stared down at it, his eyes darkened, and she found she could not quite breathe.

'How *douce* you are, Miss St Aubin,' he said quietly, roughly. 'I doubt anyone has ever seen me quite like that before.'

'How could they not?' She couldn't bear to go

on. She went up on tiptoe and impulsively pressed her lips to his, longing to know what he tasted like, what he felt like. His lips were warm, surprisingly soft, and he tasted of champagne and strawberries. Warm, so warm, so inviting.

Shocked at herself, she stepped back, staring up at him. He looked just as surprised, his green eyes wide, lips parted.

'I will take that wonderful feeling all the way back to Scotland with me,' he said hoarsely.

Mary wanted only to sink down into the grass and disappear. Now she would never, ever be able to forget him!

She had no idea what to do, so she spun around and ran away. Surely she would not ever see him again.

Chapter One

Bath,
December 1818

'Mary! If I come in here to find you working late again, I shall—I shall…' Eleanor, Countess of Fleetwood, paused on the threshold of the offices for the St Aubin and Briggs Confidential Agency, and stomped her satin evening slipper.

Mary St Aubin put down her pencil to laugh at her sister. Ella had always been so sensible and soft-spoken, angelic in her steady temper and always, always responsible. Never one to stop someone from working or ever stomp her foot.

Over a year of marriage to her darling Fred seemed to have changed all that. She was still the kindest heart in the world, but there was a lightness about her now, a glowing happiness, a constant smile. It was wonderful to see. Now it was

Mary, the one who used to always be ready for a lively dance or a game of cards, who was constantly working.

'You shall—what?' Mary said. 'Send me to bed with no supper, as you did when we lived at the vicarage?' Their mother had died so young, leaving Ella in charge, raising her sister and looking after their disorganised father.

Ella stooped to greet Miss Muffins, their exuberant terrier puppy, who lived with Mary now in the rooms above the office across from the Abbey. Miss Muffins rolled around wildly, leaving traces of pale fur on Ella's velvet evening cloak. 'I would do just that if I thought it would do some good!'

'And I would go.' Mary sighed as she scanned the close-written lines of the account book. 'An early night sounds heavenly after trying to fathom these figures all day.'

Ella frowned and hurried across the room past cabinets filled with files detailing patrons seeking their perfect matches, past pale green brocade-covered settees and armchairs, marble-topped tables holding silver vases of white hothouse roses. Every detail meant to create a sense of serene and happy romance, of a prosperous business. She ignored the view of the Abbey outside the windows draped in yellow silk, the dark blue purple of night drawing closer. 'Is it so very amiss, then?'

'I am not sure what is happening.' The agency, once so busy when Ella and their friend Harriet had been in charge, with a waiting list of patrons who had come to them seeking their perfect spouses, had grown quieter in the last few months. 'We've had fewer new patrons lately. Since you and Harry both wed, and Harry went to live in Brighton, I think. Perhaps I am simply a terrible business-woman!'

'That is certainly not true. Look at all the couples we have helped! All thanks to you and your intuition! You are so good with people, so good at reading what they need deep down inside.' Ella leaned over the desk to study the ledger. 'It must be a slow time of year, that's all. With the Christmas festivities approaching...'

'It's not that. Christmas has always been rather busy for us before. All those cosy thoughts of family, plum puddings and carols at the pianoforte while the domestic hearth crackles and children open their gifts.' She tapped the end of her pencil against the parchment. 'I think I might have an idea.'

Ella studied Mary carefully, as if she could see past any words to Mary's deepest worries. Mary had never been able to hide from her sister. 'What is it, then?'

'It was something Lady Anstruther said to me when we met at the Pump Room, on our morning visit to see the newcomers to town and pretend to sample the waters. Everyone goes there, you know, in Bath! I was so hoping she would seek our help for her niece. She had concerns about our "knowledge of such delicate subjects." Just gossip, of course, but after that I noticed a few other people who had expressed interest in a match avoiding me. It is my…lack of knowledge of marriage, I am sure. Marriage of my own.' Mary was not used to people avoiding her. She loved parties, conversation, loved her work.

'How perfectly absurd of them!' Ella cried, making Miss Muffins bark. 'You have been the only reason the agency was heard of at all. You are so good at listening to people, so gifted in seeing what they need in a match. Where would the Martin-Bellinghams be without you? Lord and Lady Langham? And dozens of others.' Ella stomped her foot again. 'Perhaps I should come back to the offices for a time. Just to help you a bit.'

'No! You're not often in Bath now, and when you are, you should enjoy yourself for a change. You have Fred and the twins, and Moulton Magna, to look after, and you've been looking forward to Christmas there this year.'

Moulton Magna was Fred's grand but rather ramshackle earldom estate, and it needed Ella's elegant, steadying hand as it revived after Fred's father's long years of neglect. And the twins, Annabelle and Edward, were crawling and too adorable for their mother to miss.

'I shall simply find a way to persuade patrons to return to us, I am quite determined on it. They shall know they can trust me, even with you and Harry gone.' She closed the ledger and pushed it away. She would not worry Ella, not now when her sister was getting all the fine things she deserved. She had always worked too hard, sacrificed too much for Mary. 'Now, where are you going this evening in such a beautiful new gown?'

Ella still looked much too concerned, but she smiled brightly, as if determined to match Mary's own determined cheerfulness. She gave a little spin, making her emerald-green gown, embroidered with delicate gold leaves and beaded vines, twirl and sparkle in the lamplight. 'It's from Mademoiselle Sandrine Dumas's shop, of course! Is she not terribly clever?'

Mary nodded in admiration. Mademoiselle Sandrine had opened her shop in York Street only a year before and was already the sensation of Bath. Everyone coveted one of her creations, which were more than mere dresses. They were dreams, of colour, texture, sparkle. Just as Mary knew how to match a couple, Sandrine knew how to bring out any lady's real beauty, her essence. She had done several wedding gowns for agency patrons, and Mary could only hope they would have more to send her soon.

'You shall be the envy of everyone there. Are you going to the opera, maybe?'

Ella tsked. 'It's Penelope's soirée, of course. I came to see if you would come in our carriage, but you're not even dressed.'

'Pen's party! Oh no.' Mary slapped her hand over her eyes. Penelope Oliver was Fred's stepmother and Mary and Ella's dear friend, who had recently married her true love Anthony Oliver and set up home with him in a grand townhouse on Greenleaf Street. This was her first party in her fine new drawing room.

'Never say you forgot. Oh, Mary. You have certainly been working far too hard if *you* are forgetting social engagements! You used to enjoy a party more than anyone else.'

'Especially for friends like Pen. We haven't even seen her since she returned from her wedding trip to Italy!' Mary had indeed always loved a party, loved being around people, hearing them chatter, swirling through a dance. She had never been made to be buried in ledgers, yet there she was. She had to prove herself, both in her own mind and to their patrons. But maybe part of that was socialising with them. 'I shall just change my gown at once, Ella, if your carriage will wait for a few moments.'

'Of course it can wait. I'm meeting Fred there, and he won't even notice I'm late once he starts a card game with Anthony.' Ella eyed the file cabinets.

'And no working while you wait! I forbid it. The agency is mine now.'

Ella laughed. 'I was only going to take a tiny peek. See who is new, who might like who. Who might—well, you know...'

'Who might suit *me*?' Mary asked wryly. She'd seen Ella watching her with a speculative gleam in her eye and suspected Ella's matchmaking skills might be moving closer to home. 'Ella, you know we do not use patrons to make matches for ourselves.'

'Yes, I know,' Ella sighed. No one would ever trust them as matchmakers if it was suspected they were only working for themselves. And Mary had no interest in marrying anyway; the agency took up all her time and attention, her affection. She had to focus on it. 'Even if they might wish for us to match them with *you*. So many of our patrons have mooned over your golden curls, my dear sister! Is Mr Overbury still in the files?'

Mary nodded sadly. 'Indeed. I have offered him any number of introductions to fascinating, lovely ladies, but he says none of them would suit. Too tall, too petite, too brunette, too poetical, too lacking in poetry, too sensible, too flighty.' But she and Ella both knew that was not Mr Overbury's problem. His problem was that he had conceived a great infatuation for Mary herself. He followed her about at assemblies, sent her poetic love letters. It had been thus ever since he came to the agency many months before. 'Surely you are not saying I should accept his suit just to get him out of our books!'

'Oh, no, never Mr Overbury. He does have a fine fortune, but those waistcoats of his! But, well, someone better. Someone you could truly care for as I do my Fred. Maybe you are right that—that...'

'That my spinster state, when you and Harry are so blissfully wed now, might really be having an effect on our patrons? That a matchmaker who can't match herself isn't trustworthy? Sadly, yes, maybe so.'

Ella squeezed her hand. 'You must never think of marrying for the sake of business. But for yourself, dearest, you might just...'

'Might what?'

'Find someone to be with. I've never felt so *right* since Fred and I married, never so exactly where I should be! To be seen and loved for ourselves—it's blissful.'

Mary shook her head. Ella did indeed deserve every blissful moment she had. But Mary had spent her life managing *other* people's lives, other people's romances. Did she sometimes wish for such a thing herself? Certainly she did. It made her rather wistful to see Ella and Fred laughing together, staring into each other's eyes as if nothing else existed. Sometimes the sleepless nights seemed terribly quiet and dark, and sometimes she wished she had someone to advise her, help her. But only with someone who truly understood her, saw her, someone she could understand and help in return. After being responsible for herself for so long, it was frightening to think of relying so much on someone else! She could only give in to that for the strongest of loves, for someone who loved and needed her. And Charles, after being married before, after having his own life, surely couldn't love her in that way.

She glanced out the window to the snowy evening, and for an instant she saw not the chilly evening but a warm springtime day, cheering Charles on as he ran about the cricket green, his long, lean legs swift as a panther. Kissing him in that garden…

Perhaps she had dared to dream that *he* might be that understanding man. But it was not to be. Charles Campbell had gone back to Scotland after that golden spring, so she had heard, and he was there now only in the dreams she saw late at night, when work and the rush and bustle of the day had given way to silent hours. She imagined him then, the sunlight on his hair, the feel of his broad shoulders under her touch. The way his lips tasted. It gave her such pangs to think of him now.

She shook her head. Distraction would be very good right then and a party just the thing. Even if Pen's husband *was* Charles's cousin, and she might hear of him there.

'I shall go change my gown now. I just wish I had a Mademoiselle Sandrine creation to wear!' Mary pushed back from the desk, a bit stiff after sitting there so long, and gathered up her shawl, dislodging Miss Muffins from where she had parked herself on the fringe. 'I promise, Ella, you do not need to worry about me. I shall find a solution to our business troubles, and the agency will soon be busier than it ever was!'

Chapter Two

'**Y**ou think I should *what*?' Charles Campbell
gaped at his cousin Anthony over his hand of cards,
not sure if he should shout or laugh. Or if he had
even heard the man correctly. He'd thought everyone had given up trying to see him wed, considering him an old eccentric hiding in his Scottish
castle.

In the end, he didn't laugh *or* shout. That wasn't
like him, he always tried to be calm and rational,
to weigh possibilities and make the most sensible
decision. He had to do that ever since he'd become
guardian to a young lady who needed his help. If
he merely proceeded slowly, the clock would tick
down to Anthony's wife's soirée, and he wouldn't
have to converse over cards with the man any longer. 'Interesting idea, Anthony.'

Anthony laughed and laid down a card. They had
known each other all their lives, since they were in

leading-strings with Charles's mother being sister to Anthony's father, and they knew each other too well. 'Of course, Charles. I am serious. What better solution could there be? Adele needs a mother to shepherd her through Society now, and you need a companion. You've become much too solemn and bearish lately.'

'Can you blame me?' Charles said. He gestured to a footman for another glass of wine. He very much feared he would need it if matrimony was to be the subject that evening. 'I wasn't such a fine hand at marriage the first time. No lady deserves such unhappiness.' Charles seldom thought of his youthful marriage now, and never spoke of it, but it always seemed to lurk there in the back of his mind, the terrible way it ended, his mistakes.

Anthony nodded sympathetically. 'Of course I remember Aileen. But you were so very young! And most ladies are not like her. She was filled with restlessness and dissatisfaction from the very beginning. You would be more careful in your choice now.'

Would he? Or would a new wife be just as unhappy with him? Charles wouldn't take that chance. 'Nor are most ladies like your own excellent wife. We can't all be so fortunate with our hearts.'

Anthony beamed, a veritable ray of sunshine as

he had been ever since he found his Penelope again after long, lonely years and became a devoted husband. 'Pen is an angel, it's true. I'm the luckiest man in the world.'

'And you think we should all be just as happy in our own domestic arrangements, yes?'

Anthony laid down another card. 'Certainly! Why not? My own days were so quiet, so lonely before, and now life is filled with possibility, with glorious moments. I care about you, cousin, about all our friends, and wish nothing but such happiness for you all.'

'And you are a good man to have such kind wishes for everyone, Anthony, which I know are most sincere.' It was true; Anthony had always had a tender heart, a generous soul, matched by his new wife. It was no surprise they wanted to spread the glow of domestic bliss far and wide. But Charles knew too well that could never be for him. 'But there is only one Penelope in the world. The rest of us are out of luck.'

'Pen is just as worried about you as I am. We know you have your hands full with Adele. It cannot be easy to suddenly be a father figure. And to such a—a lively young lady.'

Charles laughed. It was true that Adele Stewart, his kinswoman and ward, was very *lively*. She read a vast amount of romantic poetry and expected life to be just like in those pages. If it was not, then she would *make* it so. And now she fancied herself in love with one of the most unsuitable lads possible. Peyton Clark, a penniless rogue, whose uncle it was said had cut him off because of his bad behaviour. Charles had no idea what to do next, and a lady's hand on the tiller for a while would be relief. A lady who knew what it felt like to be a girl, what to do to safeguard one so heedless and romantic as Adele.

Charles feared, though, that his judgement was as clouded in its own way as Adele's. He had once thought himself so in love with Aileen, he was blind to the truth, blind to how unsuited they were. If he tried to choose another wife, he would probably only make matters worse.

'You and Pen are truly the best of friends, Anthony, and I'm grateful for all your concern and advice lately.' Pen had indeed tried to help as much as she could with Adele, taking her to modistes, arranging matters for a London Season, listening to her. It kept Charles somewhat sane. 'It was all manageable when we were in Scotland, but sadly we couldn't stay there forever. Adele needs friends, distractions. Scotland was too quiet, too chilly, and she seemed happy in Bath last year. She must...'

'Must marry one day. And so should you, Charles. There are many lovely ladies in Bath!'

'I'm sure there are. Pen and Lady Fleetwood have introduced me to several at the theatre and Pump Room in the short time since I returned.' Yet he had not seen the one lady he most wanted to meet again, Mary St Aubin, of the golden hair and dimpled smile. Mary, who had haunted his dreams since she pressed her lips to his in that garden. 'If I must marry for Adele's sake, it will have to be a quiet, responsible-minded, sensible lady to make up for my misspent youth.'

'Charles…' Anthony started to protest, but then had to shrug ruefully, for just as he and Charles had known each other all their lives, he knew Charles's youth *had* been misspent.

Drinking too much, cheap pubs, illegal gaming halls. Trying to escape from the coldness of his family, his upbringing, to push down the longing for a life, a purpose, for someone to understand him. He knew that was what that behaviour had been about, really. All culminating in his marriage to Aileen, a young lady he'd known for years, as she was their neighbours' daughter, but who he had not truly known at all in the end. He would not make that sort of mistake again.

'That was all a long time ago,' Anthony said quietly.

'Not so very long ago.' Music floated into the small sitting room where they were playing cards, signalling the party must be beginning. 'Adele needs a steady hand, and I need...' What did he need? He knew all too well what he *wanted*. Had wanted ever since he glimpsed her across the Assembly Room dance floor, her golden hair shining like summer sun, her laughter sweeter than the waltz music. Mary.

He was of no use to a lady like Mary. He had too many responsibilities on his shoulders, a niece to guide through the Season, a cold estate in Scotland. Too much to make up for—his rakish youth, his mistaken marriage. Aileen had been a bit like Mary—always dancing, always laughing—until life with him rang that out of her.

No. He was better off on his own, with no one else harmed by his choices. If he did marry again, it would have to be to a sensible, pragmatic lady who would understand the parameters of his life, the limits of what he could give. What he could truly do. His heart was guarded now, as it should have been all along. Mary St Aubin was too full of heat and mischief, and she deserved a place to expand and bloom like a summer rose.

Charles glanced out the sitting room window at the snow lightly flurrying against the purplish sky, the graceful pale stone walls of the elegant square. Summer felt like a long distance away.

'I declare even your excellent Penelope couldn't find a lady who would have me,' he said lightly, folding his cards.

'I wouldn't place such a bet. She and her friends are most renowned for their skills in the match-making arena.'

Charles was intrigued. 'Skilled in finding ladies for desperate gentlemen? You do shock me.'

A dull red flush spread across Anthony's face. 'Not like *that*, you old rake! They make marital matches. And are very good at it.'

'Many bored ladies in Society like to try to throw their friends together, I'm sure. It can't always work. It all seems so…random. As if a lady knows a single man and a single lady and nothing else about them, so they must suit. Not that Pen would do that…'

Anthony shook his head and leaned across the table to whisper, 'When I met Pen again here in Bath last year, I found out that Lady Fleetwood and her sister, along with Lady Briggs, who is now the Marchioness of Ripton, ran a sort of agency, matching people who were having troubles meeting suitable partners in the usual way. People who…wanted something more out of their marriages. Compatibility, love even.'

'An agency? Like a business? Lady Fleetwood and Lady Briggs? And…' And Mary? Mary making matches. Was that why she'd kissed him in the garden? Testing him out for her ledgers? How strange. How intriguing. 'And Miss St Aubin?'

'I know it sounds most peculiar, but they do so many people an excellent service. The Confidential Agency does nothing so vulgar as advertise, of course, or put out signs on their doors. They are strictly by referral, past patrons giving letters of recommendation to those in need. Whispers at the Pump Room or the Theatre Royal to a friend who might need a tiny push in the right direction. Bath is filled with those seeking their perfect partner, you know.'

'How extraordinary.' And it was. Charles could feel his already considerable admiration for Mary grow even more. She ran a business! A strange one, to be sure, but a business. Another reason she would not want to marry someone like him. When Aileen ran from him, he thought he saw why she would do that, why he could not make a lady a truly good husband. He'd never seen happiness and family contentment with his own parents. How could

he give that to someone else? Especially not someone as strong and independent as Mary. 'Did they
introduce you to Pen?'

Anthony shook his head. 'We had already met
years ago, you know, before she married the late
Lord Fleetwood, and finally discovered each other
again here in Bath. But so many others owe their
happy marriages to this agency. Including Lady
Pennington, who will be here tonight. She used
to be Miss Evans, remember, the rich merchant's
bluestocking daughter? Everyone said she would
only be married for her money, before Ella and
Mary found Lord Pennington and his studies, and
she fell quite in love. Now look at her! Happy, stu-
dious and doubly rich, as Pennington had his own
fortune. They say they have a new scientific laboratory at Northland Park. I supposed we'll see it
for ourselves at their Christmas house party this
month! They found Miss Evans someone just as
rich and dotty about studies as she was. They saw
the match straight away.'

Charles sat back in his chair, startled at the
thought that Mary could do such things, wave a
magic wand and make perfect matches. He was
certainly impressed by her, by her ingenuity and
by her energy for such work, but he was not sure
such fairy-tale magic could be real.

'You know, Charles,' Anthony went on, 'I am sure they are exactly the ones you should be talking to about your—your conundrum.'

'My lack of a spouse is hardly a conundrum.' And Charles was sure they were exactly *not* the ones he should talk to, even if it was. He could never speak to Mary about the truth of his past, of his marriage. 'As fine as the St Aubin ladies are, my needs are quite small after such glittering matches as the Penningtons. I wouldn't want to bother them.'

'They would never be *bothered*! They are friends to us. Lady Fleetwood has been so busy with Moulton Magna of late I'm sure she's not at their offices much, but Miss St Aubin is. Pen has been helping her a bit. She's a wonder at organising and such.' He looked awestruck at his wife's filing ability, just like everything else about her. 'She will be here this evening. And at Lady Pennington's house party. Plenty of time to seek her advice, casually.'

Mary would be there in that very house that very evening? He felt a rush of something like panic, as if he were a boy again. Yet there was also excitement, longing. 'Miss St Aubin is to be here?'

'Certainly. She's been too busy to go out in Society much of late. Must be so odd for her, she did love to dance.' As he certainly did not. She would never want to see him again if she had the displeasure of dancing with him! Even as that would give him the excuse to touch her, be close to her, he knew he could not inflict his dancing on her. 'But Pen persuaded her that the festive season should be shared! Shall I have Pen talk to her about your situation?'

'No!' Charles snapped too loudly. Anthony looked startled, and Charles felt terrible for his loss of control. His childhood had been filled with his father's sudden rages, his mother's distance; he didn't want to do that, didn't want to give Adele that sort of home. Another reason he shouldn't marry again.

'No,' he repeated calmly, considerately, and laughed. He shuffled the cards as if he hadn't a care in the world. 'Let the ladies enjoy their parties. Pen is right, Christmas should be shared. I will work out my own small troubles. No wife required.'

Anthony looked unsure, as if he wanted to say more, but Penelope came in just then, her bright blue star-embroidered gown shimmering around her. She looked rather harassed.

'There you are, Anthony!' she cried, straightening a chair, twitching a drapery. She paused to kiss her husband's cheek and studied the cards on the table. 'The guests are arriving, and you and Charles are hiding away in here. It looks like you lost terribly, by the way. Why didn't you play the ten of hearts there?'

'Pen!' Anthony said with a laugh. 'You can't let everyone know what a terrible card player I really am.'

'Well, now you can escape your bad cards and come with me to greet the guests.' She kissed him again and went to check the chairs at the next table. 'What were you and Charles speaking of, then?' She sounded suspiciously casual, as if she guessed the matchmaking nature of their talk.

'Nothing at all, I fear,' Anthony said, giving her a long glance.

'How is Adele?' Charles asked, hoping to distract them. Adele had been getting ready for the party with Pen and was hopefully staying out of trouble.

'She is very well and looks so pretty in her new frock. I let her borrow my hairdresser, and she was so excited to try the new style. How lovely she's growing! And so charming. I'd love it if she could play the pianoforte later. The heather breezes are so good for her. She will be quite the diamond of the Season this spring.'

'And unsuitable romances seem to suit her, too, I fear,' Charles muttered.

Penelope frowned. 'She harbours some unsuitable tendre? She hasn't spoken of it to me, but I suppose I have seen her looking at Mr Clark...'

''Tis just a young lady's poetic fancy, soon vanished, I'm sure. I shouldn't mind so much if that fancy found a more harmless object than Clark, though.'

'I am quite sure there is a quick solution,' Pen declared. 'I shall give it some thought tonight. And keep a close eye on Adele during the dancing, of course. I fear it is so easy to make a misstep at such an age, one not always easily recovered from.'

That was exactly what Charles feared. Adele needed help, and so did he, to navigate such rocky shoals as a first Season.

A footman stepped into the doorway, and the music from the drawing room was growing louder. 'The first carriages are arriving, Mrs Oliver,' he announced.

'Thank you,' Penelope said. 'Shall we, my darling?'

The happy couple swept out to their party, arm in arm, leaving Charles to his thoughts. And his thoughts were all of Mary St Aubin, her quick elfin laughter and bright hair. The joy she brought when she was nearby.

Suddenly, as if summoned magically by his thoughts of her, he glimpsed Mary St Aubin through the crowd. The light seemed to gather only on her, bathing her in a sparkling glow. She laughed, her face alight, her golden curls bouncing, and he couldn't look away.

He hadn't seen her in some months, so he'd often told himself she couldn't really be so beautiful as he remembered. But in truth, she *was*, or even more so, like sunshine breaking through a grey Bath sky. How he wished he could save her up, save how she made him feel, for another dark day!

He drifted behind the gathering, still watching her. She accepted a glass of wine from one of the crowd of gentlemen around her and gifted the man one of her jewel-like smiles. She chatted and laughed, her honey-brown eyes glowing. Charles was enthralled by her, by the glow of the cloud she seemed to walk on. Enthralled, bewildered and—and jealous. He watched her smile again at one of her admirers, the curve of those rose-pink lips, and he found he longed to taste them. To see if they were as sweet as he remembered from their too-brief, much-remembered kiss.

'Uncle Charles? Are you quite well?' Adele asked, and it was as if he were suddenly shoved off his delicate cloud of Mary dreams. Cold reality closed around him again.

Laughing a bit at himself, at his moment of folly,

he turned to his niece. Adele studied him with a most bemused expression on her pretty face. He remembered her as a toddler, when she would frown fiercely at the world around her as if trying to understand its every puzzling scrap. Now she did the same, though from the bright blue eyes of a young lady about to leap out into the unknown.

He smiled down at her and took her arm to draw her closer, a wave of protectiveness washing over him. 'I am quite well, Adele. Why do you ask?'

'You did look rather peculiar just then. As if you'd swallowed some wine the wrong way.' She looked around the party, twisting her lace fan in one hand. He wondered if she looked for her suitor and knew he had to distract her.

'Pen wanted to know if you might play the pianoforte, maybe before the dancing begins,' he said. Pen had only mentioned it in passing, of course, but he knew she wouldn't mind if Adele sat down at the instrument at all. She was very talented, her musical skills so expressive. She deserved so many fine things in life, more than a rake like Clark could give.

'Play?' she cried, startled. 'But I need to find my friends! I did promise I would…' She seemed to remember herself, remember to try and be discreet, if Mr Clark was indeed what she looked for. 'Of course I can, if Aunt Pen asked.'

'You are so accomplished, my dear, everyone asks for your Scottish airs at every gathering lately.' That was very true. Adele had so many admirers, if only she would look around. Just another reason he would never let her throw herself away on someone most unworthy of her artistic gifts, her kind heart, her pretty face and fine manners.

As he turned to lead Adele towards the pianoforte set in the corner of the drawing room, he glimpsed Mary one more time. She was so beautiful, so dangerous to his serenity of mind. He couldn't think of anything else when she was near.

She was a glorious distraction he certainly did not need.

Chapter Three

Mary always thought parties really should start with some sliver of excitement, some frisson that anything could happen in the next hours. Especially for a matchmaker! The thrill of watching two people dance and thinking 'Hmm, maybe...' watching two people laugh together. It gave it all such a sparkle. She greeted Pen and Anthony with a laugh, and urged Ella and Fred to go and dance, shocking as a husband and wife dancing together would be!

She carefully studied the crowd around her. The swirl of colour, the men's dark coats against the ladies in their pastel pinks, sky blues, pure white, amethyst, green. The shine of jewels in the candlelight, the laughter and chatter blending with the swing and twirl of the music. The sweet scent of hothouse roses and winter greenery in the air, along with fine perfumes. It was all very pretty, as Pen had excellent taste, but as always what really happened at the start of a party was not frisson but—ever so slight boredom. Oh, not at Pen's parties, really. She knew how to blend music, conversation, decoration to perfection. Yet it was all very much of a sameness those days. The same people, the same talk. And Mary had once so loved parties!

Now she felt a bit lonely as she took in the happy crowd around her.

'Some wine, Miss St Aubin?' she heard someone ask, and turned to find Mr Sillerton standing there, impeccable in a finely cut green coat and perfectly tied cravat pinned with a large cameo, his brown hair swirled into the latest style. She had tried once or twice to gently steer him towards an agency match, but he seemed happy as a single gentleman, as a pseudo-suitor to Mary. But he had sent her a few marriage-minded friends, and she needed all the help she could find.

'You quite read my mind, Mr Sillerton,' she said, and took the glass from his gloved hand with a smile. 'It's become quite the crush this evening.'

'Mrs Oliver is a hostess par excellence, it's true,' Mr Sillerton said, gesturing at the growing crowd around them. 'Her food and wine, and definitely the intelligent conversation of her chosen guests, is far above average in Bath! But I fear this town has become rather dull this season. That last play at the Theatre Royal was so very lifeless! And the quality of dancing at the Assembly Rooms abysmal. It's a fine thing Lady Pennington is having her Christmas house party to carry us away from it all. They say Northland Park is superb!'

Mary nodded and secretly hoped she would meet new clients there. Maybe they would be lurking under the mistletoe, waiting for their ideal partners. 'Indeed. I'm very much looking forward to it.'

'Lord and Lady Pennington were a product of your fine agency, were they not? You clever girl. They are a scintillating pair, and poor Miss Evans looked so unpromising at first.'

'Yes, they do seem quite happy together,' Mary said, proud of their finest match yet. 'I am of the hope there will be many more such people at their party in need of a soupçon of assistance.'

'I fear all the men are in love with *you*, our fair Miss SA, and won't be set on lesser lights. Much like my own pitiful self!' He clutched at his heart through his fine cream brocade waistcoat. 'This party is a mere salve to my heartache.'

Mary laughed, glad she had friends who could amuse and distract her from thoughts of Charles Campbell.

Was it a sign that marriage had been mentioned so often of late as a solution to her problems? It was true that the right alliance could set straight many things in one wave of a vicar's hand in benediction. Her business would be seen to be in safe, *married* hands. She'd always known what she *should* want, a husband and children, a house to look after. Yet what she liked was her work. It was most satisfying to see the happiness she could help create for others, to make her own way in the world after a childhood in which she and Ella were dependent on their scatter-brained father. A husband would not like his wife working outside her drawing room.

Yes, indeed; a husband might be a nice thing to have. Useful. And a family such as Ella had now looked wonderful. But she knew few households were blessed with such real love and understanding as Ella and Fred, and Pen and Anthony, possessed. Mary couldn't fathom marriage without such a meeting of hearts. She let herself be distracted by a few gentlemen clustering around her, offering wine, a dance, a stroll about the room.

The music of the dance had faded, and she heard the strains of a soft song instead, an air on the pianoforte. It sounded most enticing, and she drifted towards the sound of it from the instrument in the corner of the drawing room. She nearly bumped into a petite, slim figure draped in pink silk on the way, the wine in her glass jostling. She glanced down, and recognised Mademoiselle Sandrine, the modiste.

'Oh, Mademoiselle Dumas!' Mary cried. 'I do beg your pardon. How lovely to see you again! And how charming you look.' She studied the pink gown closer, admiring the slashed sleeves revealing puffs of beaded white satin à la Renaissance. Sandrine was often invited to social events by her favoured patrons, as all ladies in town hoped to engage her. And, being French and mysterious, she was considered most fascinating. 'That must be the very latest in sleeves.'

'Of course! My business depends on such things,' Mademoiselle Sandrine said with a laugh, her bell-like voice touched with a Parisian accent. Though she wore spectacles, and seemed not at all ashamed of that fact, she was quite pretty, with dimples and flashing brown eyes. But behind those lovely eyes lurked something like a shadow, a sadness. Mary wondered where it came from. Something in the lady's past, some grief? 'Now that we can see all the latest French fashions, we are spoiled for choices in our silhouettes.'

'I do wish there was time for me to have such a frock made up for Lady Pennington's party.'

'Oh, I shall be there, too! I'm so looking forward to getting a glimpse of that laboratory. I'm sure I could make up a new gown for you before then, if I have the correct fabric in my stock.'

'Could you really?' Mary gasped. Perhaps an ultra-stylish ball gown or walking dress would catch some attention for the business. 'You are an angel, Mademoiselle.'

Sandrine laughed again. 'I am merely a very hard worker, much like yourself. But this music—now, *that* is angelic. Such expression!'

Indeed it was. A song full of expression and light and shade, no mere succession of keys as young ladies' playing so often was. This was music with feeling and talent.

Mary went up on tiptoe to peer through the crowd gathered to listen to the music. To her shock, she saw it was Adele Stewart, Charles's niece, who played. Her head was bent, strawberry-blonde curls dangling over the keys, as if she saw nothing else, her brow furrowed with emotion. Yes, it was definitely her. And if Adele had returned to Bath, then surely...

A man stepped forward to turn the page of the music, and she saw it was really Charles. Suddenly back in Mary's own town, in her life, real once more. Everything else grew blurry around her, reality sharpening only on him, and she couldn't quite breathe.

She'd thought she could forget him when he was far away in Scotland, that he would fade from her thoughts and memories. That hadn't happened as of yet; she remembered him in the dark of night, when all was quiet. Thought of his sea-green eyes, crinkling as he smiled that warm chocolate smile of his, thought of how his touch sent tingles all through her, how his kiss swept away everything else in the world.

But she'd been sure he *would* fade, given time, as all impossible dreams did. As a girl, she had been romantic, dreamy; as a woman, she had to learn to be practical.

Now, there he was again, no dream but all too real. And even more handsome than she remembered. Not like a fashionable fairy-tale prince, but so very *real*. Maybe it was the Scot in him that gave him such an air of freshness and vitality, even when he stood still. That spark of humour and raw energy that hummed about him. That small hint of danger, like a hardened warrior off the battlefield, relaxed and smiling but liable to leap into action again at an instant's notice.

Mary pressed her folded fan to her lips to keep from laughing. She was surely too old now to indulge her young, poetical self, yet here she was, being so terribly fanciful! Making him into the hero of a novel in her own mind.

He glanced up, and with no warning, his gaze met hers. Something seemed to sizzle and crackle in the air between them.

Mary inadvertently took a step back, nearly treading on someone's train. She wanted to run, to hide from that green gaze that seemed to see everything, but she was hemmed in by the crowd with nowhere to go. And she really wanted to run forward, as well, to catch his hand in hers and stare and stare into his eyes forever.

'Who is that?' Sandrine asked. Her gaze narrowed as she studied Adele's gown, a creation of cream and gold that shimmered like autumn leaves in a breeze. 'I think the dress is one of mine, but I don't remember them.'

'Mr Campbell and his niece Miss Stewart. They left Bath not long after you arrived and must have only just returned. Perhaps Penelope loaned her the gown, it suits her very well.' Sandrine's creations were the envy of the town, transforming their wearers into rare beauties in colours and trims that enhanced their own lovely qualities. She was especially sought after for wedding gowns, though Mary wouldn't think Adele was quite ready for that. 'They live in Scotland, but he is Mr Oliver's cousin. I'm sure they must be here for Christmas.'

'A handsome family indeed,' Sandrine murmured. 'That gown looks well on her but doesn't quite fit correctly in the sleeves, *n'est-ce pas*? I just got a bolt of spring-green muslin that would suit her hair very nicely...' She wandered away, murmuring about silks and laces.

As Mary watched her go, trying to pretend Charles was not mere feet away, she felt the hard press of a stare from somewhere in the crowd. She finally saw Mr Overbury watching her, and when her gaze met his, he started towards her.

Mary pivoted on her shoe heel and slipped back into the press of people in hopes she could vanish before her unwanted suitor found her. She'd once found Mr Overbury amusing, fun to talk about poetry with even, but the more she talked to him, the more she entertained his visits to the agency and tried to find him a wife, the more he pressed closer to her.

To her vexation, though, the people she *wanted* to pay attention to her, potential patrons of the agency, seemed to see right through her! They nodded to her but would not approach for conversation. She chatted a bit with the Morleys, a couple who'd formed their attachment through the agency when everyone in Bath had said they were quite doomed to single life because of their obsession with taxidermy. They were kind, but even they only wanted to ask after Ella, sing her praises as a superlative matchmaker.

'And now her own match is to an earl! So fitting for her!'

Ella's marriage to Fred, and her semi-retirement from crafting matches, seemed to have enhanced Ella's professional reputation while everyone seemed to forget that Mary had also worked to build their business.

The crowd grew once again as the dance music struck up. Mary turned towards the doorway of the sitting room set aside for cards, hoping it would be a bit quieter, have a space for her to take a breath. Perhaps she would even find a game herself. She was rather keen on whist and hadn't played much lately. Not since that game with Charles at the Assembly Rooms. She remembered peeking over the edge of her cards to see a man coming to their table, so tall and powerful, clad in a fashionable, conventional evening coat of dark blue superfine, but he might as well have worn a kilt and carried a broadsword, he seemed so arrestingly of another time.

Yes, she could definitely use a quiet game to clear her head.

But she realised her mistake right away. Charles Campbell stood near the fireplace, quite alone—and still more beautiful than a man had a right to be. Months in his windswept Scotland seemed to have made him even more gorgeous, carving his sun-bronzed features into a Greek statue, making his eyes even brighter.

It felt as if someone had kicked the breath from her, just seeing him there in life and not in her day-dreams.

He was watching something across the room, and she thought maybe she could back away and dash off before he approached. She was too slow, though, too caught up in the sight of him, and he suddenly began towards her. A slow smile spread across his lips, making her knees tremble.

She couldn't run away now. She made herself smile merrily, as her party-loving self would once have, and went to meet him. She held her hand out, arm straight, as if she could keep him far enough away. Another mistake. He took her hand, and heat shot through her whole arm straight to her heart.

'Mr Campbell,' she said lightly, her inner self all in tumult. 'How nice to see you again! I didn't know you had returned to Bath.' *Liar.* Truly, she'd thought of little else but him since she first saw Adele at the piano and realised Charles must be in

Bath, as well. She'd daydreamed about him, thought about him in her bed at night, doodled his name in the margins of ledgers and then furiously scratched it out.

'Only recently, Miss St Aubin. I fear Adele is of an age when she needs a great deal more society than Castle Campbell can give her.'

'That is your estate?' Blast him, but even the name of his home sounded romantic and rugged!

'Yes, near Dunfermline. It's an old place, maybe a bit draughty and out of style, but with views from the ramparts for miles...' He sounded most wistful, and Mary wished more than anything she could see the place, share it with him.

'And I daresay you miss it very much,' she said softly. She imagined him there, striding the heather-covered hills, his hair tousled in the breeze. Holding out his hand so she could walk beside him.

He smiled, a bright too-quickly vanished flash. 'Aye, I'd happily spend all my days there. Adele deserves more, though. She needs far more people to hear her talent at the pianoforte, for instance, than just me and the servants.'

'Oh, yes, I heard her playing when I first arrived. She is very talented, such charming expressiveness, so much understanding of the emotions of the music. She is certainly accomplished, as well as pretty.' Mary glanced around the card room, remembering what she'd heard about each gentleman there, whether he was single, what his estate and character were. 'She should have her pick of suitors here in Bath and in London. And once she's settled, you can return to your castle, yes?' She thought of him vanishing into the Scottish mists again, never to be seen, and felt a sharp pang at the idea. Not that she should feel that way; he could never be closer to her than he was right then, anyway.

A frown flickered over his brow. 'I do fear she may have—well, I think perhaps...'

Mary had seen such an expression on worried parents' faces before. 'Has she perhaps formed a... less than ideal attachment?' she asked gently.

He swallowed. 'Have there been whispers?'

'Oh, no, not at all. Not that I have heard, and I must stay abreast of all the talk of the town.' Usually she did, though she feared not so much lately. But she did still hear murmurs and giggles when there was forbidden romance to be seen. 'I have just seen such things before, with parents and their impressionable young daughters. Are you concerned? Is this *parti* pestering Miss Stewart, pressing his attentions? I could have a quiet word with her, give her advice on seeing such unwanted admirers off without a fuss.' She just wished she could do that herself, with men like Mr Overbury. Some suitors would not be put off with gentle hints.

Charles smiled down at her. 'That is very kind of you, Miss St Aubin. I'm afraid it may be—well, that is to say...'

He did look adorably flustered, which made him seem even more handsome. Mary tried very hard to focus on his words, his conundrum and not on the way his hair tumbled over his brow. 'I see. It's a bit more complicated, then.'

'Rather, yes. I left her with Penelope, but I think I should go find her now. Would you walk with me?'

Anywhere. 'Of course.'

He offered her his arm, all perfectly proper and correct, yet she did not feel quite so proper when she touched him. The warmth of him against her hand made her want to throw herself at him and seek his kiss, like a wild creature! Somehow she managed to just walk with him at the edge of the room, slowly, just like an ordinary evening. She hoped her polite smile did not tremble.

'What is amiss with your niece?' she asked.

He frowned. 'I fear she is in love with someone quite unsuitable. Well, she says it is love, but certainly it is not.'

'I see. That sounds worrying, of course, but not so rare. Young ladies do fall into infatuations sometimes, and it always seems to be with the most terrible rakes. It usually passes. Who is this man?'

'His name is Peyton Clark. He is heir to his uncle, but they say the old man has tired of his antics and cut him off, or very near to it. He cannot support a wife, either financially or emotionally. I do not know how to persuade her that parting from him is the best thing for her.'

'Hmm, yes, I see. I have not heard of this man, but I know his type all too well. You are right to be concerned, and it does you credit as a guardian.' She scanned the floor and saw Adele twirling along the line of the dance with a young man. 'Is that Mr Clark with Adele now?'

'No, thankfully. I believe that is a Mr Bellingham.'

'Ah, yes. New to Bath. Grandson to a duke. Quite the scholar, they say, very interested in ancient Minoan culture.'

Charles laughed. 'Now, why doesn't Adele find herself someone like that? Connections, intelligence.'

'And quite nice, from what I hear. But young ladies of a poetical turn of mind, and I do seem to remember Miss Stewart was quite a reader, seldom have yet learned to be sensible. I fear I speak from some experience.'

He glanced down at her, his dark brow arched with interest. 'You were…poetical?'

'In my sad youth. I fancied myself quite the Mrs Brereton. Do you know her work?'

'I do not. But I sympathise. I was once sure I was destined to be a poet myself and grew my hair ridiculously long as I strode about the hillsides endeavouring to look tragic.'

Mary laughed as she imagined such a scene. 'Did you indeed?'

'Oh, aye. I was tiresome beyond belief, Miss St Aubin. And it took me some time to come to the realisation that a career as a poet requires the ability to write something more than just somewhat intelligible business letters. I had no Byronic turn of phrase in my fingertips.'

'Oh, poor Mr Campbell!'

He gave her an exaggerated pout that made her laugh harder. 'I know. To have my youthful dreams crushed so cruelly. My *da* said it was beyond time I ceased stalking over the hills like a bogle and applied myself to my duties.'

'I am quite sure you have many other talents beyond literature.' Kissing, for instance. Ah, yes, she remembered he was quite good at that.

'My *da* said my only true vocation was in gambling and whisky bottles.'

Mary was shocked. Her own father, the vicar, would never have said such a thing! And Charles didn't seem at all the soused sort. 'How untrue! I am sure he doesn't think so to see you now.'

Charles watched the dancers, his expression very far away. 'Perhaps he would not. I hope he would not. He passed away many years ago, and I fear that was when I realised he was entirely correct. I had a duty to the estate and its people, to my family.' He smiled at Adele as she swirled past with Mr Bellingham. 'Adele is the one who inherited any artistic talent in our family. I'm sure it came from her mother. Elspeth was a gentle soul who loved to paint and sing, just as her daughter does.'

'I did love hearing her play earlier. So beautiful, so full of emotion and imagery. Few people truly feel the music in that way. She seems far out of the common way of accomplishments! And so pretty. If you needed help finding someone, you are welcome to come to the agency. I could…' She fell silent, as she realised Adele could easily find a nice young man all on her own, if she could just learn to trust herself to see to her future. Mary wanted to help, not as a matchmaker but merely as a friend.

'You think you could make her a fine match. One high in Society?'

Mary was flustered. She had not thought Charles

would care about such things, as so many parents did. 'Of course I could try. We do sometimes have titled gentlemen come to us, even a poet or two.' Or at least they once had. She would need to find such patrons again. That was what she needed to concentrate on, not Charles's green eyes and broad shoulders. 'But someone like Adele has no need of such assistance. If you wanted a titled match…'

'I want only her happiness, her security. And I'm not sure she is in no need of assistance.' He suddenly stood very straight, a determined look on his face. 'I have been told she is, in fact, of need of a lady's help in these matters. A mother figure. I try my best, try to do as her mother would have wished, yet for a man on his own…'

Mary suddenly realised what he spoke of—marriage. Not for Adele but for himself, to give Adele a mother. 'You—you seek a wife.' She had not meant to blurt it out so plainly. Images flew through her mind, of Charles arm in arm with a veiled lady as they marched down the aisle. A lady who was certainly not Mary.

Charles shook his head. 'Not really. Perhaps. I fear I am too set in my ways. I don't know many people. Penelope does say…'

The music for the next dance set ended, and couples changed places on the dance floor. She saw

Adele claimed by another young man who led her to their spot, even as the girl studied the room for someone else. Probably her unsuitable Mr Clark. 'Well, I always think dancing is the perfect way to meet and observe new people.'

He nodded decisively, as if she had given him some assignment he must carry out. 'I quite agree. Would you do me the honour of this dance, Miss St Aubin? You could help me learn to observe, tell me what you know of the people around us.'

'I would be happy to assist, Mr Campbell.'

He offered his arm, and she slid her gloved hand over his sleeve, feeling the tense flex of his forearm beneath her touch, the strength of him. The solid warm reality. She was going to dance with *Charles*! It would be painful to show him eligible ladies, talk of his prospects without her, but she would at least have this moment to remember, to imagine when days were too dismal. That was surely something.

They took their places in the figures of the dance, yet Mary thought he looked rather…odd. Haunted maybe.

'I fear I should warn you,' he said tightly. 'I am not a good dancer. At all.'

Mary laughed. How could he not be? He moved with such an easy, athletic grace, a man who was obviously accustomed to walking and riding. And she had seen him play cricket, the flex and taut power of his back under his shirt, the swift, loping stride of his run. She shivered. 'I am sure that cannot be true. But such a hint of modesty in a gentleman is most commendable.' She often said that to men who came to the agency, a gentle hint to rein in the boasting a wee bit. Not that she had ever heard a whisper of boast from Charles.

He laughed, too, that rough, whisky-dark sound that made her feel so very hot and cold all over. 'This is no modesty, I fear, but *treowth*. I do well enough riding, and luckily can walk straight down a lane without disgracing myself falling over, but when the music begins I sprout two left feet.'

'Mr Campbell...' The music began, a lively polka, and she couldn't say any more. He took her hand and they spun away. At first, it was giddy fun, and made her laugh as the lights of the room blurred around her. But soon enough she saw all too well what he meant by 'two left feet.' He nearly sent them careening into another couple, not once but twice, and got his foot tangled in her skirt. By the time the music ended and he escorted her to the edge of the floor, she was out of breath and dizzy.

'I—you were quite correct, I fear,' she said breathlessly. 'It is not modesty.'

He grimaced. 'I did warn you, Miss St Aubin.'

'Indeed you did. But most ladies need a bit more than a warning.'

He laughed ruefully. 'They want to be swept around the floor, feeling lighter than a cloud.'

'That is one way to open a small door to a lady's heart.' And his smile was another, that self-deprecating quirk to those sensual lips. A lady would forgive much for that.

She glimpsed Mr Overbury making his way through the crowd and knew she had to talk quickly. 'Mr Campbell, may I speak freely?'

'Oh, I do count on it, Miss St Aubin. I'm a rough Scotsman, you know, delicate hints fly right over my thick head.'

Mary very much doubted that. Not much seemed to get past him. And his head was very pretty.

'Tell me, then,' he said. 'If such a hopeless dancer as myself came to your agency, would you turn him away forthwith?'

Mary laughed. They would have ladies pounding down their door if he was a patron. 'Not if they were otherwise suitable, of course not. We are here to *help* people. It's what I enjoy the most about my work.'

He studied her carefully, until she could feel her cheeks turning warm. She had to resist the urge to flap her fan. 'I can see that. You have a kind heart, and you have built a very useful business.'

'Well,' Mary whispered, 'I do think—I would recommend dancing lessons. Dancing is indeed one of the finest ways to become acquainted with someone. It's a chance to stand close, to have a quiet word together. We do have dancing masters we vouch for, along with painting teachers, French and German speakers, elocution tutors. Not that you need those, I'm sure.' She studied him again, the sharp angles of his elegant, powerful face, his sensual lips. 'Are you interested in lessons? Or perhaps a tutor for Adele? Our agency's services...'

She paused. What would she say if he did want to hire the agency for more than help with dancing? Could she find it within her to help him make a match with someone else?

'Adele is already a fine dancer. She's just in danger of being disgraced by her clumsy uncle.' His gaze swept over the crowd, and she wondered if he sought a lady he found beautiful.

And she saw that Mr Overbury, who had been providentially halted by a group of his friends, was headed her way again, scowling at Charles as if jealous. If only he had reason to be, she thought with a sigh.

Charles went on. 'I really should become a passable dancer if we're to move in London Society circles. And Adele deserves to find a good match. If I can help her in any small way...'

'With dance lessons?'

'Aye. But I would rather—well, that is...' He hesitated.

'Yes?'

'I would rather no one know of my faults on the dance floor.'

Mary smiled in understanding. '*I* know. And I certainly do not think less of you.' On the contrary. It made him seem even more endearing to her.

'Exactly. Could I engage you, or if you prefer your agency, to assist me with a lesson or two?' He smiled at her hopefully.

He wanted to dance with *her*? Mary sucked in a deep breath, trying not to feel such excitement at the thought of having her toes trod on by him again. By being close to him. 'You want me to teach you to dance?'

'Just a lesson or two. To show me a few simple steps.'

'Dancing is an art! To become skilled, one needs many lessons.'

'Many?' He frowned. 'I don't plan on dancing so very much. Card rooms at parties are much more suited. I just want to not disgrace my family name by barrelling over all the couples on the floor.'

Mary was temped. *Very* tempted. Surely it could do no harm to dance once or twice? To help out a—a friend? 'I shall think about it. Perhaps you could help *me* with something, as well?'

'Certainly. Just name it, Miss St Aubin.'

She was tempted again, this time to demand a kiss as payment. But she knew better. She was older than Adele and meant to be wiser. She had to guard her heart. 'See that man over there?' she whispered, and nodded towards Overbury. He was searching the crowd with a most determined look on his face. 'Could you just take my arm and steer me away from him?'

Charles scowled at the man. 'Is he pestering you?'

'No, I wouldn't say that, exactly.' Yet she would. 'He wishes for the agency to find him the perfect wife, and he decided long ago it was me.'

'One can hardly blame him for thinking that,' Charles said, casting her an admiring smile that made her feel terribly warm all over. 'But surely he knows a gentleman should never press his attentions on a lady once rebuffed. I shall speak to him.' He started to stride off, his face dark and thunderous. Mary wondered how Adele's Mr Clark wasn't yet scared away.

She grabbed his arm. 'No, no. I do thank you for being my white knight, but I am sure Mr Overbury will soon find a more suitable *tendre* and forget all about me.'

He frowned doubtfully, but Mr Overbury did seem rather halted in his tracks. 'If you are certain…'

'Of course. Let us just walk over there for a moment and try some of those ices.' She did not need a scandal for the agency if two men argued over her in a ballroom. But she had to admit, she felt rather glowing and satisfied to have had a defender for a moment. Especially if it was Charles.

Penelope came to them through the crowd, a worried frown on her face. 'Oh, Charles, I fear Adele slipped out of my sight for a moment, and now I cannot find her! I thought she was dancing with that nice Mr Bellingham.'

Charles's laughter turned in an instant to taut watchfulness, chagrin. 'No, Pen, it's my fault. I never should have asked such a favour of you when you have much to do as hostess. I will go in search of her. She can't have gone far. Is Clark here, then?'

'I—I don't know. He could have slipped in,' Pen fretted.

Mary thought they seemed more worried than they should. Just because Adele has a pash of sorts, she *was* at a party and could be with any number of people. 'Are you sure she has gone off with this man in particular?'

'No, but one of the footmen thinks they glimpsed someone rather like Mr Clark earlier. I just thought...' Pen shook her head. 'How silly of me!'

'I'm sure she's close by. Come on, I'll help you find her,' Mary said, and led the way through the room.

They finally glimpsed Adele near one of the windows, standing with a man whose back was to them. He touched her hand, and she smiled shyly. A smile that faded when she saw her uncle stalking towards her. The man hurried away, and Adele stared after him.

'Adele,' Charles said, 'I thought I asked you not to talk to that man again.'

Adele set her chin stubbornly and fussed with a ribbon on her sleeve, not looking at her uncle. 'It's a party! Am I not meant to speak to anyone? How unfair you are, Uncle.'

He opened his mouth as if to argue with her, which Mary knew would go nowhere. She shook her head at him and smiled at Adele. 'Will you walk with me, Miss Stewart? We can discuss the new fashion in sleeves, I am not at all sure about them.'

Adele nodded, still refusing to look at her uncle. Mary took the girl's arm and turned in the other direction, hoping she could distract her while Charles calmed himself. She had once been young herself; such infatuations had to be handled carefully. Grown-up infatuations had to be, as well, she found the more she was around Charles.

Charles watched Mary and Adele as they strolled across the room, arm in arm. At last, Adele smiled, a tiny quirk, but it was there. He felt the warmth of relief and gratitude for Mary's words of reassurance, the way she helped Adele now.

He'd been racked with worry over his ward ever since they came to Bath, and she seemed to drift further and further away from him as he struggled to understand what she was going through. He marvelled now to see how easily Mary understood, knew how to speak to Adele, speak to her as a young lady, a person, at a difficult moment that left him baffled. He was not used to such emotions—not even his own.

Mary just understood. She listened. She even laughed at how terrible a dancer he was and made him laugh at himself! That was a failing he couldn't show anyone, only her. When he looked into her eyes, saw her smile, he would trust her with anything.

And she was so very beautiful. Achingly so, with her sun-gold hair and those dimples set in peachy, creamy skin. Even the way she walked, slow and easily graceful, was lovely. She made him feel so many things he'd thought forgotten in the mists of time. Things like laughter.

Penelope came to him and took his arm, urging him to stroll with her as Mary and Adele were lost to sight through the crowd. 'Mary St Aubin is a wonder, is she not?'

Had Pen read his mind? Seen his infatuation? He looked at her sideways, trying to read her expression. 'She is very kind, yes.'

'Certainly she is that. She is also pretty and full of fun. You could use that very much.' She squeezed his arm. 'Don't worry, Charles. I am sure between us all we can steer Adele, and you, in the right direction.'

'Do you think so? I am a hopeless case, but Adele is young.' And he could not fail her, could not fail Adele's mother.

'It's not easy being her age, on the cusp of grown-up life but not there yet, so uncertain. And with her parents gone, as well.' Pen shook her head sadly. 'If she had an aunt…'

Charles laughed. 'Are you going to urge me to wed again?'

'I don't mean to be a nuisance, my dear! But to have someone to share life with can be sublime. To share worries and joys, have someone to help and advise us, to be with us in the dark of the night. Yes, it's wonderful.'

'Not always,' he said, thinking of Aileen, their quarrels and unhappiness. The way she had run away rather than stay by his side a moment longer.

'You must find the right one, just as I did with my Anthony,' Pen said. 'Third time was the charm. The Confidential Agency could be of help, if Mary herself won't have you.'

'No, not the agency,' he said, more sharp than he intended. He could not ask Mary for that. 'No, I should not wish to trouble them, they must be busy.'

Pen frowned doubtfully. 'If you say so. There are many other ways to meet suitable ladies, especially in Bath. The Pump Room, card parties, garden fêtes at Sydney Gardens…'

'I am quite well just as I am, Pen, I promise.'

'Are you?' she murmured.

He gave her a teasing grin. 'Am I such a pitiable figure, then? Am I in my dotage now and need friends to find me a kind lady to wheel my chair about?'

Penelope laughed. 'Certainly not! I had two older husbands myself, and you, our Scots *gaisgeach*, are nothing of the sort. But having someone to confide in, talk to, laugh with—and, er, other things, of course.' Her cheeks slowly turned pink, making him chuckle.

He then pictured Mary and those 'er, other things,' saw her in a firelit bed, her golden hair tumbling down over her naked white shoulders, and his laughter faded. He feared he blushed a bit himself. 'If it comes to that, Pen, I know where to look. And to find a wife, as well, but I shall not.'

'Do you know where to look, though?' She scowled at him impatiently. 'Sometimes, it is all right under your stubborn nose.'

Chapter Four

Mary often thought of the Pump Room as a sort of second office for the agency. Everyone came there, newcomers and old Bath residents alike, mingling under the chandeliers, partaking of the vile water, chatting, watching. She could meet anyone there, perusing the guest book, taking tea, getting caught up on all the gossip. One of her very favourite parts of visiting the rooms was definitely *not* trying the waters herself, but seeing a happy couple or two who had formed their match with a sprinkling of her help.

She stepped into the Pump Room the morning after Pen's soirée, ducking out of the grey drizzling day into a haven of pale green and cream and gold, of sparkling chandeliers, soft harp music. People strolled by the long tables dispensing the water and along the windows draped in green taffeta, so civilised and ordinary. She waved at a few people she knew, including Mademoiselle Sandrine, who of course had the finest ensemble in the whole room. Mary took a cup of tea in lieu of the water and went to examine the arrival book.

'Miss St Aubin! How delightful to see you here,' she heard a cheerful voice call, and turned to Lady Pennington, née Miss Evans, one of the agency's greatest successes. Her father was a wealthy merchant, new money, and her mother had determined that her daughter would raise them up in Society by marrying well, no matter what the daughter herself thought. And the daughter only wanted her studies, her own interests! Once there had been a thought to match her with Fred, one of Mary's few mistakes. But now all were happy.

'Lady Pennington! I would have thought you would be at Northland Park, preparing for your house party.' They lightly kissed cheeks, and Mary admired her gown, a walking dress and spencer of amethyst velvet trimmed with glossy sable that matched her small hat. Lady Pennington had been a most questionable dresser under the supervision of her mother, all orange bonnets and bright green pelisses with feathers, but now she was quiet the model of style.

'We leave tomorrow. The staff there is so frightfully efficient, I fear there isn't much for me to do except be in their way.' Her husband, tall and lanky with shimmering golden hair, came to her side, and she beamed up at him as he took her hand. 'We have been so eager to hear Dr Farnon's lecture on the botany of Brazil this evening before we leave. Will you be attending?'

Mary smiled. The Penningtons' scientific interests did rather make her feel wooden-headed, but it would be lovely to see their fine home, see their happiness. 'That lecture does sound fascinating. But I confess, what I am really looking forward to is your party! I haven't had the prospect of such a very merry Christmas in some time.' She remembered the festive season when she was a girl at the vicarage, before her dear mother died. The music, the scent of evergreen boughs and spiced wine, laughter. Family.

'Well, I do hope no one will leave our home without having a great deal of fun. We're so eager to share it,' Lord Pennington said. He saw one of his scientific cronies in the crowd and left his wife to stroll about the room with Mary. They walked beside the windows, looking down on the baths below, steam rising from the waters into the cold air.

'I do hope our guests will enjoy themselves,' Lady Pennington said. 'My parents always had such a lavish celebration. Ours will be quieter, more in an old style, I think, but still merry. Cosy.'

'It sounds perfect. And Northland sounds like a splendid setting for it all.' Northland Park was a grand estate, not far from Bath, which had been first built in the Elizabethan era, but had been sadly abandoned for years. The Penningtons had been working since their marriage to restore its grandeur.

'And a perfect setting for romance?' Lady Pennington said teasingly.

Mary wondered if she had noticed how she looked at Charles, and felt that terrible warm blush coming back on her again. She wished she had not worn the high-necked pelisse! It was too hot in the Pump Room by half. 'Whatever do you mean?'

'I mean, after all you did for me and my William, how splendid it has all been since we married, I want to help as many people as I can find just such a contentment. So I have invited a person or two who I think might like to be happily wed and need a bit of help. As I did.'

'Oh, Lady Pennington. How kind of you to think of them, and of my agency. I should not want to intrude on your party, though.'

'How ever could you? You are the dearest of friends, you helped me when I needed it most, and now I want to help you if I can.' She looked rather concerned as she took Mary's arm. 'Your agency is a great benefit to those of us who are a bit out of the common way, and who wish to find a sponsor who is the same. I wish to see it prosper. It *must* prosper!'

Something in her vehement tone caught Mary's attention and concern. 'Have you heard any whisper that it might not prosper?' she asked carefully.

Lady Pennington smiled gently. 'I just think your work is so very important. I hope you can help out a few friends you'll meet at my party, that's all! Oh, look, there is Lady Hanson. What a splendid hat! We must speak to her and find out who her milliner is.'

Lady Pennington hurried away through the crowd, and Mary trailed after her, trying to keep smiling, to hold her chin up. Were people watching her now, shaking their heads with pity?

That poor St Aubin girl...the last one unmarried! How can she expect to make fine marriages for others if she hasn't one herself? they might say.

She glimpsed Penelope and Adele across the room, near one of the tall windows, and wondered with a jolt of bright excitement if Charles was there, too.

As she drew nearer, she saw they seemed to be having some sort of disagreement. Adele looked on the verge of tears, waving her lace-gloved hands as Pen shook her head. Mary glanced over her shoulder, wondering if she should retreat before they saw her, but it was too late. Pen caught a glimpse of her, and a smile transformed her expression. She nudged Adele, who also looked up and smiled at Mary, her eyes still glistening with anger or sadness.

'Mary,' Pen said, 'how lovely you look today! What a beautiful pelisse. Mademoiselle Sandrine is so clever.'

'Yes, indeed. She is a wizard of taffeta and beads!' Mary answered, trying to match Pen's determined merriness, to pretend she'd seen no quarrel. 'They do say she's begun rather specialising in wedding gowns, as well, that her beautiful creations bring luck to any bride.'

'And so they would,' Pen said.

'Well, Uncle Charles refuses to let me order a gown from her for myself, even though Aunt Pen's dress looked well on me at her party,' Adele said with a pout. 'He says not until I am older! How cruel he is.'

Mary gave her a sympathetic smile, though 'cruel' was one of the last words she would use to describe Charles Campbell. *Handsome*, of course. *Rugged. Swoony.* Was that last a word? No matter, he certainly made her want to swoon when he was nearby. But cruel? No. Pulchritudinous. Yes, that was another one...

No. She wouldn't start sighing like a love-struck schoolgirl right here in the middle of the Pump Room! She had decided firmly on focusing on her work, not on good-looking gentlemen who didn't know how to dance.

'Mademoiselle Sandrine's designs *do* tend to be rather sophisticated, but I'm sure you will be able to order her creations soon enough,' Mary said. 'And this dress you're wearing is quite delightful. That shade of green suits your lovely hair so well.'

Adele glanced down at the skirt of her pale green walking dress. 'Do you think so, Miss St Aubin? Truly? I hoped that—well, that *someone* would admire it, but he—that is, *they*—are not here...'

Mary exchanged an alarmed glance with Pen. Charles had said Adele was caught in the web of an unsuitable infatuation, but she did seem to dwell on her doomed romance rather a great deal. Mary saw that it needed to be nipped in the bud. 'But I do see so many admiring glances coming in your direction, especially after everyone heard your exquisite gift for music last night,' she said, trying to keep things light and encouraging, to make Adele smile and perhaps see how many possibilities were out there for her. 'And how fortunate I am to see you both today! I was just speaking with Lady Pennington about her Christmas house party, and I know I'll see you there. I'm so excited to see the estate after they've done so much work on it in the last few months. They say it is quite a showplace.'

'It should be a most merry Christmas,' Pen said. She squeezed Adele's arm. 'And I'm sure we can persuade Charles to let you have a new frock or two for the occasion! You will be the diamond of the party.'

Adele smiled, but it looked rather sad. Mary felt for her, remembering too well how it was to be so young, so full of yearnings that couldn't be understood or fulfilled, confused and unsure but wanting so much to rush ahead. She'd seen how Ella had sacrificed for their future, to take care of Mary, and realised that was what life was about, not about romantic dreams. When she met Charles, though, those old fantasies had come rushing back. It must be even harder to be young, to be stumbling along blindly in life, with no mother. Mary remembered that, too, but at least she'd had Ella. And she couldn't let Ella down now by losing their business. 'You must tell me what you plan to order. I confess I am rather worried that my own wardrobe will not be worthy of such an occasion…'

She managed to distract Adele with chatter about

fashion, and left her with Pen and a few others while she went to fetch them some tea. As she studied the crowd around her, she heard a whisper from the two ladies in line ahead of her.

'That Stewart girl,' one of them said, catching Mary's attention with the mention of Adele's name. 'She should have a care, showing such favour to a man like Peyton Clark. Have you heard that his uncle declares he will cut him off, his behaviour has been so bad? Someone should counsel her about the company she keeps.'

'Poor girl, I do feel for her,' the other lady clucked. 'What can one expect from a girl who has lived in Scotland?'

Mary felt a flash of anger on Adele's behalf, then fear. Maybe Charles was not overreacting, if Adele's partiality for Clark was already seen. She hurried out of line to look for Adele, hurrying through the crowd so quickly she tripped over her hem and started to fall, right in front of everyone. Someone suddenly caught her arm before she could make a cake of herself, and she gasped.

She peeked up and saw it was Charles who held her. Charles, who looked down at her in concern.

'Do forgive my clumsiness again, Miss St Aubin,' he said, in that Scots burr that never failed to thrill her to her very toes. 'I've been too long from civilisation, you see.'

'Not at all,' Mary said, and was deeply chagrined to hear how breathless she sounded. She had promised herself to treat him with only politeness and professionalism, and not get carried away admiring his glorious eyes and handsome shoulders! Now here she was, not moments later, sighing over him right in the middle of the crowded Pump Room.

To be absolutely fair, though, he was staring as well. His expression was rather thunderstruck, and time seemed to hover in stillness. Mary started to wonder if she had a smudge on her nose and automatically reached up to check. The teacup she held rattled in its saucer.

'Here, let me take that,' he said, and reached for the trembling cup. His fingers slid over hers as he took the cup, warm and strong.

'Thank you. I just need to return to Pen, I promised her some tea. I was just talking with her and Adele.'

'Shall we go find them, then?' he said. 'I did tell her I would catch up with them as quickly as I could, after I saw to some business this morning. I fear Pen will start to feel like Adele's gaoler.'

'Of course.' They turned and strolled the other length of the room, Mary trying to ignore the eyes that watched them. 'Adele really is such a lovely girl. Such a sensitive heart.'

Charles smiled wryly. To her surprise and delight, a dimple appeared just above the carved line of his jaw, making him look so young, so adorable. 'Perhaps *too* sensitive. I fear I indulge her novel reading and poetry writing, there isn't much else to do at Castle Campbell, and she's convinced she must have just such a tortured love.'

'I well remember such feelings at her age. I pity her. It can be so confusing, so overwhelming, and when we are young we have no experience to tell us how quickly it passes! Especially a young lady who feels so deeply, as I suspect Adele must.'

'She takes after her mother in that. Elspeth was also a kind, romantical soul.' His eyes were shadowed by sadness as he thought of Adele's mother. 'I would never want to crush that out of Adele. To sympathise with and understand others is surely a great gift.'

'It can be, yes.' Mary thought of her work, of the satisfaction she gained in helping people find their happiness. Maybe Adele needed similar work. 'But without a leavening of good sense, it can be a danger, as well.'

'That is what I fear.' He suddenly raked his hand through his hair in a frustrated, quick gesture. 'Oh,

Miss St Aubin. I'm afraid I am failing her mother. I promised I would take care of their daughter, but I am an old bachelor who only knows how to run an estate in remote Scotland. Manoeuvring through Society, shepherding a young girl through its perils, is beyond me, try as I might.'

'I can see that you care a great deal for your niece. She is fortunate to have you looking out for her. But it's true that steering her through a first Season will be no simple matter. You must know the other families, especially their sons, know which parties to attend and which to avoid, what to converse about, how to entertain.'

'That's another thing I fear. Pen and Anthony are a great help, but I don't wish to monopolise their time and energy with my own problems. They are still newlyweds. I'm not sure what to do at times.'

'Does she seem serious about this Mr Clark, then?'

Charles frowned. 'She says so, and I do often catch her sighing and writing unfortunate poetry rhyming with his name.'

Mary couldn't help but smile at the image. 'Bad poetry. Oh, dear.'

'Indeed. But I can't tell if it's a *tendre* or...'

'Or a fantasy. Yes. I'm sure that when she can make more friends her own age, meet more young gentlemen, this will fade. In the meantime...' But assuring words failed her. She was worried about Adele. It was so easy to make a mistake at her age, to take a wrong step that led to a great fall. She would have to make enquiries about that Mr Clark.

'It's that meantime I worry about.' He stared out the window with a faraway expression, as if he didn't see the snow, the passing people at all, but a bleak future. 'You say you understand her feelings. Were you in love when you were her age?'

Mary laughed, thinking of her youthful flights of fancy. It was obvious when she stood next to him that they were not all quite behind her, not when the lemony scent of his cologne, the sight of the curl at the end of his hair, made her giddy. 'It was not all that long ago! But, yes, I fell in and out of love all the time back then, as much as I could in our little village. I even wrote poetry! I had Ella to look after me, and nothing went beyond that secret poetry. I certainly have learned prudence, learned to use all that I have seen of human nature at the agency to read people in a somewhat deeper way. Adele will do the same.'

Charles studied her closely, and Mary had that sensation he always gave that he could really *see* her, see beyond her easy smiles to the worries she held deep inside. 'I confess I'm quite curious about your youthful *amours*, Miss St Aubin. Were they much like Adele's dastardly Mr Clark?'

'Not at all. There was not much scope for dastards in our village! And for all Mr Clark's seeming failings as a suitor, I admit he does have a rather nice face and lovely golden hair. I liked that sort of thing, too. But they were local farmers and squires, perhaps a visiting poet or two, that's all. I sought an intelligent, curious mind and kind understanding as well as blond curls!'

He tilted his head, still watching her. Seeing her. 'And if you were to choose a suitor now, would you seek those same qualities? Intelligence, kindness and golden hair?' He ran a hand through his decidedly dark hair.

'I—I'm not sure,' Mary stammered. 'I never intend to wed myself. I have my business to attend to, and seeking love for others brings me my greatest happiness now. I help them find their perfect matches.'

A muscle flexed in his jaw. 'I, too, have vowed to never marry again. I was a poor enough husband once.'

Mary felt the cold touch of sadness as she watched the dark cloud drift over his handsome face. Had he loved his wife so very much, then, that no one could replace her? 'I am sorry. It's a loss to the ladies of Bath.'

He gave her that crooked little smile that made her breath catch. 'I am sure they are heartbroken. But I was a terrible husband, I wouldn't inflict that on anyone else. I never imagined I would have to act as a father to a young lady, either.' He glanced around the room, as if suddenly remembering they were not alone at all but in the midst of a watching crowd. 'Should we find Pen? I fear this tea has grown quite cold.'

'Yes, certainly,' she murmured, though she couldn't forget his words. He would be a terrible husband. She was beginning to worry that she could not agree.

Charles poured himself a brandy to take away the taste of the vile Pump Room water and listened as Adele ran up the stairs and slammed her chamber door. All the way home, she cried and declared him 'the cruellest man *ever*' for not understanding her love.

He shook his head as her footsteps pattered overhead, and took his drink to the window to study the scene outside, the park across the street, the people hurrying past the honey-coloured buildings as rain threatened again. Yet he didn't really see the clouds, the chimneys, the nodding flowers in the park; he only saw Mary St Aubin's face as she laughed up at him in the Pump Room, her face glowing like summertime. Her laughter making him want to laugh, too, making him feel young and free again.

He hadn't felt that way in a very long time. Or—ever, really. That sort of happiness, of fun, could be quite addictive.

He frowned as he tried to remember his younger days, that heady time when he first met Aileen and was so sure in his recklessness and headstrong heedlessness that he was in love. That he could never make a mistake.

Then he inherited his father's estates and had to grow up in a great hurry. The days of running around town from dances to dinners to horse races with Aileen were over, and by then he had begun to tire of it anyway, to long for something more. He hadn't been able to see the cracks, the uncrossable crevice between them. Aileen did not like the serious Charles. She wanted a rake, a rogue, a person he could no longer be. He longed for a wife to help him, make a life with him, work beside him, someone he could help in return. He couldn't go back.

He frowned now to remember those dark, confusing days, that time when he could not be what his wife wanted. It had long kept him from marrying again, even as he knew he might have to.

And there had been no other lady to capture his fascination. Not until Mary and her golden laughter.

Mary, who liked the social life of Bath, he knew that from what Pen had said, from what he'd seen in Mary's smiling ways in the card room, on the dance floor. A cold castle might not suit her, might make her unhappy as Aileen had been. He feared he could no longer trust his judgement.

A crash sounded overhead, and he winced. He also doubted his judgement in matters of parenthood. He saw too much of his old youthful infatuation now in Adele, and he ached for her. Young love was not the merry thing poetry said it was, it was perplexing and painful, and he could not persuade her it would pass. He could only try to protect her until it *did* pass. And he seemed to be fumbling badly with that.

'*Baw,*' he muttered, and tossed back the last of his brandy. He couldn't sort out matters of the heart as easily as he could an account sheet for his estate, and that was a shame. He could only enjoy Mary's company while he had it, and store it up for the return of cold, lonely days.

Chapter Five

'I don't like the look of that sky, Miss Mary,' her maid Daisy clucked as she helped her into her warmest pelisse. 'Are you sure you should go out today?'

Mary glanced out the window. It was indeed a grey day, but then it always was at that time of year in Bath. The pale, watery yellow sun had not made an appearance from behind the clouds for hours. But she longed for a nice long walk to clear her head after a sleepless night worrying about Charles and what she'd heard from enquiries about Mr Clark. 'I won't be long, Daisy. I did promise I would call on Mrs Heston and her son today.' Mr Heston wanted to wed but was painfully shy, and Mary needed every client she could find for the agency. If a house call was required, she would do it. 'I'll take Miss Muffins with me.'

The terrier perked up from where she hid under a

chair and wagged her tail at the promise of a walk. Daisy snorted and handed Mary her hat and gloves. 'Fat lot of good she'd be if it snows. She'd be buried in a drift right off with those short legs.'

Miss Muffins huffed at the insult.

'I doubt it will snow more than a few flakes. This is Bath, after all! Rain, certainly. Snow, probably not.' Though Mary was really not sure. There *had* been more snow than usual lately. But she had to go. 'I'll return by teatime, Daisy.'

She took up Miss Muffins's lead and left the cosy confines of their home and office. The day was quite dark and grey as she made her way out of town towards her potential client's house. She passed a row of cottages, a half-timbered inn, a farmhouse gate. She tried to think only of her patrons but found her thoughts turning more and more to Charles, as they had much too often of late. 'Focus, focus,' she whispered as she made her way towards the house.

By the time she left, she felt rather optimistic about the possible patrons and matches she could suggest for them, and quite pessimistic about the weather. She glanced up into the charcoal-coloured sky, the snow that was starting to fall around her, as she and Miss Muffins hurried back the way they had come. Daisy was quite right, she should not be walking alone with snow coming harder, faster every instant. She'd gone too far from her patrons' house to turn back and was too far from her own home. Miss Muffins whined and pulled back on her lead, no help at all.

'Miss St Aubin!' she heard someone shout, the words almost carried away on the wind.

From the fog and swirling flakes emerged a curricle. A solid, strong figure wrapped in a blue greatcoat sat high on the seat, like a bird of prey swooping down from the snowy sky.

'Miss St Aubin, there you are,' a man said, in a rough Scots brogue. A very *familiar* brogue. 'Blast it, but I'm glad to find you. Here, get in at once.'

'Mr Campbell?' she gaped. Indeed it was, she saw as he leaped down and hurried around to her side, his eyes glowing jewel-green in the gloom. 'What are you doing here?'

'Pen called on you, and your maid said you had gone out, and she was worried about you in this weather. What were you thinking, woman?'

Mary almost laughed at his abrasive tone. She really rather liked being called *woman* in that tone. 'I had to meet with someone for the agency. I couldn't disappoint them.' Or lose their possible custom, even for snow.

'Well, come along, I'll see you home.' He swung

her up into his arms as easily as if she weighed no more than a leaf and held her safe above the frozen ground. He settled her on the seat, Miss Muffins on her lap, and urged the horses ahead again. The snow swirled so heavily now she could barely see ahead of them. She could only lean against him, feel the heat of him as her protection against the storm.

Soon enough it became clear they could go no farther. 'There's an inn just ahead,' she called near his ear, above the howl of the wind. 'I saw it when I was walking out. We could stop there for an hour.' And then she would be alone with him at an inn. She knew it couldn't be helped, but her mind was awhirl with images of what could happen at inns.

She shook away such thoughts and gestured to the old half-timbered building as it came into view through the haze.

'You're right, I think we should rest here a while, wait for the weather to clear,' he shouted over the whine of the wind. 'It's not far back from here, but with this visibility...'

Mary peered into the swirling white ahead of them and nodded. She was certainly nervous at the thought of being alone with him, of guarding her feelings every moment, but she saw the sense in this suggestion. He drew to a halt in the small courtyard of the inn and was helping Mary down from the carriage seat when the door squealed open. A square of welcoming amber light spilled out into the gloom.

'Sir! Do come inside right away!' a woman called. 'Were you caught unawares in this storm? Frightfully sudden it was.'

'Indeed. I'm very glad we found the haven of your establishment when we did,' Charles answered. He took Mary's arm in his strong, sure grip, even as her legs wobbled and she feared she would fall. He led her towards the welcoming light of the door, keeping her close.

The landlady, plump and red-cheeked, clucked over their frozen state as she ushered them into a bright common room, warm with firelight and scented with dried herbs hung from dark old ceiling beams. If they had to land in an emergency harbour, Mary thought, this was not so bad at all.

'Well, now, you and your wife just sit down by that warm fire and I'll fetch you some hot negus. My manservant will see to your horses,' the landlady said. She waved at a maidservant.

Wife. How ridiculously thrilling that sounded, Mary thought. She'd spent so long telling herself she would not marry, that she would never rely on anyone else! Surely that flash of excitement was merely the thrill of playacting, nothing serious. A real marriage, a real attachment, would be too dangerous to the independence she'd nourished. She gave a little cough to cover her absurd delight and glanced around the room with its benches and tables, a few men playing cards and drinking ale, the maidservant who took her damp pelisse and cooed over Miss Muffins. How delicious to think they all considered her to be Mrs Campbell!

And Charles did not disabuse them of this notion. 'How kind you are, madame. I was afraid to have my lady out in this weather any longer.'

'And right you are.' The landlady poured out the steaming mugs of warm negus. 'I do have a private parlour where you might be more comfortable,' she said, scowling at the card players until they looked away. 'Nothing grand, I fear. We usually have just a few travelling merchants, some farmers going into town, who stay here, but sometimes we do have gentry on their way into Bath who use the parlour, so it should be comfortable. There's also a small room adjoining where I can send in some warm water for washing.'

Mary glanced at Charles, whose hair was tousled over his brow, a smudge of dirty snow melted on his sharp cheekbone. She feared she looked even more dishevelled after her walk, a positive ragamuffin. She started laughing and bit her lips to try and stop herself. She was quite afraid if she started laughing at their predicament, she would never stop.

Charles, too, looked very much as if he wanted to laugh. It felt all too cosy, too comfortable being with him then. As if they could read each other's thoughts. 'You're very kind, madame, thank you.' he turned to smile at Mary. 'If you want to wait here a moment, my dear, I will go make certain the room is ready. You can warm yourself here.'

'Of course, my darling lambkin,' she teased. She waggled her fingers at him as he followed the landlady down a corridor, then cuddled Miss Muffins close and sipped at her negus. How fun this could be! If they had to be trapped in the snow, this was the best way to do it. And she would get to be, had to be, alone with him. If she could trust herself, which she wasn't at all sure she could when it came to him.

After a while, she decided she would find him and order some food. The maid directed her to a small chamber at the end of the corridor, and she gathered up Miss Muffins and made her way towards the door.

'Mr Campbell, I do think—' she began, and then froze in her tracks, her words fleeing.

The door to the small washroom was open, and Charles stood there, a towel in his hand, his hair damp and tousled. His face seemed even sharper, more sculpted in the firelight. And his shirt was quite discarded.

He did not look like the marble statues that were thus far her only reference for the male form. They were smooth, nonthreatening, pale. He was burnished gold in the firelight, his skin rippling and satin-like over taut muscles. A pale pink scar was puckered over one shoulder. She could not look away, couldn't move at all, could only stare as her heart beat loudly in her ears. He was—he was *beautiful.*

Mary spun around, closing her eyes tightly. But the image of him was still there, bare skin golden in the firelight. 'I'm so sorry!'

She heard the rustle of fabric, the whoosh of the towel being tossed over a chair. 'Perhaps, under the circumstances, you should call me Charles,' he said, his voiced filled with chagrin *and* amusement. 'Especially as I'm meant to be your husband for the day.'

Mary giggled, seeing every bit of the absurdity of their situation. 'Then you must call me Mary. Or wife o' mine.' She dared turn back around. 'Oh, you shouldn't put that back on yet or you will catch the ague, and this won't be as much fun anymore.' She looked around the small room and found a grey blanket folded over an armchair. 'Here, wrap up in this, and I'll put this shirt by the fire.'

He hesitated, and she wondered if he would squeal and cover up like a shy maiden. He didn't seem at all the sort. He smiled, lazy and heated, alluring. 'If you're sure.'

'There is no sense in anyone becoming ill because of missish manners. I'm not so prim as all that, I hope, and no one can see us here.' There was nothing to fear—except her own feelings. That shivery awareness of his every movement.

She fetched a blanket and wrapped it around his shoulders, trying not to lean into his heat and hold on for dear life.

'Is that painful?' she whispered, and before she could stop herself, she lightly touched that puckered scar along his shoulder.

His shoulders tensed, and his face took on a sharp, wary, watchful expression. 'Not at all. It's quite old. A souvenir of my misspent youth. I fear I was not always so very respectable.'

She was most intrigued. The maidservant arrived then with a tray of food, and she couldn't ask. She went to the small mirror hanging on the wall by the door to distract herself, trying to smooth her tangled hair. He looked like a Greek god in dishabille, and she looked like a street urchin, red-cheeked with cold, smudged and tousled. It was not fair at all.

But there was little enough she could do about it at present. She went to sit in the chair beside his and sliced a bit of ham and cheese for their plates. 'Will you tell me about your youth, then?' she said.

He laughed but seemed to hesitate. 'I'm not sure it's so very interesting. And it would be a long tale.' Miss Muffins came to sit beside him, staring up at him with adoring eyes. Mary feared she was just the same.

She glanced out the window, which was blanketed in swirling snow. 'I think we have time, and I do love a good tale. I promise I'm not so shockable, Mr—Charles, I mean. I can't be in my sort of work. I hear so many things at the agency.' Like about Mr Clark, which she knew she had to tell Charles in turn. But right now she only wanted to hear about *him*.

Miss Muffins fell asleep, and the only sounds for a moment were her little snores and the popping of the fire. It was so warm in there, so cosy, and it felt all too *right*. Too much exactly where she should be, where she longed to be.

'Now that sounds far more interesting than my mundane stories of a rather ordinary youth of sowing wild oats,' he said.

Mary laughed. She wanted to know all about his wild oats, wanted to know everything about him. 'I will give a story for a story, then.'

'Very well. Sounds like a good bargain.' He stared into the crackling red-gold fire for a long moment. The blanket slipped off his shoulder, revealing the pink line of the scar against his fire-lit bronze skin. 'I fear it was a duel over a widow whose affections I was sure were mine alone. I was quite mistaken, but being a hot-headed youth, I could not just laugh it away as any sensible man would. So we fought.'

'And what happened?' she asked breathlessly.

'He left me this, and I left him a nicked wrist, and that was that. I was quite bored with the widow by then, and never fought a duel again. Though I nearly did over a curricle race one summer afternoon, when I was sure my competitor cheated.'

Mary deeply envied that unknown long-ago lady who had duels fought over her like a queen in a knightly tale. Envied her that Charles felt so deeply he carried the scar to that day. What would it be like to be the object of his passion in that way? 'Was the lady grateful for your gallantry?'

He grimaced. 'For a time, yes. Then she married a viscount, and I went on to win a carriage race to Brighton.'

He told a few more tales, voyages to Italy, sailing the Channel, the wild Highlands of his homeland.

'But I think it's you who owes a story now, Mary.'

She sighed. 'I am sure I have nothing to compare to duels and Italy and carriage races! I've always wanted to travel, ever since I was a child and read *La Vita Nuova*. I would sketch what I imagined the Roman ruins looked like, the hill towns of the Cinque Terre, the gondolas of Venice. I thought of the ringing of ancient bells, the smell and warmth of it all. It would take me away from the vicarage for a while.'

'Ah, yes. I remember Pen said you were a vicar's daughter.'

'And a great trial to my good father, I was!' Mary said lightly, remembering the narrow corridors of the vicarage, the constant callers, her father's closed library door. 'Especially compared to Ella, who was always perfect and did just as she should. Our mother died when I was quite small, you see, and Ella took on so many duties in our household. Our father was so distracted by his work. I was always reading poetry and wandering off to daydream in the woods. Except for the time I spent at school. I liked that so much! New friends, tea parties. But that didn't last so very long, and then I was back to reading in the vicarage linen cupboard, which was the only truly warm spot in the place.'

She closed her eyes for a moment, remembering those lonely days. She had decided long ago not to marry, not to divide her attention between the agency that was so important to her, Ella and their independence, and a husband and home. She'd seen such things could not mix, not really. No matter how much she might long for a hearth of her own, a place to belong. She'd managed to push down those longings, bury them in work.

Until she met Charles, that is. Then those old dreams haunted her all over again. She had to remember her resolve.

'You wanted a wider world,' he said quietly.

'Yes, indeed. Like Italy! Or sailing the seas, exploring Persian souks, watching the horse races in Paris, all sorts of things.'

'I admit I read too much poetry myself as a child,' he said, and Mary nodded as she remembered what he said about writing terrible poetry and wandering the hillsides. 'Perhaps that was what led me astray when I left home and went to school, then to university at St Andrews! I wanted to be someone different than my father thought me. I just didn't quite know what.'

'It's funny, I always thought you did rather look

like a poet,' she said, her heart aching at the sad wistfulness she saw on his face when he spoke of his father, his childhood. She glanced away, worried the wine had loosened her tongue, and soon she would be reaching out to smooth back that tempting stray lock of his hair, touching his face and feeling the roughness of his afternoon whiskers against her skin.

He gave her that quirky smile that always made her breath stop. 'Did you indeed? A poet?'

'Certainly. You aren't quite like all the Bath gentlemen, you know. Your hair, which could use a trim, but I hope you will not do such a thing. Your accent.'

He laughed ruefully and ran his hand through the damp waves of his hair. The blanket slipped a bit on his shoulder, making his skin gleam golden in the firelight. Mary took a deep sip of wine.

'I did try penning a verse or two, as I told you,' he admitted. 'But I fear my talents in literature, much like dancing, lay only in appreciation. Not that ladies in my younger days cared about terrible rhymes, as long as I could mention their sky blue eyes.'

'I am sure they didn't mind a jot,' Mary murmured. What would he say in a poem about *her*? She feared she'd never know.

'But I, too, longed for escape when I was young. Life at Castle Campbell was never what you'd call "lively," despite its history of battles and sieges and such. There is only farming, herding, a small village nearby, seeing to tenants. The sky is always grey, the hillsides thorny. I love it now, but back then I wanted life and noise. So as soon as I could, I ran and ran, and kept running—until my father died, and I had to take it on as my own. Then Aileen happened...' His words faded, and he looked very distant. 'Like you, I had a lonely childhood. My parents didn't much like each other and spent time apart as much as possible, neither of them often in the same house as me. I knew Aileen for a long time, and she was so beautiful, so vivacious. I thought in her I might have found a partner, someone to build a life with, you see. It turned out not to be that way.'

Mary thought building a life with Charles would be a grand thing; she couldn't quite believe a lady would run from such a blessing when she had it. Just because Mary had decided long ago not to marry herself did not mean she couldn't see the appeal, especially with a man like Charles. But she could see in his eyes, in their distant expression, in the small frown on his lips, that it hadn't worked out the way he hoped. 'It did not?'

He laughed wryly. 'Not at all. A partner in building a home, a quiet life that really mattered, was
not what Aileen wanted. She longed for parties and
theatres, a city filled with admirers, and who could
blame her. She was young, we both were. I learned
prudence and care. She did not.'

Mary nodded and turned away from him to stare
into the flickering flames in the grate. She saw that
Charles, like herself, would not easily give away
his heart. He'd learned caution, as she had. And
that meant they could not be right for each other.
'Then what happened?'

'Adele appeared, and I had to become fully respectable and dull. Aileen would have hated that.'

Mary would never, ever call him dull. They
stared at each other in the firelight, amid the silence that grew and expanded and echoed, wrapping them both in some spell. He understood her
feelings, her loneliness, and she understood his.
How she longed for more in that moment, longed to
give him everything, know everything about him!
She stood and hurried to the window before she
could act on it and reach out for him.

'I think the snow is slowing down,' she said.
'Surely we could make it back to town before night-
fall.' She hated to think of the scandal if they did
not! And yet she wanted, so very much, to never

leave their warm nest at all. To always be just with him, like that, forever.

He came close to her side. Too close, for now she was wrapped in his heat, his delicious scent. She only wanted to be closer and closer. 'I wish we didn't have to leave so soon,' he said, his accent rough and deep. 'It's so peaceful here, so...'

'Yes,' Mary whispered. It was indeed peaceful. Even the rush of her emotions at being near him felt right when they were there, a part of the world as natural as the snow.

She glanced at him and couldn't turn away. She was sure she would never be able to again, and her heart would tear in two when she was forced to walk away.

As Mary St Aubin stared up at him, her caramel-brown eyes wide and glowing pink lips parted as if she wanted to speak but could not. As she stood so close to him he could smell the sweetness of her lavender perfume, feel the silken brush of her loosened hair against his skin. It was intoxicating. Dizzying. She glowed like an angel, and he very much feared all his hard-won control was slipping beyond his grasp.

It had been a great mistake to be alone with her. He'd known it all along, ever since the instant he saw her looking so forlorn, trudging along the snowy lane. All his rescuing knight instincts had come rushing out as never before. Yet what could he do? He could never have left her alone in the snow or driven through the blinding fog until he wrecked the carriage and they both froze. He was obviously a fool where lovely Mary was concerned, but he hoped he wasn't *that* great a fool. And he would never, ever put her in danger.

Now the silence in that small, intimate room, the warmth of the fire against the cold outside, wrapped around the two of them like a shimmering ribbon that bound them together. Held them close, so close there seemed not even a breath between them. She gazed up at him with those summer sunshine eyes, her lips parted as if she felt just the same as he did, had the same longings to touch, to kiss, and he remembered what it was like when they first met. And how it was when they parted.

He did want her with that all-burning desire, wanted her beauty, her grace, her springtime perfume, her innocence and intelligence. He wanted to kiss those soft lips, taste her strawberry-like essence, feel her slim, graceful body against his, hear her gasp his name. Blast it, he wanted her in his bed! He was just a man, after all, one who hadn't had a woman for some time. Surely that was all this could be—nature.

But even as he told himself it was mere instinct, a man and a woman, Charles knew that wasn't true. It wasn't 'nature'; it wasn't just *any* attractive woman. It was this woman. Mary. It was Mary who tormented him with being so very close and not touching.

He didn't just want her touch, the rush of physical satisfaction. He didn't want to just make love to her, though—curse it—he definitely wanted *that*. Just as much, he wanted her comfort, her wry humour, her quick sense of observation and wisdom about the world around her. He wanted to hear the silver bell music of her laughter, to *make* her laugh. He wanted her body, her kiss, but also—could it be? He wanted her friendship. He couldn't have both. Mixing friendship and passion could surely only lead to temporary reprieve from the cares of life, from old memories. Once the flame burned away, one could be left with a warming glow, but it always seemed to him that it ended rather in cold ashes. He couldn't bear that with Mary. He couldn't take that chance and see it end as it once had when he realised he'd been a fool for what he thought was love with Aileen. If he saw the coldness of contempt, disappointment, in Mary's eyes, his heart wouldn't quite recover.

And that made her very dangerous indeed to his equilibrium.

'Charles?' she said softly, and it was as if someone shook him awake out of a dream. He was afraid he'd been staring at her like a love-struck lackwitted lad, and he laughed at himself.

A little puzzled frown creased between her eyes, and he longed to kiss it away. His adorable, confused angel.

'I'm sorry, Mary,' he said. 'The snow must have set me in a *dwam*.'

'A *dwam*?'

'A swoon, a trance.'

She sighed as she gazed out the window again, fraying but not breaking a bit of that shimmering ribbon of creation. Her pale, perfect cameo profile glowed against the greyish light. 'I did think maybe the snow was slowing a bit, but now it looks as thick as before.'

How he wished the snow would just go on forever and ever, leaving the two of them right where they were, alone together in their own magical spell. But he knew very well it could not last, would never last, and soon enough they would go their own ways. He noticed her shiver and guided her over to the warmth of the hearth.

'Come, let's sit by the fire again, you're cold. There's some more spiced wine, and this bread and cheese.'

She smiled at him, a sudden radiant burst that made him ache to grab her against him, hold her so very close they could never be parted. 'I'm not sure more wine is a good idea. I feel so fuzzy-headed already. But I will have one more drop.' She took the glass, and in return picked up his shirt from where it warmed by the fire and handed it back to him. She turned away as he dressed, her hair sparkling in the light, and he hated how cold it was when she was away from him.

Dressed once more, he sat down across from her at the fireside and poured out the last of the wine. As he passed the goblet to her, Miss Muffins suddenly leaped up into his lap and flopped down with a happy sigh.

'She likes you,' Mary said. 'But then, I suspect most ladies do.'

'Not at all. Adele declares I'm an ogre with no romance in his soul, who wants only to cruelly separate her from her one true love.' He tossed back the last drops of wine as his real-world troubles came back on him. 'If only I really did have a tower where I could lock her up until she's safely betrothed to someone suitable. That would make things so much easier.'

Mary laughed, and there was that bell music again, brightening everything around him. 'It would solve many problems in the world, I'm sure. But then the land would be so cluttered with towers.' She sipped at her wine and told him the gossip she'd heard about Mr Clark, that he had no money of his own, and the uncle he depended upon was on the verge of disowning him for his unruly ways. That he had pursued more than one heiress before. He was truly unworthy of Adele.

'But there may be a simpler way to help Adele than locking her up in towers,' she went on. 'Well, simpler but perhaps not *easy*.'

Charles nodded. When it came to helping Adele, he was very glad to have Mary on his side. To no longer feel so alone. 'I'm eager to hear any advice. I only want to be a good guardian.'

'Another suitor, one just as handsome as Mr Clark, but also respectable and suitable in your eyes, might do the trick. If we could find someone to sweep her off her feet and away from Mr Clark, then…' She snapped her fingers, as if conjuring a match from magic.

Charles felt a spark of hope as he looked at her shining eyes. 'Then she would forget him!'

'Hopefully. Of course, it might be his very lack of suitability and respectability that has her so fascinated right now. Feeling as if she must fight against authority, which is you, to win her love can feel exhilarating. I've seen it so often in poetry-minded girls.'

Charles was enthralled by how Mary looked when caught up in her professional work, her matchmaking. Her eyes sparkled, her hands danced, her toes tapped. He longed even more to kiss her, to feel that sparkle flow into him. 'The *Romeo and Juliet* feeling. I see what you mean. But you have seen a sufficiently alluring Prince Paris come between them?'

'I have, a few times. The trick is finding just the right one, and making sure he feels deeply in love with Juliet. Er...with Adele. And she can never, ever suspect we had anything to do with it. It must appear to be all her own discovery, her heart. There will be a greater selection of princes once she's in London this spring, and she will be so busy with the Season itself. Adele does seem the sort who would very much enjoy shops and galleries, dances and teas.'

'So we must keep her distracted until then?'

'That's the tricky bit.' She chewed thoughtfully on the edge of her thumbnail, staring into the fire as if it might have answers. 'I will look through the agency's files to see if we have any suitable young men. I fear, though, that our client list is a bit— well, not quite as robust as it once was.' Her expression shifted, turning rather sad as she glanced away, and he wanted to fix it for her, repair anything to make her smile again. 'And there is Lady Pennington's Christmas party. Adele will surely enjoy that, and who knows what gentlemen might appear on the guest list.'

And Mary would be at the party. A few days to be with her in the country amid a festive party. That was enticing—and alarming. 'I hope so. As you can see, Mary, I need a great deal of assistance in this Adele endeavour. You're so good with her, making her feel listened to, understood, while I am an old bear who keeps fumbling about the harder I try. I'm sure she would listen to your advice if you would agree to spend time with her at the party. Maybe talk to her all about the delights waiting in the Season, but not for ladies already married to rakes with no fortune.'

Mary laughed again. 'I am not entirely sure *anyone* can turn a young lady from thoughts of forbidden romance.' She tapped at her chin thoughtfully.

'It is so hard that young ladies can so easily ruin their whole lives before they even get a chance to fathom the world around them.'

Charles wondered as he studied her face, her faraway little frown, if that happened to her. He wanted to harm anyone who had ever hurt her. Before he could stop himself, he reached for her hand. Her fingers were soft, warm, so small against his, yet they held so very much. He felt the danger crackling around him, but he raised her hand to his lips and pressed a lingering kiss there, breathing deeply the scent of her perfume.

He glanced up to find her watching him with wide eyes and parted lips, as if captured by the starlit moment just as he was. 'I—I think maybe the snow really has stopped now,' she whispered.

Charles feared his heart had utterly stopped, as well.

Chapter Six

'But I love him! And he loves me. Why can we not be happy? It is so unfair!'

Charles closed his eyes and tried not to sigh as he listened to Adele's wails. It had been going on for an hour, though it felt like days, and yet neither of them seemed able to make the other understand. 'Adele, you must be reasonable...'

She gave another frustrated shriek, and he opened his eyes to see her flop down on a chaise and kick her feet. Sometimes she reminded him so much of her mother—a calm, graceful, grown-up lady— and sometimes she seemed to need leading-strings again. He loved her so much and wanted to scream along with her with his own frustration.

How he longed for Mary, her understanding, her serene smiles, her humour. When she was near, everything seemed brighter, steadier, more hopeful. Easier.

'It is so unfair,' Adele sniffled. Charles's heart ached to see her so unhappy, so lost in uncontrollable feelings she didn't know what to do with. He also laid awake into the night envisaging someone, something, he wouldn't let himself have. His feelings were his own to manage, but surely he could help Adele? Surely he could control her life as he could not his own, could make it turn out right for her?

'I thought the purpose of going to London was to find a husband,' Adele went on. 'Wouldn't it be easier if I married now and saved us the trouble? I know you would rather go back to Scotland.'

She wasn't wrong there. He did rather want to go back to Scotland. Things seemed simpler there, with the crisp wind carrying the smell of heather, with the duties he knew and understood, where there was no lady with melting caramel eyes and tempting laughter. None of this guardian business that always caught him on the wrong foot. But more than that, more than anything, he wanted Adele to be safe.

'Because Mr Clark doesn't have the income to support a family,' he said. He did wish Mary was there, she always had a better way of stating bald, unpalatable facts. 'And his reputation…'

'He is not like that now! He loves me, and he

says that's all that matters. And *income*! Who cares about such trifles when there is *love*?'

Charles struggled not to burst into laughter. 'Oh, Adele. Love, especially that of someone entirely un-reliable, won't put a roof over your head. It certainly won't buy those Mademoiselle Sandrine gowns you love so much. I promised your mother I would pro-tect you.' He knew he sounded like his own father, and he hated that, but he knew it couldn't be helped.

'I wish *you* would fall in love! Properly in love. Then you would know how it feels. The agony of it all.'

Agony. Charles thought of when he first met his wife, Aileen, how young and wild he was, how he couldn't stop thinking about her. Yes, he had been foolish once, too, had not been able to see that lust wouldn't make a marriage. It wouldn't last. At least he'd had other occupations, and Adele did not. 'I do know how you feel. But we all must learn practical-ity one day, my darling. You really are so young. You have to consider your future.'

'I am sure I will never feel differently about him,' she protested. 'Time will change nothing.'

'Then waiting a few months, going to London, will make no difference.'

Adele gave one more frustrated shriek. She

jumped up, ran out of the sitting room and slammed the door behind her.

Charles went to stare out the window at the leaden grey sky, suddenly so tired. He had begun to feel like a trained parrot, bleating the same lines to Adele all the time and never getting through to her.

I wish you would fall in love! she'd cried.

He imagined Mary, walking in the sunlight, smiling up at him, taking his hand. Making everything just as it should be, only with her presence. Yet he could not fall in love again, could not see that light in Mary's eyes fade.

He had to go and get ready for the night's assembly, though, and he found the only thing that made him want to go there at all was the prospect of seeing her again.

Mary climbed down from her carriage at the Assembly Rooms and studied the pillared portico, the golden light spilling from the windows and doors as guests eagerly flocked inside for a respite from the winter's night. She usually much enjoyed her evenings there, enjoyed seeing friends, considering potential matches, having a game of cards, dancing in the elegant pastel ballroom beneath the sparkling chandeliers. Tonight, she felt even more excited—

she might get to see Charles again! She longed to store up every glimpse, every word.

She swam her way through the crowds on the stairs, joined the river of people flowing into the ballrooms, waves of bright silks, pale muslins, waving plumes—and no Charles yet. She took a glass of lemonade from one of the refreshment tables and studied the dancers, amusing herself by making imaginary matches among them.

She glimpsed Ella and Fred dancing, swirling past in a golden haze of happiness as they smiled up at each other. So unfashionable to dance with one's own spouse! But they looked so very happy, no one who saw them could care about fashion. She imagined dancing with Charles like that, moving as one across the floor, eyes for no one except each other. Then she remembered the truth of how he really danced, and she laughed to picture the rest of the couples lying on the floor under the onslaught of his two left feet.

Suddenly, as if summoned by her daydreams, he appeared through the crowd. Taller than everyone else around him, he seemed to dwarf them with his presence. He was dressed in elegant black and white, but she would much rather he wore a blanket again...

No, she told herself sternly, and waved her fan

a little faster. She dared peek at him again and realised Adele was beside him, looking fidgety and distracted as she scanned the crowd, and Charles was frowning.

'Mr Campbell,' Mary said, ever so polite and proper. 'And Miss Stewart. How charming you look! That shade of blue does suit you.'

Adele dragged her attention from the room, and gave a little curtsy. 'Thank you, Miss St Aubin. It's not from Mademoiselle Sandrine, of course, but I did like the lace on the sleeves. If only I *could* have one of her gowns! So artistic, they would suit my own nature so well.' She slid a reproving glance at her uncle. 'I am hoping she can make some of my wardrobe for London, if I must go,'

'And my pocketbook hopes she will not,' Charles said, grumbling through a teasing grin. Even Adele had to give a grudging smile, and Mary had to restrain herself from beaming at him, letting all her feelings pour out of her at his feet.

Mary laughed. 'She is expensive, I daresay, but worth every shilling. She is much in demand. We are fortunate she set up shop here and not in London. But you do show fine taste in choosing that lace, Miss Stewart. It is exquisite.' She took a step closer to Adele, hoping to find a way to distract her from looking for Mr Clark. 'Are you very much looking forward to the Season? I am sure you will find much to delight you there.'

Adele shrugged. 'I am looking forward to the shops. And the museums and galleries, the concerts. I do love music so much. I long to see the Tower and the Elgin Marbles.'

'And looking forward to making new friends?' Charles suggested.

Adele frowned. 'I have enough friends, I think. And one *great* attachment, if only *someone* would listen to me.'

Charles exchanged a long glance with Mary, and she gave her head a little shake. Best not to let such little outbursts take on greater importance, she tried to tell him through her arched brow. She tried to turn Adele's thoughts of 'attachments' by pointing out other gowns, fine jewels, commenting on the music and soliciting her opinion on the orchestra.

As Adele joined the dance and Charles was engaged in conversation about agriculture in Scotland with a group of gentlemen, Mary drifted away to study the crowd. She noticed a mother and her daughter, Lady and Miss Tuckworth, who had made some enquiries about the agency but committed to nothing yet. Mary had rather hoped they would engage her; Miss Tuckworth needed a new coiffure but seemed quite sweet, just the sort of young lady who would suit a young man on Mary's files.

'Miss St Aubin,' Lady Tuckworth said with a sweet, sweet smile, treacly sympathy in her tone that made Mary's teeth ache. 'I'm so happy to see you out and about this evening. We must discuss dear Tabitha's prospects.'

Miss Tuckworth looked as if her 'prospects' were the very last thing she wanted to discuss. She stood behind her mother as if she wanted to hide there, twisting her gloved hands in her yellow-striped skirt.

'I would be happy to, Lady Tuckworth,' Mary said, hoping for one more on the agency's books. Tabitha Tuckworth was exactly the sort she most enjoyed assisting. Like Miss Evans turned Lady Pennington before her, she seemed someone who would bloom once away from her family. Perhaps Mr Heston, who Mary had called on the day of the snowstorm, would do? 'If you would care to make an appointment to call at the office, or I could come to you...'

Lady Tuckworth tilted her head, that sweet, pitying smile still in place, the feathers in her hair nodding. 'I am afraid, Miss St Aubin, that, competent as I'm sure you are at some aspects of such a business, I have some...concerns.'

Mary glanced at Charles, hoping his own conversation meant he could not hear her. She wouldn't want him to think she could not take care of herself! That she could not manage her business. 'Concerns, Lady Tuckworth? I'm sure I can address any reservations you may have. We do have many letters of recommendation.'

'Yet surely most of them came from when Lady Fleetwood and Lady Briggs were in charge of your files? And they are both so very well wed now. A testament to their skills.'

Ah. She *was* the problem. Mary's spinster state. She had feared some potential patrons might think that way—that a lady who cannot find her own match surely couldn't make one for anyone else. Something must be wrong with her! But Mary knew she could see what others needed in romantic attachments far more clearly because she was not blinded by her own emotions.

Not until Charles, anyway. He quite blinded her to all else but him.

'You are so young, Miss St Aubin, and passably pretty,' Lady Tuckworth said. 'You have accomplishments. Dancing, French. If you still cannot make a match for yourself, how can you do so for others? How can you move in the proper Society for making connections?'

'Lady Tuckworth,' Mary said through gritted teeth, trying to keep her smile pasted on. *Passably pretty*, indeed! 'I assure you the agency has many connections, and I have the experience to...'

Lady Tuckworth's head tilted so far Mary feared those feathers would topple her quite over. 'I am just not so very certain...'

'There you are, my dear,' Charles suddenly said. He appeared at her side and took her arm in a loose, gentle clasp. Mary stared up at him in amazement, trying to ignore the warmth of his touch through her glove, the way he smiled at her, bright and dazzling. What on earth was happening? 'I have been looking for you everywhere. Such a crush tonight, don't you agree, Lady Tuckworth? Miss Tuckworth?'

Tabitha and her mother gaped at him, just as Mary was sure she did herself. Tabitha blushed and simpered a little.

'I—yes, indeed, a crush, Mr Campbell,' Lady Tuckworth stammered. 'You are acquainted with Miss St Aubin?'

'Acquainted?' Charles beamed down at Mary, while his widened eyes begged her to play along with whatever he was doing. Her heart pounded so hard she feared the whole assembly could hear. 'We are betrothed.'

'Betrothed?' Tabitha squeaked, a spark touching her for the first time. Perhaps, like Adele, she read romantic poetry. 'How very sweet!'

'Sweet. Yes,' Lady Tuckworth said doubtfully.

Mary froze. Was this a dream? Surely it had to be. For he could not have just said…

That they were betrothed.

'It is quite the secret for now,' Charles said, squeezing her arm. 'Smile,' he whispered to her, and she felt her lips do that automatically. 'You are one of the first to know. I am quite sure we can count on your discretion before the official announcement. We simply could not wait to pledge our troth to each other. We are perfect together.'

Mary knew very well that Lady Tuckworth had not an iota of discretion in her. She beamed at them now, starry-eyed with romance and possible gossip.

Mary tried to keep smiling, to act like this was all quite normal, but she feared her face might crack with it. Had Charles suddenly gone mad? What was happening here?

'Oh, Mama,' Tabitha sighed. 'How romantic it all is!'

'Indeed,' Lady Tuckworth said. Her fan beat hard with the force of her curiosity. 'Well, I must offer my felicitations, and my apologies for misjudging you, Miss St Aubin. I must see about making an appointment to discuss dear Tabitha.'

'You are so kind, Lady Tuckworth. Now, if you will excuse us…' Mary managed to say.

'Of course. Lovebirds must have the chance of a dance!' Lady Tuckworth trilled.

Mary grabbed Charles's hand and marched him through the crowd to find an empty sitting room off a corridor just beyond the main staircase. She ignored the stares that followed them. Behind the card room, she found a small, silent storage chamber, the boxes and crates shadowed hulks in the moonlight and snow-shine from the windows. She pulled him inside and slammed the door behind them.

'What were you thinking?' she gasped, whirling back to face him in the shadows. 'Telling her we are *betrothed*.'

There, in that silvery light, he looked like magic. A Scots warrior, a powerful poet, his hair shining, his green eyes glowing as he watched her warily. But she had to remind herself he was a madman.

'I fear I wasn't thinking,' he said, his brogue thick, his expression heart-meltingly chagrined. He ran his hand through his hair, as he so often did when he was baffled. She would not think about how adorable it was right then. She would *not*. 'I just saw your face when she said you couldn't be trusted to make matches, and I—I wanted to help you. Something in me knew I *had* to help you.'

Mary pursed her lips as she remembered him rescuing her from the storm, carrying her to the inn, a gallant knight in shining armour. Was this all that was happening now? He thought to save her from gossip with that gallantry? That dear, infuriating man! She was quite dizzy with confusion.

'But now she'll tell everyone we are engaged, and then—then we'll have to deny it, and no one will ever trust me to make a match!' she whispered. She covered her face with her hands, overwhelmed. 'Oh, Charles. I know you had the best of intentions, and I...'

I love you for it.

Oh, no, no, no. She could not love him, never love him. His heart had been lost over his wife and her betrayal; hers was locked up against loneliness and temptation, locked up beyond her work. She had to focus on what was important: saving the agency. Never love. A love he couldn't have for her.

'I am sorry, Mary. Truly, deeply. Bringing you distress is the very last thing I want to do. You're good at your work, and to hear her say such disparaging things—I was just overcome with anger.'

She took her hands down and studied his face.

His gloriously handsome face. Oh, why couldn't this be real? 'What are we going to do now?'

He smiled at her, that lazy, teasing smile she could never quite resist, and came to take her hand. She *really* could not resist that. 'Mary. Is it really such a terrible thing?'

'To get married?'

'Maybe not actually get married, but to let people think we might?' he said hopefully.

'Whatever do you mean?' she said. It was much too tempting, too alluring, to think of being betrothed to him in any form at all. Especially if it involved some mischief of them against the rest of the world.

'You need to be seen as someone who knows how to make a match. I need someone to help me with Adele. It could be fun, couldn't it?' he teased, his fingers warm on hers. 'We can break it off later. I can break it off and be seen as the villain who could not appreciate a rare treasure. Just until we achieve what we need to.' He squeezed her hand, and she felt not so alone now. She seemed to have a partner in crime, and it was so wonderful. So frightening.

'But what of *your* reputation?' she asked.

He laughed. 'Mine? Never fear, I have faced gossip and disapproval before. I am sure I will have a fine match for Adele by then and will just go back to Scotland. I don't mind if there's some tutting about me after that.'

She studied him carefully, searching his eyes. It was crazy, wild! And maybe, just maybe, it was an idea with merit.

She shook her head. Oh, no, she was being tempted by *fun* again! Maybe even by a deep, secret wish to pretend he was hers, just for a time. What if her heart tumbled away then? What if she could no longer resist him, no longer resist how she felt? She couldn't bear to pick up the pieces of a cracked heart when they parted.

But there was that fun. That mischief. She'd almost forgotten that part of herself, and now it called out to her like a siren song! Of course her heart was in danger, how could it not be when he smiled at her like that? But he held out a way to salvage the agency, the thing she and Ella had worked so hard to build, the thing that was like their family now. This was all false. Playacting. She knew that going into the scheme, surely she could manage it. Surely she could just enjoy his company, store up a few memories and laugh while doing it.

Surely it could work. Couldn't it?

'Maybe it could work,' she began, and laughed. 'Or at least we could have some fun while we go to perdition!'

* * *

Charles felt quite like his old self as he walked home from the assembly, having sent his carriage home so he could enjoy the brisk wind on his face, the movement easing his restlessness. The sense of carefree mischief, of fun he carried—he barely remembered what that felt like! At least he had it for a moment, while the golden glow of Mary's laughter carried him forward like a cloud. He had to relish it before the reality of that night's mischief closed in, and he had to unknot the cord of a false betrothal. He'd almost forgotten what it was like to be impulsive, to follow something just to see where it could lead. To give in to the instinct to save a fair maiden, especially when it was Mary St Aubin.

He wanted, needed, to protect her and Adele. He would do anything to see them safe. Mary loved her agency, and he could help her keep it. Surely that meant more than any danger to their emotions? Surely, knowing this was a joke, that it would end, meant they could see their way clear to the finale. And he dared admit to himself, he would do anything to spend a little more time with Mary. To make her laugh.

He paused at the top of a steep, hilly lane to study the flickering lights of the town spread before him, flickering little spots of amber that beckoned through the winter night. It all looked so different because of Mary, and he glimpsed beauty in the cobbled streets and high walls he'd never seen before. The world seemed so wide, so filled with possibilities. Maybe it wasn't real, maybe it would end, but in this moment he felt only excitement at the thought of seeing her again.

He thought of how she'd looked at the party, her bright hair shimmering, her fan sweeping as she studied the gathering with shrewd eyes and laughed at it all. How it felt when she touched him, sparks flying from her fingertips. He'd never wanted to kiss a woman more, to taste her, touch her. The curls and coils of her beautiful hair beckoned, and he'd wanted to draw the pins from those curls, let them stream down over his hands so he could feel their softness. Feel if they were truly as warm as the sun on his skin. To kiss her neck, breathe in her perfume...

'You're daft, man,' he muttered to himself, and laughed. Surely he should attempt his youthful poetry again; it was the only way he could even begin to capture the essence of Mary in words or thoughts. But he knew he could not, because she was truly all feelings.

He raked his hand through his hair, leaving it standing on end. He couldn't remember how to woo a lady at all. Not after his marriage, years trying to forget. How would he even begin to decipher how to make this thing with Mary real? Persuade her that maybe they could actually be good for each other?

Couldn't they? Or maybe he truly didn't have romance inside him now. Nothing to offer her. Nothing to find within himself.

When he held her close, he was sure he'd never wanted anything more. All cares vanished, and there was only her. When he was alone, he didn't know anything at all. Not any longer.

He started walking again, soon running along the lane, his arms outstretched as if he could leave his worries behind. He had a betrothal to plan!

Chapter Seven

'You did *what*?' Ella and Penelope chorused, their eyes wide, teacups frozen in their hands as if they were in a choreographed scene at the Theatre Royal. It would have been funny if Mary hadn't been shaking with nerves.

She glanced at Charles, who stood beside her in Penelope's drawing room. He smiled as man engaged should. Only Mary could see the twinkle of mischief in his eyes.

Right after the ball, she'd realised the great flaw—well, *one* of the great flaws—in her impromptu bargain with Charles. It wasn't just Lady Tuckworth and her sort who would hear of their engagement, and Lady Tuckworth certainly wouldn't stay silent for long. Their own families would certainly find out, and that's what happened. Ella had run an errand before leaving Bath for Moulton Magna and heard a whisper of it.

Charles had suggested to Mary they might confide in their families, but she had feared what might happen if they did, urged that they wait, just a tiny while. She didn't want Ella to know how bad things had become at the agency, didn't want her to feel she had to leave her family at Christmas and tidy up the mess. Mary would fix it first, she had to. And deep down in her most secret heart, she wanted to have these moments with Charles, these secret little moments together. Just for a while.

Charles gently took her hand and gave it a gentle squeeze, helping her feel steadier, more sure this craziness just might work in the end. She'd recalled their meeting at Mollands, the way he made her laugh, made her see brightness around her again, and she had a box of her favourite violet creams tucked into her reticule, a present from him that showed her he remembered, too. He was with her in this—for now, anyway.

'You are *engaged*?' Ella whispered. She carefully placed her delicate cup on the table, delight replacing shock on her face. 'Oh, Mary! I did not realise the depth of your feelings for Mr Campbell.'

'Or his for you,' Pen added.

Mary peeked up at Charles. He looked rather expressionless for an instant, as if he were as unsure as she was how to convey 'depth of feeling,' but then he squeezed her hand again and smiled, as dazzling as a summer day.

'It's marvellous, truly,' Pen said, and clapped her hands.

'Marvellous,' Ella echoed, but she did not sound quite so sure. She glanced between Mary and Charles, a tiny frown between her brows, and Mary felt the pierce of the most awful pang of guilt.

'It is not, well, *official* official yet,' Mary said. 'We aren't having the banns read or applying for a special licence. We're just…seeing how this feels. For now.'

'But I am sure we'll hear wedding bells soon!' Pen said. She jumped up and rushed to hug both Mary and Charles. 'You are both such wonderful people, you deserve all happiness. You deserve each other. We shall be one great family.'

Mary hugged Pen back, yet deep down she felt quite the wretched creature for letting her dearest friends believe their tale. Yet she was sure it was a necessary evil. She had to save the agency and see to Adele's future happiness. Surely it would all be well in the end?

'What a merry Christmas we shall have,' Pen said.

Ella also hugged Mary, embracing her extra close. Mary felt the prickle of tears as she thought of all Ella's care for her, how much she wanted to make her sister proud and happy. 'Shall we just take a turn about the room, my dear?'

Mary glanced at Charles, who nodded, though she feared he looked as doubtful as she felt. Pen chatted up at him, drawing him away and leaving Mary alone with her sister. 'Of course.'

Ella linked her arm with Mary's, as they had so very many times, and they strolled by the windows in the meagre sunlight, looking down at the crowds hurrying past towards the shops, the outline of the Abbey in the distance against the flurries of snow.

'I had no idea you had such fondness for Mr Campbell, Mary,' Ella said. 'You must tell me everything!'

Mary glanced over at Charles, at the way the light turned his glossy hair to the darkness of midnight, carved his cheekbones and the elegant blade of his nose into a classical sculpture. It was true no one would wonder at her feelings for him; she just feared they were becoming all too real and would bite her sharply in the end. 'I wasn't so sure myself. I suppose I couldn't quite put it into words, even in my own mind.'

That part, at least, was so very true. Whenever she was with Charles, or thought of him, which happened far too often, her emotions whirled around like a rainstorm, leaving her tossed about, confused, giddy. 'As we said, we are merely seeing how matters progress right now. Long engagements can be good.'

'That sounds wise. Remember all the patrons of the agency we might have advised thusly? One must be very sure about marriage, it's all for one's future. Mr Campbell's a fine man, of course, handsome and well mannered, connected to so many people we care about. But—you *are* truly fond of him, I hope? That is the only thing that really matters.'

Mary thought of how it felt when Charles touched her, kissed her, the flames that roared and crackled, sizzling over her whole body, all her thoughts. The way everything else vanished when he was near. She thought of his pale, pure green eyes, how he looked at her as if he wanted to devour *and* protect her all at once.

'Yes,' she whispered simply. 'I am fond of him.' And, oh, it was the truth! The honesty of those words hit her too hard. She was fond of him; she relied on him now, more than anyone else, and she worried all her care over the years, her independence, was crumbling away. Had she made a mistake? Should she turn back?

Yet it seemed too late. Ella gave a relieved smile,

and Mary couldn't put a burden on her again. 'That is all I could want for you. You deserve all the very best, Mary my darling, and I've prayed you would find happiness such as I have with Fred.'

Mary nodded, remembering how Fred and Ella looked at each other, as if they were the only people in all the world and saw only each other. 'I don't think it is quite like what you have with Fred. But I am very happy right now.'

That, she found to her surprise, was also true. She *did* feel happy, lighter, more optimistic than she had in a long time. Having a partner in mischief was—fun. She felt quite like the old Mary again.

She would not think of where it would all lead. Not yet.

'You'll tell me if things do change, won't you?' Ella took Mary's hand and looked into her face searchingly, earnestly. 'I'm always here for you, Mary, no matter what. I want to know how you're feeling.'

'And I am always here for *you*, Ella,' Mary whispered. 'You have always been the best thing in my life, my safe port. What would I have done without you?'

Ella blinked against a sudden brightness in her eyes, and Mary feared she would start crying, too. 'I am so proud of you, Mary, truly.'

Mary hugged her sister tightly, hoping deeply that the pride would still be there when this ended. 'Oh, now you have made me a complete watering pot, and that will never do!'

Ella took out a lace-edged handkerchief and dabbed at her eyes before doing the same to Mary, gentle and motherly. 'Not on such a happy occasion.'

'You must go and celebrate a wonderful Christmas at Moulton Magna with Fred and the twins, and not worry a jot about me. I promise I will let you know the instant anything changes.' Such as the ending of a faux betrothal. Mary's heart ached a bit at the thought.

'I must be the one to organise your wedding breakfast! Once you decide on where to wed.' Ella tucked away her handkerchief and took Mary's arm again to continue about the drawing room. 'You shall have such fun at Lady Pennington's party. I want a full report on her lovely new home.'

'Certainly. Every carpet and painting and Christmas pudding. She was one of our great agency successes!' And it was to have more such successes that Mary was doing this, she reminded herself.

An hour later, Mary and Charles escaped Pen's house and stepped out into the crisp breeze of the grey-sky day, snow drifting lazily over their heads. 'Do you think they believe us?' she whispered as they hurried away. He offered his arm, and she slid her hand over his elbow, leaning close to his warmth.

'They seemed to,' Charles said, but she thought he sounded rather doubtful. 'Ella did look at you rather piercingly at times, she knows you so well.'

'Indeed she does,' Mary sighed. 'I wish we did not have to humbug them so, they care about us both so much.' They turned down a cobbled lane towards the gates to Sydney Gardens, quiet now in the cold day. They could walk there and not be overheard.

'They did appear terribly happy at the thought of a wedding,' he said.

'Who wouldn't? Lace and orange blossoms and cake, what's not to like?'

He slanted a glance down at her, shadowed beneath the brim of his hat. 'You've attended many weddings, I'm sure.'

'A fair few. The good thing with agency couples and their nuptials means they are nearly always happy and excited to begin their lives together. It's a very jolly way to spend a morning! Not like some other wedding processions I see, where everyone looks so grimly determined.'

'I know just what you mean,' Charles muttered, studying a shop window they passed with a far-away expression she wished she could read. Did he think of his own first wedding? Of the ghost that haunted his heart, stood between him and giving his love away once more? Then he smiled again, shaking off whatever wistfulness had passed over him, leaving Mary aching to comfort him. 'Shall we walk in the gardens for a while, then? I think the snow is ceasing.'

'I'd like that.' She longed to just walk with him, laugh with him, forget about work and schemes and everything else, as she only could with him.

Sydney Gardens was indeed wonderfully quiet and peaceful, with the pathways dusted with glittering snow, the fountains silent. But a few passers-by did rather stare, and Mary worried the secret was now out.

'After your great experience of such events, what would you want for your own wedding?' he asked lightly.

Mary laughed. 'Oh, I do like planning parties and such! When I was young, I would hide at the back of my father's church and watch him preside over weddings. Like many little girls, I would imagine myself as a bride, what I would wear, how I would feel...' Her words faded as she recalled that dreamy girl she'd been, the visions she'd had of clouds of romance, brightness and fun. Now she thought she didn't want to belong to anyone or have them belong to her, to rely on their happiness for her own. She'd seen such things go awry as often as they'd gone well at the agency. She'd seen her mother leave her behind, seen her father bury himself so far in work he couldn't see his children. Even Ella left in the end, though for the best of reasons, Fred and the children. Nothing in life was within control. A lady had to depend upon herself.

Yet she was so tempted to lean on Charles, confide in him, hold on to him, and that was dangerous.

'You never wished to wed, then? You would surely be an expert at it all.'

Mary laughed wryly. 'Never an expert, no. I am good at helping others find mates, seeing what would make them happy. But I grew up seeing how lonely a match can be when it's not exactly right, or when something terrible happens.' She thought surely he could understand that, after his sad marriage, and she dared to tell him a bit of her truth. 'My mother died when I was a child, and my father could not bear it. He buried himself in his work, and Ella was left to help me. I saw that one can only really rely on oneself in life.'

The glance he gave her from beneath the shadowed brim of his hat was strangely sad, and Mary feared he pitied her. She could never bear to have Charles, of all people, feel sorry for her. 'But,' she added lightly, 'I do enjoy a fine wedding.'

'What would be your dos and don'ts for a wedding, then?' he asked.

Mary made herself laugh lightly. 'I should be a wedding planner, then, as well as a matchmaker? I think I would be rather good at that. I do so like to *organise*.'

'And I hate it,' he said, with a dramatic grimace that made her laugh more. He did always make moments so much more fun. 'I am a great shambles, as Adele likes to remind me. I lose things in my office all the time, forget appointments, neglect social obligations.'

'It does sound as if you need a tidier-up,' Mary said.

'Indeed I do.' He gave her one of his crooked little smiles, the ones that made her heart thunder so, and she wondered suddenly if they *could* be a good match. She could run his castle; he could make her laugh. They could kiss all the time! And it could be...

No. It couldn't be. Running away never seemed to solve problems for anyone, and it would mean leaving behind her work or, worse, handing it back to Ella. She deserved a happy life with her family, which was why Mary needed Charles's help now. It didn't matter how much she'd like to see his castle, see the place that made Charles—Charles.

She turned away and stared hard at the icy fountain, imagining its cold in her own heart.

'Now, my advice for weddings…' she said. 'I would have Mademoiselle Sandrine make my gown, of course. She should make every Bath bride's gown.'

'Mademoiselle Sandrine? Oh, yes, the modiste. Adele is always saying I should let her order gowns there.'

'And so you should! Her creations are amazing, more than mere ribbons and fabric. They are created to suit each woman uniquely, make her feel lovely. It's also a joy to visit her shop. So inviting and elegant. I would definitely get my wedding gown there, if I required one, so I would feel like a—a confident empress on my day!'

Charles laughed, the sound so deep and rich, like summer sunshine. That's what he always made her think of, summertime. 'An empress? I picture you more as a fairy queen, I think.'

Mary shivered with a sudden golden glow at such words. He thought of her in that way? It sounded so fanciful, so…romantic. 'A fairy queen? I'm sure I feel too prosaic for that.'

'You, Mary? Prosaic? Never! You are all dances and merriment.'

She felt the heat of a blush stain her cheeks. Those extraordinary eyes of his—green as the sea one minute and deepest, most mysterious jade the next—looked at her with such intensity she could feel the shaking of it all the way to her toes, in every part of her. He seemed to see *all* of her, as no one else ever had.

She dug her nails into her gloved palms to keep from leaping on him right there on a public pathway.

She looked away to the silent fountain of a Grecian goddess. If only she could stay as cold and emotionless as her, distant from the world and its dangers. 'I am sure Mademoiselle Sandrine could make a fairy queen gown, too. One with tulle and lace and maybe silver spangles. Flower wreaths.' Ah, yes, she could picture it, floating and ethereal, drifting her through a flower arch like a cloud. And she could picture Charles there, too, tall and powerful, smiling at her from an altar…

'There would be roses and lilies,' she said quickly, trying to distract herself from thoughts of his smile as he held out a hand to his bride. 'So I suppose it would have to be in summer. An arch around the church porch all white and pink! A bouquet of rosebuds tied with more pink ribbon, rose petals scattered by little girls into the air. And green, of course, emerald ivy leaves...'

'To match the fairy queen's emerald crown?' he teased.

To match his eyes. 'Exactly. And a wreath of roses. No bonnets with veils! I would want to see everything that happens. Only a few guests, people who truly care about the match. That's the best luck at a wedding.' And her family had grown small, too, with no parents to weep with joy and wistfulness. There was Ella and Fred, and she knew they would be the ones crying with joy for her. She pushed away that pang of guilt that always came when she thought of Ella. 'But there would be more! At my father's cold church, the ancient but quite adorable Mrs Fristle played the organ. She'd been doing it for simply decades, and though she sometimes let others play for Sunday services, she insisted on doing it herself for Easter and weddings. She always played "Gentle Patience Smiles on Pain" for some reason, one wouldn't have thought it quite right for a wedding, but it wasn't an event without it.'

He laughed. 'So you would have the estimable Mrs Fristle play that song?'

'Oh, no, she passed away years ago, I'm afraid. But maybe that song in her memory. And some Mozart! I do love Mozart.' She suddenly realised it was *Charles* she pictured at the altar, his smile, his glowing eyes. His hand reaching for hers. She shook her head hard, reminding herself this was only a fantasy, a game. She couldn't have such feelings, and even if she did, he could never return them. She had to rein in her imagination, that was all.

'And what about the wedding breakfast?'

She peeked up at him, wondering if he teased her, but worse, he looked terribly serious. Almost as if he, too, pictured a wedding where they held hands.

'Oh, more guests than at the church, of course, for I would want quite an enormous cake,' she said, trying to keep it light and dreamy. 'And there would be salmon mousse and white soup and mushroom tarts. A flower-bedecked carriage to carry the couple away at the end. Somewhere simple and quiet...'

She looked up at him, and he stared back at her as if they both envisaged what might happen in a quiet cottage after a wedding. She turned away, warm-cheeked, flustered.

'But we need only concern ourselves with managing an engagement,' she said with a nod. An engagement that needed to look convincing.

'Indeed,' he said with a little cough. 'Lady Fleetwood and Pen know now. I shall have to tell Adele before we go to the Christmas party. Hopefully it will distract her from Mr Clark.'

'I do feel so dreadful for deceiving them now,' Mary admitted. 'But if I am to save the agency...'

'And if I can keep Adele safe and happy...' He nodded. 'But I do understand. I feel the same.'

'We should decide now how to get out of this in the end, without hurting anyone,' Mary said. She did fear now *she* would be the one hurt when she couldn't be with him, see him anymore. It was looking more and more as if their impulsive scheme was a danger to her. 'A broken betrothal could obviously look bad for the agency.'

'I shall make it look entirely my own fault,' he said, determined and stony. 'You can declare you could not bear to live in a quiet, cold old castle in Scotland when so many here need your help.'

'Yes. Indeed. I could not.' She pictured a medieval fortress of a place, grey and tall against the heather. Strolling the ramparts arm in arm with him...

No. Focus on the 'grey and cold,' not the 'cosy with Charles' bit. 'And I could say what you suggest, that the agency and its patrons need me,' she went on. 'It would be a source of gossip for a few days, but then hopefully the glittering new matches I make would erase any doubts. I just need to prove myself. But I'd love to know what your home is like, really. I only know such places from novels.'

They stopped at the edge of the slushy river, and Charles studied the water with a most thoughtful, faraway expression on his face. 'It's a harsh beauty, aye, but the most profoundly true beauty. In the mornings, the mist comes up and wraps around the old stones of the house like…like shreds of grey lace. Such mists have come upon the castle from its earliest moments, the same as what we see now, and in those moments I feel close to all my family that has come before me.'

Mary could just envisage it, morning light trying to break through the fog, casting gleams and shadows on the walls, grey and silver and purple. 'It sounds wonderful. My own family…'

'Yes?'

'Well, it was just me and Ella for so long, I don't know about any other family at all, really. To see things as my ancestors once did, know that we are connected—that would be wondrous.'

He reached out and gently touched her hand, as if he recognised her bittersweet feelings at such a thought. 'And when the mist vanishes into the daylight, you can see the hills all around, silver and amethyst with the heather. You could wind some in your hair and be a fair lass indeed.'

Mary laughed. 'I should enjoy that. It's been an age since I made flower chains for my hair!' She had a vision of dashing up the hills with him, the sharp green scent of it all intoxicating, flowers wound around them. But that would never get them what they had vowed to find together, solutions to problems they had right here and now. It would not erase the past or the present and all that came between them. 'But what shall we do now, to make people think our betrothal is real?'

'We could quarrel at an assembly,' Charles said after a moment's thought. 'And then make up!' His green eyes glinted with mischief, making her laugh. It almost made the magical Scottish mist vanish from her mind. Almost.

'And you could sing beneath my window at night!' Mary cried. She started to feel herself rather enthusiastic for the theatricals. 'No dancing, though. But for now, we must look engaged. You must take my hand often, as if you can't help yourself.'

She impulsively grabbed his hand, and immediately realised her mistake. Even through their gloves, she felt the strength of him, the heat of his fingers. Yet she could not let him go. Those sparkling, shimmering bonds she'd so often felt between them seemed to tighten around her, pulling her close to him.

'And I could press your hand to my heart.' He matched his words to action, taking her hand and holding it close over his coat. She could feel the steady rhythm of his heartbeat there. 'And kiss it, thus.'

Staring into her eyes, he raised her hand to his lips and pressed a lingering kiss to her fingertips, warm through her gloves. It was all she could dream of, all she longed for, and all she couldn't have in reality. He smelled of lemons and sunshine, and she felt like soaring up into the sky on a cloud. All heat, excitement, fun.

There was a laugh in the distance. Mary was startled, dropped to the cold, hard ground from that shining cloud. She suddenly felt the chilly wind again. She broke free from him and stumbled back a step. She stared up at Charles, stunned, dizzy. He stared back.

'I—I think we need some rules,' she said hoarsely. She could still feel him, taste him, even as they stood apart, not touching at all.

'Rules?' he muttered.

'Yes. If we are to keep up our show.'

He smiled, slow, lazy, and she had to hold herself back from throwing herself against him again. 'I would say anyone who just saw us would think we were engaged.'

Mary couldn't help but giggle through her daze. 'That is the problem. We must maintain control, if we are to preserve the story of our betrothal—and its breaking off. And control over *ourselves.*' She nodded. Yes. She had to simply control herself and her impulses.

And that had never been her strong suit.

He straightened his coat, picked up his hat from the ground where it had fallen in their kiss. 'What rules would you suggest?'

'Well…' She tried to organise her swirling thoughts. 'No kissing. That should be number one.'

He frowned. 'Where is the fun in that?'

She pursed her lips to keep from laughing. 'So, rule number two. No fun.'

'Ach, now you're just being daft. I barely remember what being betrothed is like, I was quite young and callow the first time, but I am sure it was not *fun*. It should be!'

'A real engagement, yes.' Though she *was* having fun, she was startled to realise. She loved thinking of rules she wasn't sure she could keep, loved seeing his teasing little smile, loved having a scheme. A secret. 'But it is Christmas, and we're going to a party. I suppose there could be *some* amusement. But not too much.'

'Just a tiny bit.'

'A tiny bit, yes.' She tapped her finger on her chin, planning. 'So, rules. No whispering in dark corners. No walking alone in the evenings. I will help you dance, but no enjoying it. No twirling about.'

'I think I can safely promise not to enjoy dancing. I could never keep up with a fairy queen's light step.'

'And no flirting!' she cried. She felt such a terrible, happy little glow when he called her that.

He clapped his hand over his heart. 'I vow I never flirt. Not now. I am an old, responsible, stodgy bachelor.'

'Now you are the one being daft. No one would ever call you stodgy.'

'So, what about holding hands? I assume that's allowed.'

Mary reached out and tentatively touched the tips of her fingers to his, waiting for that lightning strike. The more she touched him, the more she craved it. 'Maybe. But not like this!' She wrapped her fingers around his tighter, clinging on as if she were drowning.

He smiled down at her, slow, sensual, and wrapped his other hand over her fingers, holding them together. '*Och*, Mary, you are *delichtsome*. Like—I don't know. Fireworks. Fizzy champagne. I've never known anyone quite like you.'

Mary smiled. *Delichtsome* sounded quite a wonderful thing to be. 'I thought you never flirted now.'

'I don't, but you bring it out in me. The old me. You make me remember how bright the world once seemed.'

And he made her see he could be the storm in her heart and the shelter from the world, just the same. It was sorely, deeply tempting. 'So, shall we agree to have just a little fun being engaged, then?'

He raised her hand to his lips for a lingering kiss. 'Some fun, it is. And a few simple rules.'

'It's a bargain, then.'

After all, how hard could pretending to be engaged really be? Terribly hard, she was afraid. The more time she spent with Charles, the more she cared about him, and the more you cared about someone, the more there was to be lost. She dreamed of love, of a life with someone like Ella had, but the reality of it was frightening. It was better to be alone than unhappy with the wrong person. And Charles, after his marriage, after his youthful follies did him false, could never return love, surely. After all the fun and laughter, that would be too painful.

She glanced up at him now, at the way the pale sunlight sparkled on his hair, the half-smile on his beautiful lips. Surely with only a false betrothal, there was no risk, nothing to lose. But she feared she was about to step foot off a cliff into an unknown blue-sky future, and she shivered.

The string of little silver bells on the shop door sang out a joyous welcome as Mary stepped inside Mademoiselle Sandrine's shop the day after her discussion of rules with Charles. As always, it felt like an oasis of serenity and elegance, of lightness and brightness against the winter day, against a sleepless night thinking of Charles, and she let out a deep breath as she looked around.

Everything—from the gilded letters on the small sign on the door to the pink-and-blue pastel floral of the carpet, the scent of rose pot-pourri and lavender in the air, the blue satin draperies at the bow windows, and the frescoed ceiling of goddesses and cupids on clouds—seemed ineffably, perfectly *French*, in the old regime way. Just like Sandrine's musical accent, her perfect way with stylish accessories.

The blue brocade chairs and small marble-topped tables holding porcelain trays of tiny pastel cakes, the attendants in their blue dresses and crisp white aprons waiting on patrons, told everyone they could expect nothing but the most fashionable and tasteful there, and the gowns on a few mannequins dotted around the floor confirmed it.

Mary felt delighted as she studied a pale lilac and white striped walking gown, with a matching pelisse trimmed with swansdown. A ball gown of creamiest, heaviest satin that glowed. A display of gloves fanned out on a glass counter, blue, pink, butter yellow, snowy white. She longed for all of it, every single bead and embroidered flower! She wondered what Charles would think of her in that sophisticated dancing dress of burgundy silk and lace, daringly cut low over the shoulders...

But no. She was not there for herself that day, not there for something to entice her 'fiancé,' even if she was terribly tempted. She was there on a mission.

Mademoiselle Sandrine herself appeared from behind a blue velvet curtain, which Mary knew led to the studios and offices that produced such magic.

Like her shop, Sandrine was the perfect image

of elegance and calm. Tall, slender, clad in mulberry silk with an embroidered shawl draped over her shoulders and a neat chatelaine at her waist, her dark hair twisted in an elaborate chignon at the base of her swan-like neck. Everyone in Bath hoped for gowns created by her, yet it was true no one knew much about her, knew anything about her life in France or why she came to Bath. The mystery just seemed to make the gowns more enticing.

'Mademoiselle St Aubin,' she said with a smile, 'how lovely to see you! Have you come to look at some of the new fashion plates for springtime? I just got a lovely book from London. There is much to suit you there.'

'Oh, you are a wicked temptress!' Mary said with a laugh. 'I do love the springtime frocks the best of all. The bright colours and light fabrics.'

Sandrine nodded. 'It is my favourite, too. But I have your gown ready for Lady Pennington's party, as well. We shall look at that book, then I'll wrap it up for you. Do you have time for tea or maybe some chocolate?'

'Yes, thank you,' Mary said. She was in a hurry to return to the office, to making matches. Everyone who had arrived that morning had wanted only to ask about her engagement!

'Sophie, fetch the tea, *s'il-vous plait*, and those

new cakes from Mollands,' Sandrine said to one of the blue-clad assistants, and led Mary to two chairs set in a cosy little window nook, near a display of—what else?—a wedding gown of palest sky blue silk overlaid with organza, a matching veiled bonnet on a stand beside it.

As Sandrine poured the tea and offered some of those luscious little cakes, Mary studied the fashion plates. She smiled at a very stylish tartan pelisse, thinking of Charles and his Scottish castle.

'These are indeed very *a la mode*,' she said. 'I especially like this spencer with the braid on the sleeves, so cunning, and this organdie theatre gown.'

'And that, perhaps?' Sandrine said, rather slyly, as she gestured to the tartan. 'It is called the Auld Alliance. For the friendship between Scotland and France, of course, though I am not sure a Parisian lady would wear such a fabric. Which is too bad, this dark green is beautiful.'

Mary frowned. Were rumours of her engagement already flying around the crescents of Bath? 'Why would you say that?'

Sandrine laughed. 'Oh, *mon ami*! Bath is a small village, isn't it? And people do like to whisper and confide here in the shop. That's the point; this is a safe space for them. A tiny bird told me you and a certain handsome Scotsman are secretly betrothed.'

'Not so secretly, I see,' Mary murmured.

'The bird brought her baby chick with her to order a new gown in this pale green taffeta. She said you especially advised it once at your agency.'

'Ah. Lady Tuckworth, I see.' She *had* advised the green for the Tuckworth girl before, when they asked her advice in attracting a style-minded gentleman. Funny how only now did they think of her advice.

Sandrine made a locking motion at her lips. 'I am silent on my sources. But is it true? He is so very handsome! Like an—an ancient warrior. Defending his castle from the Vikings, leading his knights into battle...'

Mary laughed. 'Yes, yes, I see what you mean.' And she thought exactly that when she looked at Charles, that he didn't quite belong in their modern world. She studied Sandrine and wondered if she should be jealous. Other women would admire him, certainly, and Sandrine was very beautiful. Very mysterious.

'We are—fond of each other,' Mary admitted. Such lukewarm words for the burning emotions she felt when he was near! 'But we have not called the banns yet. In fact, he is rather the reason I'm here.'

Sandrine clapped her hands, looking terribly gleeful. 'You wish to order a wedding gown! And maybe a little trousseau?'

Mary glanced again at the frothy wedding gown on the mannequin, the pearl-edged veil, and sighed. 'If it comes to that, of course. There is no one else I would trust more with such a creation. But today I wanted to see if you might have something that would suit Miss Adele Stewart, his niece. She is about to have her first Season.'

'Ah, yes, Mademoiselle Stewart. Such a pretty young lady, and her playing at Mrs Oliver's was so enchanting. She came here one day with Mrs Oliver, I remember, and seemed truly wistful over that display.' Sandrine nodded to a gown in the other window, a pale pink and creamy white muslin trimmed with satin roses. 'Yet she did not order anything.'

'She says Mr Campbell won't let her. That she is too young. Yet you might have noticed she did borrow one of Penelope Oliver's gowns for the party, and looked so beautiful. I'd like to help her gain some confidence before she goes to London, and how better than with one of your perfect dresses.'

'Hmm.' Sandrine tapped at her chin, her eyes narrowed as she seemed to go into herself where there were visions of every lady's perfect gown.

She got up and looked through a tray of ribbons, a rack of lace shawls. 'This one, maybe?' She held up a white-on-white embroidered shawl and shook her head. 'Not quite right. The frock in the window is a good start, but I want to do something just a bit different. A bit unique.' She turned to a rack of rolls of jewel-like fabric, rich satins, delicate silks, ethereal muslins, and got caught up on a pink chiffon embroidered with slightly darker roses. 'This as an overskirt! And a wreath at the shoulder. Young, spring-like, just like her.'

'Yes, perfect!' Mary exclaimed. The colour would be delightful on Adele, taking her creamy skin and red-gold hair and making them positively garden-like. 'You always do have just the right garment for each person.'

Sandrine swirled around the chiffon in a blur of sunset-pink. 'Just like what you do, Mademoiselle Mary! You find each person their perfect match, the one who will make them stronger, braver, even more themselves. And then they come here for me to make their dream days complete.' She sat down across from Mary again and smiled. 'I'm glad to hear you have found your own dream.'

'What do you mean?' Mary asked cautiously.

'You and Mr Campbell. You and your sister have

helped so many people through your agency, you deserve your own happy ending.'

Mary bit her lip. 'Such nonsense. I hardly need *him* to do my business.' But wasn't that the whole point? She did need him, right now anyway, to build up the agency.

'Certainly you do not. We females must put up with so much in this life, manage so many things and hide so many emotions. Who better to run a business?'

'And it is not exactly a dream. Mr Campbell and myself.' Though it could be. Wasn't that why she stayed up so very late thinking about him? That was why she was beginning to wonder if this was such a good idea, no matter how it seemed in the moment. She just had to remember it was fake.

'But I am sure it's quite wonderful. It's all over your face! I can always tell when a love is worthy of one of my gowns, and yours assuredly is.'

'So, your gowns are magic?'

Sandrine laughed. 'Something of the sort, yes.'

Mary took a long sip of tea, hiding her embarrassment at being so obvious behind the cup. 'Have you never been tempted to make such a gown for yourself?'

It was as if a grey cloud skidded across Sandrine's elegant face, and Mary felt terrible for bringing up something that obviously caused her friend some sort of bad memory. 'I have never met anyone who could match one of *my* gowns for a wedding day. I shall not marry. I *cannot* marry, I have my shop to think of.'

Mary nodded. Did she not feel the same? A business and a marriage could seldom match, and the agency meant so much to her. 'Well, if you change your mind, the agency would love to be of assistance,' she said, setting down her teacup. 'You would be the great prize of our books! So beautiful and elegant, you would have your pick.'

Sandrine waved this away. 'Nonsense! I am merely passable, it's my gowns that lend elegance.' She ran her fingers over her own dark satin skirt. 'I am just an old spinster and shall remain so now.'

Mary wondered what really could lurk in Sandrine's past, but she knew her friend would never say. Never tell of her old life in France. 'Perhaps you will find someone at Lady Pennington's party,' she suggested. She would so love to think of someone's romance besides her own for Christmas!

'I doubt it. But I shall definitely have the gown ready for Mademoiselle Stewart. I have Mrs Oliver's measurements on file, and they are much of a size, so I can use that to make a start. To make a woman's clothes is to give her armour and be her secret keeper.'

Mary sensed the first secrets Sandrine kept were her own, hidden behind the beautiful facade of the shop, and she would say no more that day. 'Marvellous. And while I'm here, I'll just take a pair of those pink gloves.'

'And put in an order for the Aulde Alliance? I could get a bolt of Campbell tartan. It could make a wedding gown as well as white muslin or blue silk...' Sandrine laughed at Mary's expression and rose to pack the new gloves in fine tissue. 'No, no, I see you will make no such order today. But just in case you need it later...'

Chapter Eight

The Crown Club on Milsom Street was always a masculine haven of silence, far from noisy homes, social obligations with demanding wives and the pressures of business. It was filled with deep, dark velvet upholstered chairs, carved black marble fireplaces and rooms where deep play could take place.

It was also a good hiding place.

Peyton Clark sat slumped in a leather settee near a crackling fire, hoping no one would look for him in such a quiet corner. 'Quiet' was not often a quality associated with him. He lived in chaos and motion, gambling, racing his carriage, betting on horses, finding a willing woman or two. And he certainly did not *enjoy* quiet. It was very boring. Now he found it was forced on him.

He drained his glass of port wine and gestured to a footman for more. He'd had a few glasses before that one and was feeling rather fuzzy-headed, but it wasn't as pleasant as usual. Worries pierced even through wine fumes. And wine was really the only pleasure left to him for the moment. He dared not add to his gambling debts, and Mrs Tolliver's fine establishment of beautiful, obliging women—and a few men—was firmly off-limits. Mrs Tolliver had tossed him out for not paying what he owed there last time and threatened to set her burly watchmen on him if he came back with no coin.

Peyton had hopes that this sad state of affairs wouldn't last much longer. He'd been in utter despair, a black rage, when his stupid old uncle declared he would cut him off.

'Not a single shilling more until you reform your way of life!' Morton Clark had raged as Peyton stood before him, hat in hand, boiling silently with fury that the old man would treat him thus. 'I have tolerated far too many outrages because of what I owe my late brother, your poor father's memory, but no more. This is the last straw!'

So much fuss for one tiny little indiscretion. One little scandal. How was he to know how young the lady had really been? Surely, as Uncle Morton's only remaining family, he was owed some consideration and respect! To throw one's own nephew practically out on the streets was beyond the pale.

At last, Uncle Morton's prosing sputtered off,

and he slumped into his chair, staring up at Peyton with burning eyes sunk in his wrinkled face. 'I can give you only one chance.'

And then the sun pierced that crimson anger. A touch of relief. Of course! Peyton was due another chance. 'Oh, Uncle, you won't be sorry! I will reform, I will…' He calculated how fast he could get back to the nearest gaming hell.

'I certainly will not be sorry. Because there are conditions.'

'Conditions?' What did that mean?

'Yes. I will release your allowance, with a substantial increase, as well as purchase a house on King's Crescent…'

'How very generous, Uncle!' That crescent was quite fashionable, the perfect place for a gaming party.

Morton had cut him off with a sharp wave of his walking stick. 'As soon as you marry with my approval. A lady of respectable family and utmost virtuous character. A lady of fortune, a necessity for *you*, I'm sure. One of sturdy morals, who will guide you on a better path.'

Now, he drained his glass again and stared morosely into the fire. Maybe, just maybe, matters were not all *that* dire. He could borrow a bit more, just enough to hold him over, albeit at a criminal rate of interest. And now there was a prospect. One his uncle might even approve of. Adele Stewart.

He remembered when he met her at an assembly, begged for a dance. So young and pretty, with golden-red curls and wide green eyes that stared up at him so admiringly, as if she saw only him. Listened only to him. Exactly what a chap wanted in a wife, someone obedient and sweet. So enticingly innocent.

It was a perfect plan. Except for Adele's monster of a guardian.

Peyton scowled as he thought of Charles Campbell. The man guarded Adele like a dragon, not letting anyone near her. There had to be a way around him.

'Someone sitting here, old chap?' a voice asked, and Peyton glared up to find Percy Overbury standing by the other chair near the fire.

Peyton had enjoyed the quiet for his brooding thoughts, but Overbury was a good enough sort. 'Not at all, do join me,' Peyton said, waving towards the chair. 'Some port?'

'Please. A great deal of it.' Peyton noticed for the first time that Overbury's face looked rather glum under his artfully floppy waves of hair.

'That bad, eh?' he said as he gestured to the footman.

'Dreadful. I was so ecstatically looking forward to the Pennington party, and now—now I am in utter despair about it all. I am done in by true love.'

'True love?' Peyton could not fathom such a thing, though he did understand *fake* romance well enough. It was exhausting to keep it up. 'What happened, then? Some gel throw you over? They all seem to swoon over those books of yours.'

'Worse. I can't even catch her first so she could throw me over! She slips away from me like a—a silk scarf in my hands. Like a summertime breeze. A ray of silver moonlight…'

'Not amenable to poetry, then? No adventure in her? No barque of frailty?'

'She is the most virtuous! The most perfect angel that ever was seen. The most beautiful goddess I have ever beheld. My heart aches to make her mine!'

'Offer a diamond bracelet from Rundell and Bridge and an account at Mademoiselle Sandrine's shop. That usually does it for me, right quick.'

Overbury looked horrified. 'She is not that kind of female! She is a *lady*. I want to marry her, to possess her fully. But she eludes me.'

'I sympathise with you there, Overbury.' It seemed they both had to fall into the parson's mousetrap, yet the satisfying snap of it evaded them. 'I also cannot secure the hand of the lady I seek.'

Overbury looked astonished. 'You—*you* want to get married, Clark?'

'A sad prospect but a necessary one. My uncle has put his gouty foot down, the old villain. It's marriage or no more allowance.'

'So you are not in love?' Overbury seemed as if he could hardly believe such a thing.

'Oh, I like her well enough. She's a pretty little thing.'

'A pretty little thing? Oh, Clark, you have no poetry in your soul at all! *My* lady is a bright-plumed bird of rarest—'

'Yes, yes,' Peyton cut him off impatiently. 'But it seems that at bottom we both have the same dilemma. Our ladies will not have us. Or rather, her guardian will not let me have her.'

'Mine simply doesn't wish to wed, even as I offer her all the world and my heart.' Overbury looked as if he might break into tears, so Peyton quickly poured him more wine. 'I am going to try my very best to woo her at the Christmas party. It seems an ideal season for romance, don't you think?'

'Perhaps.' The snow was dashed inconvenient for slipping off into dark gardens, but the cold wind could close people in cosily by the fire. But the

Pennington party… 'You might be on to something there. Something relaxed about a Christmas house party. I shall be there, too.'

'You?' Overbury asked doubtfully. 'But Lady Pennington does not approve of rakes.'

'No matter about that. I am going with Lord Mountley. They'll be too polite to turn him away. My lady will be there, and I must win her before the New Year.' He had to pay his debts by then, or there could be trouble he would much rather avoid.

'So will mine. My goddess! If I can get close to her…'

'Corner her under the mistletoe?'

'Something like that.'

If Peyton could get Adele under the mistletoe, he'd do more than stealing kisses. If he compromised her, her uncle would have to let them marry. 'So, who is this goddess of yours, Overbury?'

'Miss Mary St Aubin.'

'Hmm. She's pretty, I'll give you that. And seems a merry enough sort. Too marriage-minded, if you ask me. I've heard she makes matches all over the place.'

'Yes, indeed. I only wish she would see her match with *me*. I am becoming quite desperate.'

Peyton sat up straighter, a sudden thought striking him. Mary St Aubin was connected with his

Adele! 'I think she knows my lady, too. Adele Stewart.'

Overbury stared at him with wide eyes. 'I say. A bit young, isn't Miss Stewart?'

'She's old enough for her first Season,' Peyton said, disgruntled. 'Plenty old enough to wed. Maybe we could find a way to help each other, you and me.'

Overbury tilted his head, looking dubious but intrigued. Peyton was very familiar with that combination. 'How so?'

'I'm not entirely sure yet, but the two of them are connected, and they will both be at the party. Listen here, Overbury, I'll tell you what I think...'

A Journey to the Western Islands of Scotland; *The Evergreen* by Allan Ramsay; *Highland Topography and its Effects on its People.*

Hmm, Mary thought as she studied the titles on the shelf at Brunton's Bookshop. The clerk had directed her to this dimly lit corner when she asked about volumes on Scotland, but she wasn't sure this was quite what she was looking for, lovely as the poetry was.

She took the Highland study down and looked through some of the engraved illustrations. Rolling hills, ruined castles, deep lochs. In her mind, though, she saw Charles's face as he talked about his castle, the gentle pride of it, and she longed to know more about his home, about what created such depth of feeling in him.

She shook her head and put that book back to take down the poetry. Charles did take up far too much space in her thoughts of late, space she needed for thinking about her business. Instead of balance sheets and finding new clients, she thought of his terrible dancing and wonderful laughter.

Farewell to Lochaber, and farewell, my Jean,
Where heartsome with thee I hae mony day
been...

Such beautiful words, she thought. Maybe that was it. Maybe the essence of Charles, the glowing spark she saw when he spoke of his Scotland was just poetry.

The sun in glory glowing, with merry dew be-
stowing
Sweet fragrance, life, and growing, to flowers
and every tree.

Yes, that was it. The sun in glory glowing, that was him. She flipped to the next page, losing herself in the words, the misty images of rocky valleys and castles overlooking promontories. The shop, the rainy town outside the grimy window, it all quite vanished in silvery heather.

'Lost in a wee *dwam*, are we, lass?' a whisper sounded in her ear, making her jump.

She whirled around, the book raised high to defend herself—only to find herself facing Charles himself, stepped out of her daydreams. A Charles with a delighted, teasing grin on his face.

His ever so handsome face, with its craggy cheekbones and bright green eyes.

'You frightened the wits out of me,' she gasped, and indeed they were still flown far away. Being alone with him in a dim corner would do that.

'So it seems. It must be a fine book to have you so enthralled.' He slid the volume from her hand and studied the cover. 'Ramsay, eh?' He looked up at the row of leather bindings behind her. 'All things Scottish, I see. A new interest?'

'Don't be so egotistical, it's naught to do with you,' she said sternly, and took back the Ramsay. 'I need to be informed about all sorts of cultures for my work, don't I? And…'

One dark brow quirked as he studied her. 'And?'

Oh, how distracting he was! He made every coherent thought fly quite away. 'And—well, yes. Talking to you about your home made me quite curious.' She opened the book and read aloud the words that had just enthralled her.

Overcome by longing for a life, a place she didn't know, for all that was contained in the 'sweet life' of Charles himself, she peeked up at him to find he watched her intently, his eyes very dark.

The book dropped from her grasp as he took her hand and drew her behind the shelf, deeper into the shadows. She leaned into him, breathed deeply of the summer lemon scent of him and curled her fingers into the lapels of his fine wool coat. It always felt so *right* to be with him, even when it was so very wrong.

She couldn't let that perfect moment go. She kissed him, and he met her with such hunger, such eagerness, she knew it did have to be right. He tasted of summer, too, of sunshine and brandy and mint and that wonderful essence that was only him. Their 'no kissing' rule flew right out of her mind. She knew this thing between them had a finishing date, that such moments as this couldn't keep happening, but she couldn't stop what was igniting between them now.

His arms locked around her, and he drew her closer and closer. His mouth hardened on hers, his tongue tracing the curve of her lips before plunging inside to join them even more fully. She wanted, needed, more of that kiss. More of *him*.

He pressed her back against the shelf, his open lips sliding from hers to trace the curve of her jaw, the arch of her neck above the frill of her spencer collar, making her shiver. He lightly nipped at that sensitive little spot just below her ear, and she whimpered.

How could he *do* this to her? She was never herself when she was around him! She never could seem to stop this flood of feelings.

She reached up to twine her fingers in his hair and dragged his kiss back to her lips. He went most obligingly, eagerly, kissing her with a hot artlessness and need that fired her own.

She pressed even closer to him, wanting to be ever nearer and nearer. Wanting she knew not what. She wanted the poetry that was only him.

And she knew that soon, very soon, she would have to let it go. Not just there, in that bookstore, but in her life entirely. The desire that flared between them when she first kissed him in that garden had only grown stronger, hotter, in the time she'd spent with him since then. It would surely be painful when they parted, when she didn't have him with her any longer, but it was so hard to hold on to caution when they were together. She had only this kind of stolen moment, and she meant to make the most of it all now.

Chapter Nine

The Olivers' carriage turned in at a pair of ornate iron gates touched with gilt at the spiked tips that made them gleam in the winter light. Northland Park was in sight at last.

And soon Mary would see Charles. She slid to the edge of the tufted velvet seat, her toe tapping in her kid half-boot as she tried to see ahead. This fidgety excitement was *not* at the prospect of seeing him, she told herself sternly. Certainly not. It was just having her feet on steady ground again, after the jolting and sticking of the wintertime road. That was all. It had nothing to do with the memory of her kiss with Charles, surely. She had to plant her feet on the ground again, remember her goal, move forward.

Yet she still felt herself trembling with eagerness to see him again.

'I am quite agog to see Northland,' Pen said. She

leaned to look out the window beside Mary, Miss Muffins perched on her lap. 'They say it was quite a ruin before! Such a shame, it was rather a show-place, built by a courtier of Queen Anne, I think. I heard the Penningtons have worked wonders.'

'Just as they said the agency worked wonders with the former Miss Evans,' Anthony said, shooting a smile Mary's way. 'She barely said a word when the Evanses first arrived in Bath, now look at her.'

'She didn't need "wonders" worked,' Mary protested. 'She was always beautiful and intelligent. Maybe a bit caught under her mother's thumb. She merely needed to find someone who truly understood her. Valued her, her true self.' Just as everyone should. Just as Mary sometimes longed for, deep in a lonely night. Someone to really look at her, *see* her, as it seemed Charles did whenever her turned his green eyes onto her.

'And surely that was Lord Pennington,' Penelope said. 'They are like two cooing lovebirds in a tree! Perfect for each other.' Anthony took her hand and smiled down at her tenderly, making Mary's heart ache. 'It was so kind of them to open their home. What a lovely Christmas we'll have.'

Mary wondered how lovely it would all be if she had to fight off daydreams of Charles all the time.

She'd just have to determine to focus on her work, that was all. Yes. Work.

'Oh, look, there's the house now,' Pen said, and Miss Muffins gave an excited little yip.

Mary peeked out the window again. The drive through towering old oaks was cunningly curved to reveal enticing glimpses of the house and outbuildings, including a round summer house atop a hill and a crumbling brick tower, dappled in light like a painting until the carriage suddenly tumbled out of the woods towards the house itself.

It was quite vast, the centre section of the old Elizabethan manse, with stone walkways, towers, wavy old glass windows, brick chimneys. Covered walkways connected to newer wings on either side, perfect Palladian style in contrast to the rambling old house, with tall, symmetrical windows, pale marble faced in darker brick that echoed the older section. Somehow it all came together perfectly, just like a house Mary would want for herself.

The gravelled drive circled an elaborate Italian fountain, silent now beneath the figure of Diana with her bow raised, past the old house to one of the new wings, two staircases sweeping up to a row of columns and a shaded portico leading to open front doors where rows of liveried footmen waited. She glimpsed gardens beyond, neat beds and mazes sloping down to dark woods. The agency had done well by Miss Evans indeed. She couldn't help but feel a bit proud.

The carriage jolted to a halt at the front of the double stairs, and footmen in green and gold Pennington livery rushed forward to open the doors and let down the steps. Mary climbed down after Pen, holding Miss Muffins under one arm as she studied the dozens of sparkling windows, the Grecian columns, the forest of chimneys, with awe. How happy she was for Lady Pennington. How splendid to have a true home.

The hostess herself rushed out the front doors and down the marble steps to greet them, drawing a fur-edged shawl close against the wind. The skirts of her blue-striped silk gown, surely a Mademoiselle Sandrine creation, swayed around her. 'Oh, you're here at last! We were so afraid the snow would come in again and keep you away. But here you are, and Miss Muffins, too.' She took the delighted pup from Mary and kissed the top of her head as she led the way back to the house. 'Almost everyone is here, except for the Sandfords. We're having tea in the yellow drawing room, you must be famished after your drive.'

The drawing room was a long high-ceilinged space lined with tall windows on one side, looped and draped in pale yellow satin, with paintings on the other wall, gold frames against yellow and white striped silk paper, portraits and still-lifes and grand landscapes. The painted ceiling, inlaid with yellow and cream and pale green, had gods and goddesses and cupids peeking down from fluffy clouds, laughing at human foibles. The faded blue-and-green antique carpet was so thick Mary's boots sank into it, and it was dotted with conversational groupings of yellow brocade chairs and settees. Lord Pennington stood near the huge marble fireplace, talking to guests about his latest scientific experiments. Holly and evergreen boughs around the picture frames and fireplace scented the air with winter and Christmas.

It was all most welcoming, but Mary's heart quite sank when she saw Mr Overbury among the gathering. His expression lit up when he glimpsed her, but luckily he was in conversation with a group near the windows and could not escape. Yet.

'Miss St Aubin, I don't believe you know Mr Clark? An unexpected guest for Christmas, thanks to a cousin of my husband,' Lady Pennington said as they stopped next to a couple on a settee by the window, along with the odious Mr Clark.

Mary's eyes widened at the sound of that name. Adele's unwanted suitor, here, where she could not escape? She pasted on a polite smile; it would never do to give things away by letting him know she saw his game. He took her hand and bowed over it with a wide grin he no doubt thought of as charming and flirtatious. She had to force herself not to snatch her fingers back.

'Miss St Aubin. Delightful to meet you. You're as charming as everyone reports,' he said. Yes. Definitely slippery.

'Mr Clark,' she answered, taking a step back. Miss Muffins growled, and scurried off in search of more congenial company.

They only had to chat for a moment more, before Lady Pennington took Mary's arm and they strolled onward. 'I am afraid there is something about that Mr Clark I cannot find agreeable,' she whispered to Mary. 'But my husband's relations did insist on bringing him, and I didn't want to seem ungracious.'

'I am sure all will be well,' Mary whispered back. But she realised she had to say something to warn her hostess. 'I would just make sure he's not very near Miss Stewart when she arrives.'

Lady Pennington frowned. 'Has he been pressing his attentions on her? Oh! Poor girl. I think I did hear a whisper of some unfortunate young lady in Bristol last year. If I had known…'

'We'll be here to keep an eye on matters,' Mary said, trying not to let her worries show.

'Yes, I shall be vigilant. But I forgot! I did hear you were quite engaged to Miss Stewart's uncle. I was so happy to hear the news! After all the joy you have brought others, you deserve it doublefold yourself.'

'How did you know?' Mary whispered. 'We have made no announcement yet.'

'Such a small neighbourhood, is it not? Everyone loves such happy news. Though I think they love *bad* news even more.' Lady Pennington leaned closer. 'He is ever so handsome, I must say. Almost as much as my darling Pennington! How lucky you are.'

'Yes. Lucky.' Mary once again had to worry if their impulsive plan was such a good idea after all. The 'romance' of it all seemed to be doing the trick for the agency's reputation, but what would happen after? What would she tell her dear friends? And what of herself? She knew she should step back, away from him, guard herself against the moment when they would part. Yet a tiny sliver of her heart, the heart that belonged to the old, romantic Mary, longed to cling onto this connection for just a bit longer, before she resigned herself to industrious spinsterhood.

'So many are bragging that you helped *them* in their fine marriages, that obviously your eye for a happy match is like magic,' Lady Pennington said. 'Just as you did for me. They will be battering down your office doors.'

They stopped at the tea table, its white damask-draped length lined with enticing trays of cucumber and salmon sandwiches, pastel cakes, white-iced Christmas pudding, along with gleaming silver pots and thin china painted with primroses. Lady Pennington handed her a gold-edged cup. 'Will you have time to help them after you are wed?' she said, as she held out a plate of salmon mousse sandwiches. 'I hear that Mr Campbell's estate is in Scotland.'

'We—we haven't yet set a date or made firm plans,' Mary improvised.

'Of course! You want to make sure you perfectly suit, very wise of you.' She smiled as Mademoiselle Sandrine came into the room, glamorous in fur-edged dark blue velvet and matching turban. 'But one thing I'm sure of, Mademoiselle Sandrine will make the gown. All Bath will be so eager to see it.'

'Certainly I will go to her, if it comes to that. Yet, as I said, we have no firm plans yet. We just want to enjoy Christmas in your lovely home. So kind of you to invite us.'

Lady Pennington grimaced. 'I was quite nervous, I must admit. I've never hosted such a large gathering, but I wanted to show what we had done to the estate.' She glanced across the rooms at her parents, Mr and Mrs Evans, looking so proud and so in awe of their daughter's grand drawing room. 'I do hope everyone will find something to enjoy. I have planned games, charades and hide-and-seek, excursions to some local ruins if the weather will hold for us, and a ball for Christmas itself.'

'It all sounds most delightful.'

'I must give you a tour of Northland later. We've been working so hard on it, choosing colours, restoring floors, buying artwork. I wanted to keep the essence of it all, the history, especially in the park and gardens. There's a long gallery in the oldest part of the house, which was Elizabethan, and we can walk there if the snow comes in. And our laboratory, of course! Lord P. is working on his experiments there.'

Mary smiled to see how happy Lady Pennington was, how she glowed talking of her husband and home. And it was true, the agency *had* helped to bring it about. Maybe all would work out after all.

Lady Pennington refilled her teacup. 'I daresay Mr Campbell's home in Scotland is even older than

Northland! They say it's a castle. Does it have a moat? Dungeons? So stylish now.'

Mary laughed at her friend's enthusiasm, though she did feel a bit discomfited. She found she didn't know as much about Charles's home as she would like, just the mist and the heather that sounded like such magic, and she wanted to know *everything* about him. His childhood, his favourite food, favourite book! *Everything*.

After chatting for a few moments, Lady Pennington went to greet some newcomers, and Mary wandered to look at a painting hanging near the windows, a beautiful summer scene of children in a garden, laughing and leaping about with their dog. She was lost for a moment in the happiness of the painted scene, and thus did not notice she had left herself vulnerable to Mr Overbury.

'Miss St Aubin,' he said quietly from behind her, making her jump.

She whirled around, and found him lingering close, blocking her exit from the corner. 'Mr Overbury. What a surprise to see you here!'

'It has been much too long since we met.'

Mary made herself smile. 'You did call at the agency only a fortnight ago, Mr Overbury. I was so sorry we had no new entries on our files that would suit you.'

He leaned even closer, his flowery cologne threatening to engulf her in its cloud. 'You know my very high standards. My very high artistic needs for the lady I can truly love. My sensitive nature could never tolerate anything less than perfection.'

'I am aware,' Mary murmured. When he first arrived at the agency, when she and Ella thought he was a true prospect, they had sent him a few very suitable and beautiful ladies to consider. Then he decided he wanted Mary herself, and that was that. Yet he *was* a well-known poet, connected in Society, and they'd felt they could not toss him out. That his infatuation would fade. What a mistake that had been.

She wished she truly was in possession of a castle with a moat, to keep such suitors at bay. She pictured tossing failed agency applicants into the murky waters and smiled.

Unfortunately, Mr Overbury seemed to think the smile was for him. He stepped even closer, touching her hand. She took another step back but ran into the silk-papered wall. He pressed closer, making her feel a cold rush of panic, the need to flee. That cologne engulfed her, so different from the light crispness of Charles's alluring scent. So different from Charles's *everything*.

'I did so much want to share my new poetry with

you,' he said cajolingly. 'There is one verse in particular I hope you will like. That will touch your heart. "When Marian Walks across My Soul."'

'It—it sounds charming, Mr Overbury,' she said, trying so hard to sound polite, to escape without a scene. Polite but discouraging, in a way that would not wound his sensitive feelings and make more trouble for herself. 'About church, is it?'

His eyes widened in a flash of anger. 'No! It is about *love*, worldly love. True, pure, radiant love. For one lady, the only lady. It is most...'

The drawing room door opened, and Charles and Adele came in. Mary felt that cold panic fading away, and she only wanted to run to him. 'Do excuse me, Mr Overbury. I see someone I absolutely must greet,' she said quickly. She slid past him, ignoring his reddened face, the hand he held out to her.

She hurried towards Charles, her feet feeling so light they could surely skim the carpet to carry her to his side. But some of her quick rush of joy faded when she saw Adele notice Clark, saw the flustered blush that spread over the girl's cheeks.

'Miss Stewart,' Mary cried, taking Adele's arm to move her attention away from Clark and subtly draw her across the crowded room. Charles gave her a little nod to show he understood. 'I'm so happy you're here. I know you enjoy Gothic poetry, and there is this painting over here you would most enjoy, it reminds me of such tales. I should love to hear your thoughts on it.'

'Miss St Aubin,' Adele said, glancing over her shoulder in longing. 'Of course. Yet I was just going over...'

Mary inexorably led her around, still chatting about paintings, books, snow, whatever she could think of. Charles shot her a grateful look that made her feel warm all over. They were operating as a team to a good end, a feeling she enjoyed far too much.

'Mademoiselle Sandrine is here, as well,' Mary whispered to Adele. That seemed to catch the girl's full attention. 'I'm sure you would like to converse with her.'

'Oh, yes!' Adele enthused. 'You are so understanding, Miss St Aubin. Charles is kind, and I think he does try, but he is so—so *teuchle*. He doesn't understand how I long for beauty in the world, for emotion and truth, as others—well, as you do.'

Mary gave her a sympathetic smile. She did indeed remember how it was to long for something bigger, wider, more meaningful, to be young and filled with restlessness and desire. And she remembered that Charles, too, had once wanted to write poetry and find a grander world. Surely he could find it in him to connect with Adele now. They both had such good hearts.

'Oh, my dear,' she said, taking Adele's arm. 'I think you must not underestimate him…'

'And how is the servants' hall here at Northland, Daisy?' Mary asked as Daisy helped her prepare for dinner. She studied herself in the dressing table mirror as her hair was curled and pinned, fastened with a ribbon bandeau. Miss Muffins lounged on the large soft bed with its yellow satin counterpane and yellow-and-blue-striped hangings, trying to loll on the precious gown that lay pressed and ready to be donned. It was a lovely, comfortable room, the bright colours bringing a bit of summer into the winter chill, with several cushioned chairs ready to curl up and read in, a fire crackling in the white marble hearth.

'Oh, ever so nice!' Daisy said as she frowned at an errant curl and pinned it firmly in place. 'It's a grand house. You did well for Miss Evans.'

'She did well for herself, standing up to her parents in the beginning.' If only other potential patrons could see what Mary could do for *them*! With or without her own match. 'It is a beautiful house, true. Perfect for Christmas.'

'It's nice to get away from Bath for a time, isn't it, miss? Meet some different people, hear some different conversation...'

Mary thought of the large gathering in the drawing room, of Adele—and Mr Clark. 'Indeed. If we can avoid certain guests and spend more time with the best ones.' Like Charles. She wouldn't mind in the least if the party was *only* him! The two of them talking, walking in the snow—kissing. She turned her head as she studied herself in the mirror, wondering if he would like her hair that way, then scolding herself for even caring. 'Daisy, do you think I need to do something new with my hair? Cut it, maybe? Or grow it longer?'

Daisy's eyes lit up with a challenge. 'Your hair looks lovely as it is, miss, but with this colour and the curl of it, you could do ever so much! Perhaps like...this?' She twisted some up, leaving other curls dangling enticingly against her neck. 'You would be the diamond of the evening!'

'Then let's try it. And it should go well with the new blue gown. Very fashionable.' She wanted to look her best, to gather people interested in the agency and convince them she was *au courant* in all matters. Not for Charles. No, definitely not. Assuredly not.

But what would he really think?

Daisy had just added the final touches to the new coiffure, making sure it tumbled 'artlessly' like some fashionable milkmaid, when there was a knock at the door. Adele peeked her head in.

'You asked if I could come see you, Miss St Aubin?' she asked shyly. Mary smiled and held out her hand, hoping she could help in some way.

'Oh, yes, Miss Stewart! Do come in, I was just finishing my toilette for the evening.' She stood up and tightened the sash of her dressing gown as she gestured to a chair by the fire. 'I won't take up much of your time before dinner, I just had a small gift for you. A sort of early Christmas.'

Adele's eyes widened. 'A gift for me?'

'Yes. I do hope you'll like it, if not we can find something else to suit, I'm sure.' Mary took out a long white box tied with pale blue ribbons and handed it to Adele. She waited anxiously to see the girl's thoughts.

Adele eagerly pulled off the lid—and gasped. Her hand flew to her mouth as she stared down at the treasures tucked there in tissue. 'Oh, Miss St Aubin! It's—it's…'

'Do you like it? If the colour is wrong…'

Adele clutched the gown to her as if it would be snatched away. 'It is *perfect*.'

Mary smiled in relief. 'Sandrine can make adjustments if it doesn't fit. She says it will be the height of fashion in London with those cap sleeves, but I thought you might want to wear it first for the Christmas ball here at Northland.'

'My very own Mademoiselle Sandrine gown,' Adele whispered. She held it up, and the firelight danced on the small spangles caught in the rosy chiffon. 'But what will Uncle Charles say? He declares I am too young!'

'Leave him to me,' Mary said.

Adele hurried to the mirror and held up the elegantly draped folds of the skirt to her, twirling around. 'Oh, yes, for you are to marry him! I don't see how you can, he's such a stuffy old ogre, but I am very happy you'll be here.'

Charles, a stodgy old ogre? Mary thought of the fire of his kisses, the music of his laughter, and wanted to giggle. He was hardly old. Or stodgy. She wasn't sure about the ogre. 'I hope I can be of some help to you both.'

'You bought me a Mademoiselle Sandrine gown! You are an angel of helpfulness.' She twirled into the chair again as Daisy helped Mary with her own gown, clutching the rose-pink silk and chiffon close. 'I do so miss my mother sometimes. She was so good, so wise. I wish she was here to tell me how to be like her, instead of so confused all the time.'

Mary nodded sadly. She understood that feeling all too well. She'd lost her mother too young, before they had many such moments between them, and she wondered what it would have been like to confide in her, choose gowns together, to whisper and laugh. When her mother was gone, so much light went out of their little family, and she didn't want to hurt that way again. 'I, too, miss my mother. She died when I was just a child. Ella was wonderful, but I know she also yearned for our mother's counsel.'

Adele carefully smoothed the gown, staring down at it. 'Miss St Aubin...'

'Mary, please.'

'Mary. How do you think our mothers would have advised us about—love?'

Mary glanced at Daisy, and they exchanged cautious nods. 'What about love, my dear?'

'How does a person know that they are really in love?'

Mary stared at her for a moment, rather dumbfounded. Surely describing love was rather like trying to explain the colour blue? Impossible. She thought of all the couples she'd met through the agency, what had made her sure they would suit one another.

'Surely it means the way one longs to see the person, counts the seconds until they are there?' Adele said, and touched her heart. 'And the flutterings just here! The longings!'

'It is lovely to first meet someone special and feel like that, yes,' Mary said, squeezing Adele's hand. 'You see someone in a ballroom or across a teashop, and they are handsome and charming, and make you feel warm all over. As if you could melt with delight! Yet this feeling lacks what true love needs to grow—vulnerability to another person, showing them our true self and glimpsing theirs in return. Understanding each other. Knowing one's soft heart, the one we usually hide away, is safe with them.'

She thought of Charles, of how when he studied her so closely, she thought he could see everything, that she could say anything to him.

'And those butterflies we can feel?' Adele asked.

Mary laughed. 'They are lovely and very important, of course. One must have passion. Attraction. But also a real, heartfelt friendship. That feeling does not fade but only grows deeper. It takes time, yet you'll want to stay deep in conversation with them, day after day, hear them, look into their eyes. Be together even when there are difficult times. They will help make everything easier. You want to know their dreams and desires, everything about them...'

'And they will desire that, too?' Adele asked doubtfully. Maybe Clark did not wish to converse with her, know her more deeply. Maybe she was realising that now.

'Yes. That is how two people come to be their true selves with each other. To see and accept imperfections...' Mary shook her head, as if she could clear it of her own dreams and hopes, hopes she feared could never really be. 'And if you love things in your own life, art or music or family, you want them to be a part of all that, and they will want that, too. To help and support you. Love does not leave you confused or unhappy. It is like—being on the same cricket team. Making one's life whole.'

Adele giggled. 'I cannot play cricket. But I do like the idea of working together. Very much.'

'As do I,' Mary whispered.

'That's the second gong, miss,' Daisy said, and tied off Mary's sash, smoothing the short sleeves. 'We should finish getting you dressed.'

'Oh, I've kept you too long, Mary.' Adele jumped

up, holding her treasured gown close. 'I should go and let you finish.'

'Adele.' Mary reached for her hand, worried, hoping beyond hope she had given her something to think about, warned her subtly away from men like Clark. 'You will think of our conversation? You are so young, and your first Season is about to begin. You have so very many possibilities open to you, you must consider so carefully what *you* really want.'

Adele frowned doubtfully. 'How will I know it's what I want and not what everyone says I must want?'

Ah, yes, there was the rub. 'I have often wrestled with that dilemma myself,' Mary admitted. 'Just— listen to yourself. Make a space of quiet where you can really hear. And remember, you do have time. Don't rush.'

Adele quickly, as if on impulse, kissed Mary's cheek and hurried out.

'There is a sweet girl,' Daisy said as she smoothed the blue organdie skirts of Mary's dinner gown.

'Sweet, yes. And confused, I fear,' Mary murmured in worry. She wondered if this was an inkling of what real mothers felt as they watched their children try to take wing. It was terrifying.

'You'll help her, miss,' Daisy said reassuringly.

'If anyone can help, it's you. Look what you and Miss Ella have done for all your agency folk!'

Mary nodded, but she simply wasn't sure. When it came to her patrons, she could see so clearly what they needed, what they longed for. When it came to herself, things were so much cloudier.

Mary thought she had never seen a more perfect evening before.

Dinner in the elegant Northland dining room had been a delight, white soup and haricot lamb, salmon mousse and cinnamon apples, all amid laughter and talk of all the delightful plans for this party. She'd rather forgotten all her worries, felt like her old, carefree self again.

Now she strolled beside Charles along the windows of Northland's long gallery, the chalky silver moonlight spilling through the old wavy glass of the windows to cast dancing shadows on the dark panelled walls and faded floral carpet runner. Suits of old armour and portraits of people in huge ruffs and wide skirts watched them as they passed, laughing together.

The convivial sounds of dinner went on in the sitting room at the end of the gallery, Adele playing Christmas carols, coffee cups clinking. Best of all, Mary was there with *him*, practically alone at the darker end of the old gallery. They'd been separated at dinner, yet close enough to cast each other glances that seemed to say they understood exactly what the other was thinking about the conversation, about their fellow guests. Now she could feel all the cosiness of winter closing over them like a downy blanket. The cold weather always seemed a time for firesides, quilts, books, cuddling and intimacy. She'd been lonely so long! Maybe all her yearning for Charles was for just this sort of thing, a place to belong, cosy family moments. She feared she was coming to rely on him too much, to long for him. Would she struggle when he was gone? Feel even more alone?

She stopped to stare out the window, wishing she could press her flushed cheek to the chilly glass, to banish the images of cosiness and domesticity. They were much more dangerous than any lust could be, more alluring. But she knew the winter night wouldn't cool her, because he would still be there, right next to her.

'I can see why the Penningtons are so happy here,' she said. 'It's like a fairy-tale house, a dream. Just look at the moonlight on that old tower! And the snow blanketing everything, sparkling under the night sky. It could have been written in a romantic novel and brought to light.'

Charles stepped up next to her, studying the beautiful scene. 'Lord Pennington was telling us at dinner that the tower was built in the 1200s. A maiden of the house was not allowed to marry her true love, and when she heard he was killed in battle, she flung herself from the tower. Only he was not dead but wounded, and came back seeking her. When he found she had perished, he jumped from the highest window to join her. Their souls have walked the gardens ever since.'

'How very sad! I'm glad there's so much happiness here now.' She glanced across the room at Lady Pennington, whose husband stood behind her, his hand on her shoulder, the two of them laughing together. 'Such joy surely banishes old sorrows.'

'Oh, I don't know. They say there's a ghost here.'

'A ghost!' Mary cried with a delicious chill.

Charles laughed, as if he sensed how very much she enjoyed a spooky tale. 'Probably several, in a place so old. But this one is about lost love.'

'Oh. How can I bear such heartbreaking tales on such a fine evening?'

He smiled as if he knew how much she really loved them. Such romance. 'I would have thought a haunted medieval tower perfect for your poetry-reading heart.'

'For poetry, maybe. But not on a night like this.

Christmas just seems made for being cosy, don't you think?'

He looked out the window, a shadow seeming to pass over his eyes, darkening them to moss. 'I don't think my childhood Christmases could have been called cosy. My father was always gone, and the house was very cold in the winter, very silent.'

Mary's heart ached to imagine him so lonely, as she once was. 'Your father was away often, as mine was?'

Charles grimaced. 'In a way. When he was home, he was often in a rage, followed by icy silence. It was often better when he was gone. His estate was his priority, just as your father's parish was his, and that work overcame all else.'

Mary understood such feelings very well. 'And you had no fun at Christmas at all?'

'It wasn't entirely bad. At Christmas, they told ghost stories in the servants' hall, and I would sneak down to listen to them. If I was very good, cook would give me some extra mince pies.'

'Ghost stories?' Mary's heart ached to imagine him as a lonely little boy. She longed to hold him close, make him feel safe as he always did for her. She laid the edge of her hand against his, and he touched her little finger with his, a small, secret link.

He smiled, the wistfulness dissolving. 'A fine old Scots tradition, ghostly tales at Christmas. Didn't you do that?'

'My father was a vicar! He wouldn't have approved. Christmas was all church services, visiting parishioners, serving tea. But when my mother was alive...' Mary looked back out the window, and for a moment she saw not snowy gardens and medieval towers, but the warmth of her mother's firelit sitting room, the sound of the pianoforte playing carols, the sweet cinnamon scents of cakes, and laughter as they tried to play snapdragon. 'She loved Christmas, and when her duties were done there were games and special sweets, gifts and books and music. Ella and I tried to do what we could after she was gone, to remember her, but it wasn't quite the same.'

Charles smiled understandingly, and all the sadness seemed gone like a cloud. She wasn't so alone now, the walls around her heart not quite so high. 'And since you came to Bath?'

'We go to church at the Abbey, of course, and then have a fine dinner and give gifts. But I'm glad to be at Northland now. Just listen to that music! And so many people making merry. Very Christmas-like, and yet nothing like any Christmas I've had before. I enjoy the idea of finding new traditions.'

They walked onward, and when they turned a corner into a silent, dark window nook, he gathered her into his arms. 'What would you choose to do, then, in an all-new, Mary-approved Christmas?'

'Hmm, let me see.' She tapped at her chin, pretending to be deep in thought. 'Make sure everyone has someone to kiss under the mistletoe! That should be on my agency books to instruct everyone.'

He laughed deeply, warmly, making her tingle all down to her toes. 'A new branch of your agency? Christmas instructions?'

'Yes! The Mistletoe Branch. No one should be alone for Christmas.' She twirled around a bit, feeling suddenly lighter, more fun, whimsical thoughts tumbling through her head. 'There must be plum pudding. And charades. And definitely flowers and music!'

Charles took her hand and spun her about until she giggled dizzily. 'That is what you recommend for promoting a Christmas romance?'

'Of course. And dancing! That's the most important of all.'

They listened for a moment to the strains of a

waltz drifting from Adele's piano. 'Then I would fail miserably,' Charles said.

'Not with my help. That's what the agency is here for. I did promise you dance lessons.'

'How about now?'

'Right now?' she laughed.

'No time like the present.'

'Very well, then. Take my hand and bow. I know you can do that.'

He took her hand with a flourish, and bowed so low his head nearly brushed the floor, making her laugh. 'I did that well, yes?'

'Very well,' she answered through her giggles. 'Now, step like this—no, to the left. And around. Faster.'

'I can do that, too!' he said, and twirled her around, taking both her hands to send her into a loop. Faster and faster, into and out of beams of moonlight, closer and closer.

Mary threw back her head and laughed giddily as they twirled and spun. How light she felt, how young and free! He held her safe, and she could soar.

They skidded to a halt, both of them breathless. 'See. You are a better dancer already.'

He stared down at her, intent, serious as their giggles faded away. There was that look only he ever gave her, as if he saw everything. Understood everything. 'Only when I'm with you.'

Mary couldn't breathe. 'I—I'm sure everyone would believe us betrothed, then.'

'So we should hold hands more? Sigh and shoot longing glances across the room?'

'Maybe we could—try this?' She held up her hand, palm out, and he pressed his own hand against it. She went up on tiptoe and kissed him. It was soft and tentative at first, just an impulse. But the taste of him, the way his mouth felt on hers—it made her fall down and down into a blurry abyss of sheer need.

His hands closed over her shoulders, and for an instant she feared he might push her away. Then he groaned, a wild sound deep in his throat, and he dragged her close against his body.

His mouth hardened on hers, his tongue tracing the curve of her lips before plunging inside to taste deeply. She only wanted more, more of this kiss, more of *him*.

How could he do this to her? She seemed to lose herself when she was with him, yet she was more truly herself than ever. It was too wild, too uncontrollable, and she loved it.

She twined her fingers in his hair and held him

closer. He went most willingly, kissing her with a heated artlessness and sheer need that fed her own.

A sudden burst of laughter from around the corner startled her, making her jump back from him. He stared back at her, tousled, startled, his eyes very dark.

'I'm sure that was against the rules,' she gasped.

He ran a shaking hand through his hair, leaving the glossy dark strands awry. 'Entirely.'

'We are to be friends.'

'Yes. Friends.'

'And partners in seeing the agency and Adele succeed. That is all.'

'Completely.' He paused. 'Yet, we do seem to break our rules often.'

Mary remembered the bookstore, their sizzling kiss there, and she sighed. 'So we do. It must stop. Immediately.'

'Immediately.'

They stared at each other in the crackling, taut silence. She was altogether doubtful that was a bargain she could keep.

Charles had always been a man of his word, even in his wild youth. A promise was a promise. Now his word was slipping out of his grasp. How could he ever keep his bargain with Mary? How could he ever walk away from her, from their 'betrothal,' and never think of it again?

Friends! Friends with rules, like no kissing. Those rules hadn't lasted long at all.

And how he longed to break them, every one of them, one after another. To catch Mary up in his arms and stride from the room, away from the crowds, to lock her up alone with him until they could work this strange intoxication, this glittering magic that seemed to fly through the air whenever she was near, out of their systems. Surely what he felt for Mary was just desire? Never mind how he loved to laugh with her, talk to her, just look at her, if they could truly be together for just one moment, his feelings would vanish. That had to be it, because he could never bear to make her unhappy in any way, as any wife of his would surely be.

He took a glass of wine from the tray of a passing footman and stood there half hidden in the shadows of a window drapery as he studied the party, feeling so apart from all their merriment.

Mary and Pen stood by the pianoforte, listening to Adele as she played carols. Adele did seem much happier with Mary, more at ease, laughing as they sang a rousing chorus of 'Good King Wenceslas.' Mary turned the page of the music, laughing at something Pen said, breaking up their lyrics. She looked like sunshine in the moment, like happiness personified, and he was captured by it.

He felt that enchantment anytime she was near. She made him feel like himself again, like the weight of the world was slipping off him and he was, or could be, free.

He was still grinning like a foolish schoolboy now as he studied her across the room, as admirers flocked around her. She did have so many suitors, whether she wanted them or not, and none of them seemed to worry whether she could make matches as a 'spinster' or not! They only wanted to be near her, as he did. Seemed to long for her laughter, the warmth of her smile, her attention.

He noticed a young viscount among the circle, a baron who handed her a glass of punch and then lingered. Aye, Mary had declared she was committed only to her business, but anyone could see it didn't have to be that way. She could have any life she chose—any man she really wanted.

So what could she want with him? He had a respectable estate, a fine income, a rebellious niece and more years behind him than he cared to think of.

He glanced at a group of ladies who sat near the vast old fireplace, whispering over their teacups as they studied the gathering at the pianoforte. It struck him that perhaps it was not the gentlemen who stayed away from the agency, who were wary of it, but the ladies. Afraid their matchmaker would take all the attention?

Charles almost laughed aloud. Of course. It all made sense. Mary was ethereally beautiful, with her golden hair and luminous skin, her wide smile. But she also had the kindest heart, the shrewdest, clearest judgement about matches. They were only harming themselves if they wouldn't trust her. He had to fix it all. To help her.

He turned back to watch the pianoforte. Mary had slid onto the bench with Adele, and the two of them played a lively duet, their hands flying together over the keyboard, laughing, their faces alight with fun. Mary glowed with the performance, brighter than the ice-sharp stars beyond the windows, filled with such life. She made him feel alive, too. Made him look forward to things again.

He realised how easily, how very easily, he could fall in love with her, tumble down deep and never be found again. Yet he could not. He knew he did not make a good husband, and he couldn't bear to see any of her glow dimmed.

'Mr Campbell,' a man said, and Charles tore his rapt attention from Mary's laughing face to see Percy Overbury watching him. He scowled at Charles's greeting smile.

Suddenly he remembered what Mary had said about the man's courtship of her. 'Mr Overbury?'

The frown deepened. 'You know who I am?'

'Of course. The poet.'

He ducked his head, as if trying for modesty. 'I see my work does precede me. I do try to circulate my verses only to a few friends, but they will persist in showing them to others.'

'And you know me.'

The man's eyes narrowed. 'Not well, no. The Scots are not regular *habitués* of Bath, are they? I'm surprised you can tear yourself away from the lochs for our theatres, dances and soirées. How strange it must all seem.'

Charles smiled. 'Oh, I am ever surprising, Mr Overbury. A man of many interests.'

'And I think one of them is Miss St Aubin.' The man's chubby white fingers curled into fists.

'It is,' Charles said simply. 'She is a fine lady indeed.'

'She is a goddess! And she deserves far more than some run-down ruin in the Highlands.'

Charles quite agreed about Mary's goddesshood, though his house and park were not really falling down and were not in the Highlands. As for what

Mary deserved—Overbury was not wrong there. She deserved everything. All the things Charles couldn't give her, and he thought Overbury certainly could not. She would have plenty of suitors when they parted ways, if she wanted them. She would have her business. He could help give her that. Yet he longed to give her so much more.

'Surely that is all up to her,' he said, trying to sound supremely careless.

Overbury suddenly grabbed his arm, and Charles stared down at him coolly, even as his heart seemed to pause to see if there was to be a fight right in the Northland gallery. 'She belongs with me! I can give her all she needs, all she requires. I adore her! I have ever since I first glimpsed her. We are twin souls.'

Charles arched his brow at the man and slid his arm away. 'As I said, that is up to her. I see no ring of yours on her finger.'

'Nor I yours, though they whisper you are engaged. Surely her true fiancé would have presented her with the largest, greatest jewel.'

'No jewel could ever compete with the light in her eyes,' Charles snapped, and he realised that little flight of his own poetical fancy was very true. Nothing was brighter, more enticing than her eyes as they laughed and danced. *Lud*, but he was as bad as Overbury now! Mary did bring out the romantic fool in him. 'Our friendship is surely none of your business.'

'My business!' The man's face turned an alarming shade of scarlet. 'I *love* her, and I have since long before you arrived. I deserve her. No one can ever understand her as I can. I am warning you—'

'No. I am warning *you.*' He seized Overbury's arm, holding it with seeming lightness as the man's eyes widened with a flash of pain. 'Miss St Aubin wishes to choose her own friends, and they do not include you. You have tried to play the game, and you lost long ago. If I catch you pestering her again, I shall not be accountable for my actions.'

Overbury tore himself away and fell back a step. 'Just like a barbaric Scot! Miss St Aubin will not stand long for such behaviour, I'm sure. Then she will remember who her true friends are. I shall see to that, with the help of others concerned with her happiness.' He smoothed his bright green coat.

'Others?'

'You will find she is not as friendless as you might think, as you try to take advantage of her kindness! There is Mr Clark, and—and others…'

'Clark?' Charles said sharply, suddenly alarmed. What did Adele's unwanted suitor have to do with it? 'Is he your friend, then?'

Overbury seemed to realise he had made some sort of mistake and glanced away. 'He is a man of refinement and feeling, he defends wrong wherever he sees it, just as I do. Those of us with chivalry in our blood will not let you so mistreat ladies, Mr Campbell. You had best stay far away from me! Your threats mean nothing here.' He fled into the crowd.

Charles scowled after him. What did this man and Clark have to do with each other? What did Overbury think he held over Mary? Charles glanced at Adele and Mary at the pianoforte, the two of then laughing together, and a wave of protectiveness washed over him. He would let no one hurt them, ever. They were too precious.

Lady Pennington came up to him with a smile, the plumes on her satin headdress nodding. 'I do hope you are enjoying yourself here, Mr Campbell?'

'Very much. Your home is very beautiful, Lady Pennington, and your cook superlative. How could anyone not enjoy themselves?' Though he did wonder about her taste in other guests, if Overbury and Clark were samples.

'I am so glad you and Miss Stewart could come. I've so enjoyed getting to know her this winter.' She studied Adele at the pianoforte, her head tilted with concentration. 'Her music is sublime. And she does seem to be enjoying herself, now that she is past a bit of shyness! I did worry Northland might be dull for one so young.'

'She always tells me she is not young at all, and I must cease treating her like a child.'

Lady Pennington laughed. 'She sounds like I did with my own parents! You are so good with her, and I will make sure she has a merry Christmas. Mrs Oliver tells me she needs to learn a bit more about Society before she goes to London. And I'll make sure you have a nice Christmas, too.'

Charles thought of dancing with Mary, and knew he'd never had a better Christmas before. 'I just enjoy watching the fun.'

'But you cannot just watch! The Christmas spirit will catch you, Mr Campbell, I promise.' She gave him a sideways, searching glance. 'Miss St Aubin looks beautiful tonight, does she not?'

'She is always beautiful.'

'Indeed she is. And so kind. My husband and I owe everything to her. But tonight she has such... such *radiance* about her. Don't you think?'

He studied Mary again, his very favourite pastime those days, and smiled to see her smile. The golden aura that seemed to shimmer all around her.

And yet there were those blasted rules.

'Very much,' he murmured, and knew he was in deeper trouble than he'd ever been before in his life.

Chapter Ten

'Your home is extraordinary, Pennington,' Charles said as Lord Pennington led him towards the breakfast room after a morning tour of Northland's chambers and corridors, the laboratory where the Penningtons worked side by side. They'd transformed a large cold, old place into a haven of warmth and intimacy, and he wished so much he could do the same. Find just such a home. He'd always longed to create such a feeling in his own castle, his estate, but despite his care for it, it never felt warm. Never felt like the home that hovered just beyond his reach all his life.

Lord Pennington smiled proudly. 'It's almost entirely due to my wife. She has improved my life so much, Campbell, I can't even tell you. My life was quite desolate before I found her! She's transformed it all.'

Charles smiled, even as he felt a pang of jealousy.

He'd never wanted to make a home before, never wanted someone to share it all with. Until now.

Pennington pushed open the door to the yellow and white breakfast room, where the long, gleaming table was set with tea and toast, the sideboard groaning with chafing dishes and covered platters, quiet laughter in the air. He saw Mary and Penelope sitting at the far end, whispering together, and his heart ached at their smiles.

All of that warm contentment faded in one icy flash when he glimpsed Adele, sitting at a quiet corner of the table with Mr Clark. Their heads were bent together, their expressions solemn as they whispered. The man touched her hand.

Charles stalked towards them. 'Charles...' he heard Mary say, a warning note in her voice. He ignored her, a haze of anger and—was that fear?—wrapping around him. He strode ahead to get his niece away from that bounder.

Adele looked up, and her eyes widened. 'Uncle Charles!' she choked out, pulling her hand away from Clark.

He took her arm and gave it a little tug. 'Come and sit with me now, Adele.'

She tried to draw away. 'Uncle Charles, really, we were just talking. Surely I am allowed to have friends! To sit where I choose at breakfast.'

'This man is not your friend,' he said. He was aware of the others in the room, the way they watched while trying to pretend not to see, and he couldn't seem to back away. Couldn't just leave her there.

Mr Clark rose to his feet, a smirk on his lips. 'Mr Campbell. If we could just talk, if you could come to know me, I'm sure we would understand each other. This miscommunication could be quickly cleared away. I have nothing but respect for your niece.'

Charles studied him carefully and could see something of his old self in the man's eyes. The sense that he was the only one that mattered, it was of small concern if others got hurt as long as he had what he wanted. Charles hated his old self, the rakish young man Aileen thought he would always be, the one so irresponsible and careless, and he would not let Adele be caught up in the darkness of such a man. He had to try to be worthy of her now, worthy to take care of her. 'Just leave her alone,' he said as cold and steady as he could make himself. 'I shall not say this again.'

Clark stared at him a moment longer, just a beat too long, before he bowed and left the room, not looking behind him.

'Uncle Charles,' Adele whispered. 'How dare

you! How can you ruin my chance of happiness this way?' She, too, ran from the room, and Penelope followed.

Charles was suddenly even more aware of being watched, and he feared he'd ruined what he and Mary hoped to accomplish with their 'betrothal.' He left the breakfast room and made his way towards the library, where he doubted anyone would be at that hour. He had to think clearly, decide how to protect Adele and fix everything. Make it right once more, for the women he cared about so much.

Mary pushed open the library door, Miss Muffins at her heels, and saw Charles standing by the window, staring out at the snowy scene of the garden. The other guests had gathered there to explore the white-dusted pathways, laughing and jostling, tossing snowballs. He looked so lost in stormy thoughts she wondered if she should interrupt.

'How is she?' he asked roughly. He didn't turn around, just seemed to know Mary was the one who stood there. She longed to go to him, take his hand, reassure him, so she did just that. His fingers were warm in hers, and after an instant he squeezed back.

'She will mend.'

'Will she?' he asked doubtfully.

'Of course! She was already smiling when I left her, and Sandrine is looking over fashion plates with her. Adele has a wonderful eye for colour and line, she will be distracted for quite some time.'

Charles glanced down at her, his eyes unreadable. 'What did she say about me?'

Mary smiled up at him. 'That you are a cruel monster, of course, bent on shattering love's young dream.'

He laughed, though it sounded a bit rusty. 'Aye, that's me. I shouldn't have reacted that way. They were only talking, and others were nearby. But when I saw him with her, looking so *small*, I just lost my temper.'

'You were quite right to do so. It's only a small step from a bit of flirtation over the breakfast table to arranging a meeting in—in that summer house over there, maybe.' She gestured to an elegant little folly atop a slope in the garden, its windowless space perfect for liaisons. 'Now Clark can be in no doubt you are watching him. That people know his wiles.'

'And push her closer to him? What was it you said about forbidden love?'

Mary shrugged. 'She is young. I remember what that was like. We need only get her to London this spring, and she will see how paltry Clark looks compared to all other possibilities.'

He tilted his head, watching her closely. 'We?'

She felt the heat of a blush touch her cheeks and turned to the window. 'Well, *you*, I suppose. But I am here to help you now. Was that not our bargain?'

'Ah, yes. The bargain.' The bargain that was meant to help save her business, at least in the short term. Buy her time. For if there was no business in the short term, there could not be in the long term, so the risk of how people would see her matchmaking skills if her own betrothal ended was worth it.

It had been meant to be all so businesslike. Now all she wanted to do was help him, be beside him, take all those shadows and worries from his beautiful eyes. The risk had turned out to be to her heart. 'Yes, certainly.'

'Adele likes you. I'm glad she can confide in you.'

'I'm glad, too. It isn't easy being between two worlds as she is, not a child but not yet quite a grown-up lady. I'm happy to help if I can.' She made herself laugh. 'And your end of the agreement seems to be working! I've had a few people ask me about the agency, for relatives or friends who wish to find a good match.'

He leaned back, crossing his arms. 'Is that so?

Any spectacular matches in mind yet, like the Penningtons?'

'Not quite so grand, but I have hopes. There was a viscount last night during the music, he would like to find a suitable wife who likes riding to hounds as much as he does. And the Penningtons *are* very happy, aren't they?' So happy they positively glowed with it. It made her feel so satisfied and also so, so envious.

'That they are. Lord Pennington showed me his laboratory early this morning and bragged about his wife's intelligence in the sciences. I've never seen a man so in alt about his life.' He shifted on his feet, staring at the crowd outside. 'I admit I was a bit jealous.'

Mary laughed. 'Me too. They are so sickeningly perfect together. They have made such a home here together. A place to belong.'

And she found she wanted that, too. Especially when she was near Charles as she was just then. 'I could—could find you such a thing. Through the agency.'

'Wouldn't that be an odd thing to do for your own fiancé?'

'Once we are…ended. I could help you.' She hated that thought, it made her want to scream and stamp her foot in protest! But that was what a person did for friends, surely. Looked for what was best for them. Even when it hurt.

'Can you, then? Even for such a monster as myself?'

'Well, it would not be easy. I might have to charge quite a sizable fee.'

He laughed again, and she loved to hear it, loved making him laugh. 'Whatever you charge, it isn't enough for such a difficult case as mine.'

Mary sighed. 'I must admit, since Ella and Harry left, I feel rather confused about so many things. They mostly took care of the business side of matters—accounts, ledgers, ordering. I just looked for patrons, thought up matches. Now I must learn it all, and fast.'

'I understand.'

'Do you?' She glanced up at him, at the halo of pale light around him. 'You seem good at everything. Confident. Racing, cricket, riding...' *Kissing.* No, no, there should be no thoughts of kissing at all.

'Before my father died, he'd pretty well cut me off from most things at the estate. His passing was rather quick, and suddenly I was in charge of it all. Staff and tenants, accounts, decisions. I had to grow up in a great hurry, when I realised I could never let them down. I found that my name, my home, really did mean something to me after all.'

'What did you do?'

'Listened, mostly. In many ways, I think a castle is like any other business—like a matchmaking agency. You must put the right people together to get the task accomplished in the best way. Must stay organised. I did it, and you can, as well.'

'You think I could?' she asked.

'Of course! You are one of the most energetic people I've ever known, Mary, one of the smartest and most intuitive. You want to help as many people as possible, I can see that. Just as I do at my estate.'

He did see her, did see what she longed to accomplish. He believed in her. Mary felt like dancing. 'That is true. I want everyone who feels—well, *unique*, different, everyone who is lonely and wants to be seen, to know they can come to me and I will help. I want branches of the agency all over the place! London! Edinburgh! York! All filled with happy couples like the Penningtons that *I* have helped.'

'And you will certainly do so. Employing ladies like yourself everywhere.'

Mary studied his face in the light, all angles and shadows, his jewel-green eyes written with nothing but confidence and admiration. Confidence in *her*.

It was a strange feeling, an intoxicating one. She'd

always been the younger sister, the flighty one, the one who had to be looked after. But Charles believed in *her*. Believed she could do more, do what she dreamed of. He treated her as if she were competent and smart. And it made her feel, deep inside, that she really was.

It also made her ache to kiss him. To throw her arms around him and hold him ever so close.

A snowball suddenly smacked into the glass of the window, reminding her they were not entirely alone after all.

'Well, there is still one part of our bargain we haven't completed yet,' she said.

His brow quirked in question. 'And what's that?'

'Dancing! I did promise you lessons. I cannot stake the reputation of my agency on a man who cannot dance.' She held out her hand to him, palm up.

'Right now?'

'When better? We have this vast room, no one is watching, and Lady Pennington says there will be dancing after dinner tonight. Don't you want to impress all the fine ladies here with your elegance? Sweep them off their slippers?'

'Not treading on their slippers would be a start,' he muttered. But he did take her hand and let her lead him into the centre of the library, under the doubtful stares of the portraits on the walls between the bookcases.

'There's no music,' he said. 'Maybe we should try later…'

Mary held on to him firmly. 'No time like the present. We must seize the chance, before the party ends. It will all go well. You will dazzle the whole gathering!'

'Do you think we will fool everyone into thinking I am the Louis XIV of the Christmas ball, leaping about in a graceful ballet?' he said.

Mary laughed and blew a stray curl from her eyes. 'Well, I suppose we must not get ahead of ourselves. Every journey begins with one step. A chassé step, to be precise. Come, let's try that one.'

As they made their way to a clear space on the carpet, she had to remind herself sternly they were there to dance. To make everyone believe they were betrothed—and then possibly find Charles a true match later, thanks to his dazzling new dance skills. Not to fall deep into the blissful forgetfulness of his kisses again.

'Now,' she said, trying to sound brisk, practical. 'We can do a basic waltz step first. One, *two*, three. Right, left, glide. Right, left, give a little hop here. Like this.'

She demonstrated, and he followed her smoothly enough, landing rather heavily but quite acceptable.

'Very good,' she said with a laugh. 'Are you sure you really don't know how to dance?'

'You've seen me.'

'Indeed. Hmm. Well, let's try to add a few flourishes, then.' She stepped closer, and his warm, clean scent enveloped her, surrounding her, making her dizzy. She swallowed hard and reached for his hand. 'Now, place one hand at my waist, like this.' She laid his right hand close, his touch pressing against her, warm through her gown. She was beginning to think this was a huge mistake. 'And the other can go against my back, lightly, just above my—my…'

A tiny smile touched his lips. 'Your *what*, Mary?'

'Here.' She dared to press his hand into the back of her waist. Suddenly she grew so tense she could barely move, barely breathe, and he stared down at her.

Don't faint, she told herself.

She peeked up at him and found his eyes had darkened in that intense way that always made her forget everything. She could feel the crackle between them as a palpable thing.

'I—now, step,' she whispered. 'I turn thus, we

take a forward gliding step. Both with the same foot at the same time, to turn. One, two, and...'

But Charles got ahead of her, stepping forward before she did. His leg tangled in her skirts, and she tilted off balance, falling towards the floor.

'Oh!' she cried, and clutched at his shoulders. He held her close, turning at the last second so he landed on the floor with her on top of him, their bodies pressed closely together. She tumbled off, and started laughing helplessly, laughing until tears ran down her face, and she heard the rumble of his own laughter next to her.

'So, now I'm ready to dazzle them all?' he said breathlessly, helping her to her feet.

Mary gave in to temptation, and reached up to smooth his tousled hair, feeling the silk of it against her fingers, the warmth of him all through her. 'You have the makings of a dancer, I vow it.'

He twirled her in a circle, making her laugh again. 'I shall dazzle them all! My fallings-down will charm all the young ladies, aye?'

Mary was so charmed by his smile, *too* charmed. She just wanted to jump on him, kiss him, muss his hair even more! Forget the dratted bargain.

'It's just the first lesson,' she whispered. 'You surely did not put your estate in order in one day! Have courage, persist.'

'I shall persist!' he shouted, and launched into some sort of impromptu Scottish leaping dance that made her ache with laughter.

'I am sure that woke up any layabouts here at Northland,' she giggled. Charles seized her hands and spun her in a wild circle, as Miss Muffins stared from her settee. They whirled and whirled until they almost fell down with it all again.

'I think we should find Adele and distract her with carols at the pianoforte,' Mary gasped as they slowed to a halt, and her head kept spinning. 'Show her your reels! She will be astonished.'

'You mean I must sing *and* dance? Ach, lass, you're killing me.'

'So, you cannot sing, either?'

''Tis worse than my dancing.'

'Oh dear.' Mary smoothed the edges of his coat and smiled. 'I think what we need, Mr Campbell, is a Christmas miracle.'

Charles watched Mary as she turned Adele's pages at the pianoforte, smiling at the merry strains of the music, her slipper toe tapping under the fluttering hem of her gown. How beautiful she was, the loveliest thing he'd ever seen. He didn't know how he'd been able to resist her bright pull, like the sun drawing him ever closer into her orbit. He'd almost given up even *trying* to resist it, to step away from her.

He almost laughed at himself and reached for a glass of wine instead of doing what he most longed to—move closer to that glowing circle she created around herself. Lose himself in it. He'd almost begun to think there must be a way to make this permanent, make the betrothal real. Mary was surely worth the risk of marrying again. Days of laughter and nights of passion would make a fine life, surely, for both of them. Even if his heart was guarded, as he sensed Mary's was, they could build a future worth having. The thought made him smile.

But now—now he saw that she deserved more. And her offer to help him find a match after their 'betrothal' ended was just a reminder of that. It made some of that new glow fade, made ice creep in at the edges, just waiting to engulf him again when she was gone.

Did he dare risk his inner heart now? Even if she did not want a real betrothal as he did? Charles had never felt more of a coward—nor braver. He gulped down the wine and resolved to find out once and for all if Mary was worth the risk. If he could begin to give her all she deserved. For she deserved the world.

Chapter Eleven

'How do I look, then, Daisy?' Mary asked, twirling in front of her looking glass in her dinner gown. 'Presentable?'

'Like a Christmas angel, I'd say!' Daisy answered as she clapped her hands in approval. 'All the gentlemen will have eyes only for you.'

'Oh, we can't have that! We're meant to pair up others, make many matches.' But she had to let herself preen just a tiny bit. Her newest Mademoiselle Sandrine gown, spangled silver tulle over paler grey satin, trimmed with silver gilt leaves at the shoulders, draped and swirled just right. Her golden curls were swept up in Daisy's new coiffure, bound with silver ribbon and white silk roses, and seemed to shimmer in the candlelight. She almost wished she had jewels to compare to some of the other ladies—Lady Pennington's new emeralds were scrumptious—but she thought her mother's pearls looked quite well.

Would Charles like it all? That was certainly her main concern—even though it definitely should not be. He was in her thoughts no matter what, he would not be dislodged.

There was a knock at the door, and Mademoiselle Sandrine appeared with her workbox. She cast a professional eye over the silver gown and finally nodded approval. 'Very nice, Mademoiselle Mary. Very nice indeed. You are a credit to my work. Now, let's adjust that hem a titch…'

She knelt down to pin the gossamer hem, tsking over a small tear, pinning and nodding.

'How is Adele faring?' Mary asked, remembering that Adele had gone to look over the new fashion plates with Sandrine that afternoon.

'Pauvre petite,' Sandrine murmured as the turned a bit of the silk. 'First love is so very difficult. Especially with someone like Mr Clark.'

'You suspect he is not good for her, as well?' Mary asked.

'Of course not!' Sandrine stood as she lowered her voice to a whisper. 'He owes me for *two* ladies' wardrobes, which he signed the bills for when they were ordered. So expensive! I told him his lady loves would have to go elsewhere from now on. He was quite angry.'

Poor Adele, indeed. Mary shook her head sadly. 'We shall have to keep a close eye on her.'

'Indeed. I made sure her new gown fits perfectly and showed her sketches of a few others I thought she might like for her Season.' She tilted her head in thought. 'If her guardian is one who pays his bills on time...'

Mary laughed. 'I think you need have no fear of that. Charles—that is, Mr Campbell, is most scrupulous. I'm sure he'll want to keep Adele most content now, as well, so I say show all the tempting sketches and swatches you like.'

'I am glad to hear it. I have heard it said he was not quite so responsible in his youth.'

'Where did you hear that from?' Mary whispered. She glanced over at Miss Muffins on the settee, as if she could overhear and spread gossip. The pup just chewed assiduously on her bone.

Sandrine shrugged. 'A modiste hears all sorts of things, *mademoiselle*. Ladies are eager to spill all the scandal broth onto my carpets! They said he once overturned an expensive curricle racing, that he enjoyed cards and ladies and brandy quite excessively. But what man does not in his youth?

And he never opened an account for a woman at my shop.'

Mary studied herself in the mirror, studied the shimmering silver tulle that seemed to make her seem taller, more radiant, more elegant. She was glad to hear Sandrine had never worked her magic on a female on Charles's behalf. 'They would certainly have been lucky to have an account with you.' Lucky on all sides, romantic *and* stylish. 'You do the most exquisite work.'

Sandrine packed up her workbox, studying a length of yellow ribbon, a bit of silk thread. 'A gown is like armour, yes? It makes us as we wish we could be; it makes others see us that way, and hides what we do not want seen.'

Mary thought of the shabby muslin frocks of her youth, the way they hid nothing of her circumstances, nothing of her soul. Not like this new silver gown. 'Armour. Yes. I do feel more confident in your gowns than any other, somehow. As if I am perfectly seen *and* invisible at the same time.'

'Our work is very similar, isn't it? We women must always help each other in this world, or we would be utterly lost.' She plucked and straightened the sleeve, arranging a silver leaf so it emphasised the delicacy of a shoulder. 'There! Now you are ready to conquer the world, *mademoiselle*.'

Mary nodded and wished that was true. The world seemed out of control even more than it ever had before.

To Mary's delight, her beautiful armour of silk and sequins would not go to waste, for she was seated next to Charles at dinner. And it did not go unnoticed. He stared at her in silence for a long moment, as if thunderstruck, before he nodded and a slow, lazy smile spread across his lips.

'How elegant you look this evening, Mary,' he whispered warmly close to her ear as the wine was poured and the soup was served.

Mary smiled up at him in return, trying not to giggle. He, also, looked very elegant, his hair dark in the pale amber candlelight, his eyes shadowed. 'Not a dusty old spinster who can't be trusted to make a match?'

'More like Aphrodite, goddess of all romantic matches.'

She laughed in delight. 'Now you certainly exaggerate.'

'Never! I am a blunt old Scotsman. I cannot tell a lie.'

'Mademoiselle Sandrine does make beautiful gowns.'

'It's not the frock, pretty as it is. It is your eyes.

Or maybe…your hair.' He surreptitiously touched the end of one curl, his finger brushing her bare neck, and she shivered.

A footman offered a tray of the next course—chicken fricassee in mushroom sauce—and Mary sat back, feeling as if the portraits on the walls watched her. Eyes seemed to burn from somewhere nearby. 'Should we have another dance lesson soon?' she whispered. 'Lady Pennington seems very excited about her Christmas ball.'

His eyes crinkled at the edges with mirth. 'Are you brave enough? Do you have a large supply of slippers with you?'

'You are making great improvements. And there are many ways you can, er, distract a partner from what one's feet are doing. Smile, laugh, compliment…' *Kiss.* Give a lady speaking, searching looks.

He seemed doubtful. 'I can't imagine what I could do to make a lady not notice she's been tripped to the floor.'

'You are learning enough not to fall over! Just move a bit and stare deeply into her eyes. She'll notice nothing else, I promise.' She demonstrated by staring into his eyes, and immediately wished she had not, as she felt quite dizzy and warm. She kicked off her slipper beneath the floor and wiggled her stockinged toes, hoping for some cool air.

'What if there is no one I want to do that with, except you?' he whispered deeply.

And Mary knew she did not wish to dance with anyone else but Charles. She had waltzed and reeled and minuetted with good dancers, excellent dancers, but they'd never made her feel as he did.

She couldn't speak for a long moment, couldn't look away from him. Chatter and laughter went on around them, but neither of them turned from the other. She had no idea what went on near her, no idea anyone else was in the world at all. She stared up into his sharp, handsome face, a face of such masculine power in every carved line, in his strong jaw, his blade of a nose over full, sensual lips, the fierce, dark glow of his mossy green eyes as he stared back at her. His long sun-browned, scarred fingers wrapped tight around the stem of his wineglass.

Yes, a great, masculine beauty of a face, drawn with the tightest of control. She would always be safe with him, or maybe she just imagined she could be. It had been so long since she felt safe, she couldn't even be sure of the feeling any longer. Couldn't shake away the old clinging fear.

She turned away, flustered, fidgety. She needed

control, as well. 'What of Adele, then?' she said, trying to keep her tone light, humorous, turn their attention to matters other than that heated sparkle between them. 'She will need more suitable dance partners than Mr Clark.'

They glanced towards Adele, who sat farther along the table between the viscount and a young baronet's heir, most suitable. She seemed deep in conversation with the viscount, surely a good sign. Mr Clark was seated far away and ignored his own neighbours to glare at Adele. Luckily, she didn't even seem to notice between the attentions of her dinner partners and the delectable cheese tarts that had just been served.

'Mademoiselle Sandrine tells me at least two ladies whose bills were meant to be paid by Mr Clark have been left in arrears,' Mary whispered.

'Just as I would expect,' he growled.

Mary watched Adele laugh with the viscount. From all she'd heard, he was a young gentleman with a fine estate, as well as a title and a good reputation as a fair and caring landlord. He did seem to admire Adele very much, surely a good sign for her future prospects.

She turned to study Mr Clark, who was gesturing for yet more wine and still glowered. They only needed to keep Adele away from him long enough for her to see the truth for herself. A tall order, but Mary was determined.

As the fruit trifle was served, she reached her toes out to find her discarded slipper, and accidentally knocked it beyond reach. She searched for the feel of its satin, but it was lost. What would happen when she had to stand and everyone saw her scandalously naked toes?

'Oh, blast,' she gasped.

'What is amiss?' Charles asked.

She leaned closer and whispered, 'I fear I have done something quite dreadful.'

His eyes seemed to sparkle as he looked at her. 'Oh, please do tell.'

'I lost my slipper.'

'Lost your slipper?'

'Under the table. I took it off, and now it's gone.' Somehow, it didn't feel so embarrassing to tell him that. It was as if she could tell him anything, share any silly story with him, and he would not care. He would just join in. It was strange...and delightful.

He laughed, low and rough. 'Never fear, Cinderella. I am here to help.'

For only an instant, he dipped below the edge of the tablecloth, and Mary held her breath as she felt him press close to her leg through her silk skirts. He found her shoe and then took her foot lightly, delicately, onto his palm and slid it into the abandoned slipper. His touch lingered warmly, caressing, along the edge of her stockinged leg, the arch of her foot, and she gasped. Yet it was all over in a flash, and he reappeared next to her to give her a teasing smile.

Mary's shoe was safely replaced when Lady Pennington rose from her seat after the fruit and cheese were finished, her gown of emerald satin rippling in the light. So very different from the girl in garish clothes chosen by her mother who first came to the agency! Mary could only wish for such a thing for Adele. 'Ladies, shall we take our coffee in the drawing room? Don't linger over your port too long, gentlemen; I have a Christmas surprise planned.'

Mary smiled at Charles, feeling such a wrench at leaving him. He seemed to feel the same, trailing his hand over hers under the edge of the damask tablecloth. She pressed his fingers back before she rose to follow Pen and Adele into the drawing room. Lady Pennington poured the coffee as everyone scattered to cosy nests of chairs and settees near the fireside to chat.

'Do sit by me, Mary,' Lady Pennington said, patting the brocade cushions of her settee. 'We have had no time for a quiet cose! I'm dying to know if you have many happy matches in your queue.'

Mary could only hope there would be, very soon, thanks to her scheme with Charles. She told Lady Pennington about a few couples who had come to her recently and her hopes for them.

Lady Pennington gave her a teasing little smile over the painted edge of her coffee cup. 'But surely the happiest match will be your own! Mr Campbell is so handsome, and he has that delicious accent. We're all so envious. When is the wedding?'

Mary felt that terrible heated blush, that curse, flood over her cheeks, and she looked away to the lavishly luxurious room. 'Not as fine a match as your own. And I am not sure about the wedding yet.'

'I'm sure all of Bath will be invited! So many of us owe you so much.'

Luckily, Mary didn't have to stammer over her 'wedding' any longer, as the drawing room doors opened and the gentlemen returned. Lord Pennington came to his wife's side as Mary watched Charles join Adele and Penelope.

'So, what is this surprise, my dear?' Lord Pennington asked, as his fingers entwined cosily with his wife's.

'A game I loved when I was a child at Christmas,

though maybe some would think it rather vulgar,' Lady Pennington said with a laugh.

Her husband grinned in delight. 'Even better.'

'What is it?' another guest demanded.

Lady Pennington clapped her hands. 'Hide and go seek! Northland seems just like the sort of home for such games, so many corridors and hidden spaces.'

'Surely it's a child's game?' Miss Tuckworth whispered to her mother.

'No matter! We are all children at heart, *oui*?' Sandrine said.

'Especially at Christmas,' Lady Pennington said.

Adele blushed with joy, peeking across the room at Mr Clark, and Penelope quickly said, 'Dearest Adele can play a tune to help everyone hide! Anthony and I will turn her pages.' Adele's smile faded as she trudged to the pianoforte, and Mary noticed Mr Clark slip out of the room. She could only hope he was departing for good, but they could not be so fortunate.

'The ladies shall hide first, the gentlemen seek,' Lady Pennington said.

Her husband laughed. 'The way of life, eh?'

'Very well, then, ladies! Adele, are you ready with a song to count?' Lady Pennington asked. 'Get ready, get set—everyone hide!'

Mary was caught up in the stampede of guests running from the drawing room, parted from Charles by the stream of dashing people. She couldn't glimpse him above feathered and ribboned headdresses.

'One, two, three,' Adele called as she played a lively polka. Amid giggles and shrieks, everyone scattered in various directions, up the double staircase, down to the kitchens, into the shadowy corridors, leaving only a cloud of laughter and perfumes behind, the patter of eager footsteps.

Mary wasn't at all sure where she wanted to go without Charles nearby. What if she was 'found' by Mr Overbury instead? The man had been keeping his distance rather oddly in the last couple of days, but could her luck hold? She looked around and headed up the stairs.

'Nineteen, twenty,' Adele called, playing even louder.

Mary suddenly noticed Overbury watching her, his lips set in a most determined fashion. Mary twirled around and ran up the next flight of stairs, lifting her delicate skirts until she reached a hallway on the top floor. Silence closed around her like a winter cloud. It was dim there, lit only by flickering lanterns at each end, revealing rows of closed doors and a dark green carpet runner, the glow of snowflakes drifting past the darkened windows.

She heard furtive giggles, the snap of shutting doors. Footsteps clattered, and she hoped Overbury would not dare follow her there.

She ducked behind some heavy tapestry curtains into a window nook and tucked her feet up under her, pressed back to the wall. It was chilly there, the cold from outside seeping into her delicate tulle sleeves, but she didn't care. It seemed quite private and safe.

She closed her eyes and held her breath. The quick patter of her heartbeat slowed in her ears.

And suddenly she was no longer alone. She heard a whisper of movement, felt the breeze of the curtain parting, the heat of someone beside her, banishing the winter.

For an instant, she felt a flash of panic that Overbury had found her, but then she smelled the fresh, springtime warmth of lemony soap, and she knew very well who it was.

Charles.

And her heart pounded in an entirely new way.

She opened her eyes and glimpsed Charles's broad shoulders silhouetted against the lamplight before he dropped the curtain and they were quite alone.

'Are you unwell, Mary?' he whispered, his breath stirring the curls at her temple. She shivered.

'I thought maybe Overbury was following me. I imagined I could be alone here.'

'Shall I go?' He moved as if to leave.

'No!' She grabbed his hand. 'I do feel safe now. With you.'

And she did. She'd never felt so safe in her life. She swayed towards him, drawn to that quiet strength, that delicious warmth he always brought with him. The wonderful way he smelled, the brush of his hand on hers.

His arms closed around her, drew her even closer, as if they were the only people in the whole world. And she felt so wonderfully *un*safe. She felt reckless, wild, excited—joyful.

She threw her arms around his neck and held tight. She pressed her forehead against his shoulder, the fine wool of his evening coat warm on her skin. She closed her eyes and listened to the steady, reassuring music of his heartbeat.

She knew she shouldn't be so close to him in there, knew it was against their own rules of fake courtship. Who knew *what* she would do with such temptation! But she couldn't let go, not yet. It felt all too good. She held him even closer.

She felt the soft press of his kiss on top of her head, and she tilted her face up to his. His eyes, those wondrous emerald eyes, glowed in the darkness. His lips touched her brow, the pulse that beat frantically at her temples, the tip of her cheekbone. Tiny drops of flame on her skin, trailing dizzying desire with every touch. Flames that burned all the way to her heart.

Mary stretched up on tiptoe and pressed her lips to his, giving in to that insistent desire. It was a small, questing kiss at first, but the soft heat of his lips made that flame roar out of control. He moaned, the sound ragged against her lips, and he dragged her so close there was nothing between them at all. How perfectly they fit together! As if made to be just so.

Her lips parted at his touch, and his tongue slid lightly over hers. He tasted of wine and strawberries, and that darkness that was only him. He seemed to question, to seek, and as if finding whatever he sought, he delved deeper.

She curled her fingertips in his rough silk hair, trying to hold him with her forever. He gave no sign of running away. The kiss plunged even deeper, and she fell down into hot, blurry *need*. Mary felt she was on fire, and she swayed as if she would tumble to the floor her legs were so weak.

Charles pressed her against the wall, and she felt his lips trail from hers in a ribbon of fire over the arc of her throat, the edge of her collarbone along the edge of her gown, nipping and teasing with the tip of his tongue to soothe the little sting.

'Oh, Mary, *m'usghair...*' he whispered roughly, his brogue heavy. She blinked open her eyes and saw that he rested his forehead against the wall beside her. His own eyes were closed, his brow furrowed as if he were in pain. His shoulders shuddered as he drew in a ragged breath. He seemed to struggle with the raw, hot longing between them, just as she did.

She reached up and touched his cheek, feeling the stubble over his satin-smooth skin. He turned his head and kissed her palm.

'Oh, Charles. I think, that is, I—'

Suddenly, the real world seemed to crash and clang into their secret little haven. Footsteps and muffled laughter echoed from the corridor, and she remembered the party, the games.

And this little game, this masquerade of a betrothal, didn't seem like a game at all any more. It felt like a heartbreak about to happen.

She knew she couldn't stay there wrapped up in him a moment longer, or she would never want to let him go at all. She softly, gently kissed his cheek. It felt rough and delicate all at the same time, just like he was. She slid away, but his hand seized hers as she passed, strong and hot.

'Just one more moment, Mary,' he muttered. 'Please.'

She was deeply tempted. She leaned against his shoulder, resting her cheek on him. His whole body was rigid, perfectly still, except for his hand on hers. His iron control was still there, but she could feel it cracking almost like she heard it, a whiplash in the night.

'You know Shakespeare?' he asked.

Mary was quite surprised by the change in topic. 'Shakespeare? Of course. I am a poetical sort of female, you know.'

'This party seems to have run mad. We need Puck's reverse remedy to set it right again.'

'Are you saying it's a love potion?' She laughed. 'My grandmother, when I was a very little girl, used to tell tales of spirits hiding in the Christmas wreaths, and that was why we put out holly. To keep them at bay. I can imagine them now.'

A smile wrinkled his brow, despite their situation. 'Spirits caught in the holly boughs?'

'Yes. It could very well be Puck or Oberon, or Queen Mab. Everything feels quite topsy-turvy lately.'

It certainly did feel like something had been set free inside of Mary, something wild she'd spent her whole life fighting against in order to be safe.

To be responsible. She had to find a way to catch it back again, to put it back into the jinni bottle before her life, her heart, shattered. She couldn't afford to fall in love with Charles Campbell. She needed the agency; he needed a proper wife and to help his niece. That was that.

'But if I remember correctly, Puck's schemes only create more chaos! It's Christmas, yes? We only need a little time, for reflection and planning, and all will be well. We cannot lose control.'

He turned his head to look at her, his hair tumbling over his brow, shadowing his eyes. 'My sweet Mary, I'm sure we need more than this one Christmas to set things right. My mistakes are—'

There were more voices outside, lighter, closer, more raucous, as if the Penningtons' cellar had been dipped into deeply. Mary trembled and edged away from Charles. Her whole being urged her to *stay, stay, stay!*

She smoothed her hair and dress, and tried to paste on a careless smile. It was truly as if the mad Christmas spirit had taken over her world—security, control, was flying apart. She remembered too much when she was younger: the fun, the longing for adventure, the passion. All the things she'd thought packed carefully away in order to take care of herself, build her independence. Now, with

Charles, they were soaring free out of Pandora's box! And she loved it. She loved feeling like her old self again, even if just for a moment.

She didn't want to leave, but she knew she had to, for both their sakes. She kissed his cheek one more time and slid her hand out of his. She tiptoed out of their little alcove and blinked at the sudden flare of light after the shadows, the rush of people dashing past.

On the top step of the staircase, she glimpsed Adele—standing with Mr Clark. Adele did not look guilty or defiant now; she looked horribly shocked and chilled, her arms wrapped around herself, as if Clark had tried something with her.

Oh, how terrible Mary was for being such a bad chaperone, she scolded herself as she hurried forward, no time to summon Charles. 'Adele!' she called, sharper than she intended.

Adele jumped, a startled expression on her face, followed by a bad sign—stubbornness.

'Did you become lost? This house is quite a maze.'

'I—yes, lost. I am so glad to see you, Miss St Aubin!' she said, and as Mary drew closer, she saw that Adele was shaking. Not so stubborn after all. What had Mr Clark been saying to her?

He smiled innocently, smoothly, and Adele would not look at him.

Mary slipped her arm around the girl's trembling shoulders and noticed a rip in her embroidered sleeve, a red mark on her shoulder. She sucked in a deep breath, trying to contain her fury until she could get Adele away. If she was caught looking like that, Mr Clark would not be the one blamed but Adele herself. 'Come along, it is late. Let's see if I can find something warm to drink, and we can have a chat.' She glanced back at Clark, who looked rather infuriatingly smug as Adele trembled against Mary's shoulder.

'He—he kissed me,' Adele whispered as Mary led her into her own bedchamber and wrapped her up in a soft blanket. 'I thought it would be wonderful, but...'

'It was not?' Mary asked gently. She rang the bell to summon Daisy to bring some tea and sat down next to Adele.

Adele just shook her head. 'I don't want to talk about it, I pushed him away and he reached for me just as you appeared.' Her eyes widened. 'Uncle Charles! He will be so angry.'

'Oh, my dear,' Mary whispered. 'He would be angry, yes, but not with you. And he need never know. We can keep it between ourselves if you feel the need. Come, tell me about it, and I know we'll find a way to help you...'

Chapter Twelve

'Oh, the holly she bears a blossom as white as the lily flower...'

Mary laughed as the wind caught at her pelisse and made her cheeks sting with the cold. Was it really the best day to look for fresh greenery to deck Northland's halls? But it *was* pretty outside, she had to admit as the cart lurched along the path that wound through the park and out the gates, led along by their singing.

The pale gold sunlight, peeking through dove-grey clouds, shimmered on the dusting of snow, and everyone laughed and sang louder as they jostled amid picnic baskets, warm blankets, tools for cutting the greenery.

Best of all, she sat beside Charles on the narrow bench. His hand brushed hers, lingered, and she remembered the overwhelming bliss of him kissing her behind the curtain.

'Oh, the holly she bears a berry as red as any blood!'

The cart suddenly jolted around a corner, and Mary tumbled against his shoulder. He caught her, his arm coming close around her. She laughed and clutched at the edge of his coat as if she would fall. She wished she *could* fall, right into his arms.

Mary studied the scene around them, finding it more and more like a party under an enchantment. Even Adele laughed today, enjoying herself with Mr Clark nowhere in view. The trees grew thicker, the shadows more dappled, the little dome of the elegant summer house peeking above the branches. The notes of the song echoed as if floating along down a long corridor.

'How lovely it all is,' she said, and pointed out the summer house to Charles. 'Couldn't you just go inside there and stay forever?'

'Not much like town life, is it?' he said wistfully, and she wondered if he missed Scotland so much. 'Do you long for streets and shops here?'

Mary considered this. She'd always been rather a town sort of person, liking people and activity, but this peace was addictive. 'Not really, no. Yet I always thought I was a town mouse! After my childhood in a country vicarage, I yearned for parties and fun. But this is too enchanting. Like a fairy story, I almost expect to see gnomes around this corner. I could get used to this beauty. Are you missing Scotland and your castle?'

He quirked a smile down at her. 'I can't miss anything at all when you're here.'

And just like that, Mary couldn't breathe.

Before she could find words to answer, or even remember what words were in her jumbled, confused, lustful thoughts, the cart lurched to a halt in a clearing surrounded by circles of trees. Like a fairy ring for her story, where elves would dance. She stared around her, dazzled.

'Now,' Lord Pennington announced as he hopped down from the drivers' seat and helped his wife to alight, the two of them smiling into each other's eyes as if no one else existed and they saw only each other. 'I command you all, as lord of this demesne...'

Everyone laughed and teased him, and Lady Pennington gave her husband a playful shove.

He laughed, too. 'I do command you all to go out and find as much greenery as possible to deck the halls of Northland for our ball. The winner shall have the first glass from the wassail bowl! And I assure you, our cook mixes her wassail very strong indeed.'

A great cheer went up, loud and raucous as if

they'd already been dipping into the wassail, and everyone scattered into the woods like a flock of brightly plumed birds in their pelisses and cloaks and greatcoats. Adele wandered off with Penelope and Anthony, who kept her close, and Mary noticed Mr Overbury starting towards her in a most determined fashion. But before he could get far, Charles held out his hand to help Mary down from the cart and held on to it, making Overbury back away scowling and kicking at the snow.

Mary's flat boot sole slid on the rung of the cart, and Charles quickly caught her around the waist before she could fall, her stomach clenched in sudden panic. She held on to him, breathless at the sparkling jolt of pure, clear, bright pleasure his touch gave her, wiping away any fear. It made her tingle all the way to her toes.

He slowly, oh, so slowly, slid her to her feet. He felt so warm, so strong, so safe. She wished with all her strength she would never, ever have to let him go again. Never lose that heady blend of protection and excitement he always brought. She wanted him to twirl her free in the winter light, spin her in a dance—kiss her. To let the fizzing Christmas spirit take over.

But she did have to stand on her own two feet. As she always did. 'Th-thank you, Mr Cam—Charles,' she whispered as she stepped back from him and felt the cold wind on her skin again. She glanced around and saw no one paid attention to them. They had scattered on their own errands, their own flirtations. 'So clumsy of me.'

He watched her carefully, intently. 'Not at all. I fear it is *I* who must beg *your* assistance.'

'My assistance?' She wondered dazedly what he could need. If he might *need* their kisses, as she feared she now did. She remembered thinking she should enjoy these moments together, these bright, fleeting days, and she knew she could do just that.

'I see a fine patch of holly over there just begging to be a mantelpiece decoration, but I don't have quite the adept nature I once had, and it's rather high. I think teamwork is needed.'

Mary laughed, distracted and charmed all at once, as she always was with him. 'I'm sure between us, we can defeat the holly and bear it home in triumph.'

Charles offered his arm, and she smiled up at him as she slipped her gloved hand through the curl of his elbow, feeling him press close to her. They followed the others between the thick stands of trees, hearing laughter bounce off the bare branches and twine into the sky. Mary found it easy to chatter with him, to talk about light matters such as favourite Christmas carols, Christmas traditions in Scotland, as if they had known each other forever. A cold wind swept through the trees high above them, swaying the branches, making the voices a mere blur. It felt like they were all alone, together.

'So, what are Christmases like in your castle, then?' she asked. She paused to clip a clump of low-hanging mistletoe, pearly with white berries, perfect for enticing someone into Christmas kisses.

'There's the ghillies' ball. I always looked forward to that as child, it was the only time there were people and noise and music in the place! I must organise it myself next year, with reels and lots of food and drink.'

Mary looked around at the silent trees, the pale, quiet sky, and imagined dancers in tartans twirling and spinning. 'This must seem rather dull after such a thing! Just a plain English country Christmas.'

'Oh, Mary,' he said, slanting her a sad little smile. 'An English country Christmas is one of the finest things I could ever imagine. Especially right now.'

Mary looked away, feeling shy, flattered—hopeful? Yet, what was there to be hopeful about? After this perfect Christmas, they would go their own ways. 'Shall we conquer that holly, then? I see some with particularly luscious red berries twined just up there.'

She took his hand in hers, revelling in the feel of his warm palm through their gloves, and led him to the holly bush, dark green against the snow. She held up the branches as he sawed them off to fill their baskets. They would surely bring back more than anyone else, and the wassail would be theirs! She could hear the voices of everyone else on the wind, far away, and she was just there wrapped in his warmth.

'It does remind me of some Christmases when I was a girl,' she said. 'Ella, Papa, and I would find decorations for the vicarage and the church. It all smelled so delicious, of evergreen, and we would sing as we searched. And in the evenings, my father would read us the nativity story, and sometimes we could even get him to talk of our mother, of when they first met. Christmas was her favourite time of year.'

'It sounds wonderful,' he said wistfully. 'Like a family.'

'What did you do at Christmas, then? Besides the ghillies' ball, and the cook's mince pies and ghost stories.'

'That is just about it. When my mother was alive, she was usually in London, and I seldom saw my father. He did not enjoy Christmas, or anything that might dare to try to be fun.'

'Oh,' Mary whispered, her heart aching for the lonely boy he'd been. He smiled as he spoke, as if it were all of no consequence, a normal sort of life, but she knew there was sadness behind the words. She pictured a little boy wandering the stony halls of a castle, longing to hear carol music. 'And what about later?'

'When I was married, you mean? Oh, Aileen loved any chance for a party, but she usually found them much more easily in Edinburgh!' he said, and snipped off another branch of holly. 'In truth, I knew very soon after we wed that we were not compatible. But had to figure out a way ahead. *I* had to figure out a way.'

'And did you?'

'For a time. She liked the idea of being mistress of a castle, more than she liked the reality, and who can blame her. It's not easy. But she seemed to enjoy it for a while, and I was happy to have some-one to share the work, as I thought. Then she found someone far more to her liking and stayed in Eng-land more and more until she did not come back.'

Mary gasped. 'She eloped?'

'You could say that. She declared I could never understand her, never give her the excitement she wanted. She imagined when we married that I would be someone else entirely, would be my young, reckless self forever, when I could not be. And she could not be other than she was, too. So she lived with her lover and died not long after, from a lung disease they said. So you see why I have been rather reluctant when friends urge me to marry again. How could I do such a thing to another woman? I am no fine husband.'

'Indeed, I can see why you would hesitate. But you are so very wrong about being no good husband material,' Mary murmured. She longed to take his hand, to hold him, to heal his past, even as she knew she couldn't. All she could do was try to give him a bit of help. 'You are a good guardian to Adele, you worry about her, watch over her. Her unhappiness is not your fault, she is just young and unsure. Just as I once was.'

'You, Mary?' he murmured, his eyes filled with understanding and concern as he watched her. 'Unsure?'

'Yes, certainly. The world is new to her, it all looks strange and frightening. I had Ella to help me, and I think that's why I love the agency so much. It's a way to give back to Ella for all she sacrificed for me and a way for me to find meaning in myself. Adele will find such a thing, too, with you to back her up.'

'And is the agency all you really want?'

Mary stared up into his eyes, and something hit her like a boulder to truth. No, it was not *all* she wanted; she had other longings, other dreams that she'd buried for a long time. She'd thought she'd never have to see them again, until Charles. 'No,' she whispered. 'I want…want…' She paused, tilting her head as she considered, as she let the enormity of this moment between them wash over her. 'I fear I may be about to do something rather naughty. That's what I want.'

He smiled lazily and leaned closer. 'I am all attention.'

'See that beautiful cluster of mistletoe up there? Every house must have plenty of mistletoe for Christmas. I'll climb up and fetch it.'

'Climb it?' he said doubtfully, tilting back his head to take in the tree that soared up into the winter sky. 'Mary, I don't think—'

Before he could stop her, Mary ran to the tree and found the perfect foothold in the bark. She remembered her childhood, running with Ella and Fred at Moulton Magna, playing in the woods, and it was wonderful to feel that free again, even if only for a moment. She reached up to grab at a thick branch.

'Ella and I used to climb trees all the time when we were children and no one was watching. I'm sure I remember how to do this.'

He frowned and rushed towards her, his arms outstretched to her. 'Mary, it looks dangerous.'

'Says the man who used to race his curricle! And not so dangerous as going back to Northland with not much greenery to show for it. We want that wassail, don't we?' She kept pulling herself upward, her shoulders aching with the long-forgotten strain, yet it felt marvellous. Strong and free, even when her hat tumbled from her head and spiralled to the ground.

She felt a strong, warm touch on her leg, heated through her stocking, holding her steady while helping her upward. Charles, ready to catch her if she needed it. To hold her safe even as he grinned up at her with shared mischief.

She reached up and snapped off the alluring cluster of mistletoe. As she climbed back down, the toe of her boot caught in her hem, and she tumbled backward again in a flash of clumsiness. But, as he always did, Charles was there to catch her. He held her high in his powerful arms for a moment, above the rest of the world, just the two of them. Breathless, she held on to his shoulders, safer than she'd ever been before.

'Thank you,' she whispered. 'How clumsy I have become lately! You've saved me once again.'

'I have to find some way to make myself useful, aye?' he said, and gave her a playful little bounce that made her laugh. 'Rescuing fair damsels seems as good a job as any.'

'You are very good at it, indeed,' she said as he slowly, slowly slid her to her feet. He didn't seem to want to let go yet, either, and they stood there holding on to each other. 'And just look at our lovely mistletoe! Not a single berry lost. Surely it was worth the danger.'

They smiled widely at each other, letting the fun sweep them into the wind, the moment of lightness.

'There you are,' Lady Pennington called. Mary reluctantly stepped away from Charles and turned to see their hostess marching towards them through the trees, Adele behind her. 'We're setting up for luncheon near the old summer house, a fine reward for all our hard work. Oh, look at all that beautiful mistletoe you've found, marvellous! Adele here has been helping me look for evergreen boughs, but we found nothing so beautiful as that. And what we did find was all on her.'

Adele held up a branch and smiled shyly, and Mary was glad to see she'd stayed away from Mr

Clark, that she seemed to be stepping forward from what happened.

'More than a few romantics will find their way beneath it, I'm sure,' Lady Pennington laughed. 'This is our destination.'

They had made their way to the round pale stone summer house atop the hill, its rotunda roof a beacon in the grey sky, its high small windows glittering. A white tent lay at the foot of the hill looking up towards its beauty, luncheon waiting beneath it.

'Talk about a fine place for a princess,' Mary said. 'It is beautiful.' She remembered the story Charles told of a maiden and her knight who perished for love at the old medieval tower, and she wondered if the doomed pair of spirits ever came here for a little rest.

'I'm quite sure I can never return to prosaic old Bath after all this loveliness,' Adele said wistfully. Mary took her arm and gave it a reassuring squeeze.

She found them spots near the end of one snowy linen-draped table, near Charles, Sandrine, Pen and Anthony. They were laughing, merry, trading tales of Christmases in their youths, and soon even Adele was giggling, and happily whispering with Sandrine about fashion. Charles squeezed Mary's hand under the edge of the cloth, and she was sure she'd never had quite such a golden afternoon in her life.

* * *

After luncheon was over, the guests lingered around the table in a late meal lassitude, sipping the last of the wine, nibbling the fruit and pastries. Adele rose from the table and strolled outside the tent, away from the sweet-scented braziers, and was hit by the cold wind tugging at her fur-edged pelisse and making her eyes water. She thought about running back inside again. But she couldn't bear to hear her future marital state laughed about again. She knew she only had a few moments before her protective guardian and Mary came after her.

She gathered the folds of her coat closer around her and plunged into the circle of trees, taking comfort in their silent dignity, in the scudding grey clouds sliding overhead. None of them cared about her matches, about what she wanted and didn't want, didn't care about her confusion. She just needed to be alone to *think*. She was tired of being so blasted confused!

She was careful not to wander too far; the sun was fading, and she had no desire to be lost in cold night woods, nor to make her friends upset again. She paused beside one of the carts and sat down on the narrow seat, close enough to hear the chatter from the tent, far enough away she wouldn't be immediately seen.

Especially by Peyton Clark.

She drew up her knees beneath her chin, as she had when she was a child. She'd so hoped for romance when they returned to Bath! Charles's castle was filled with romance, of course, but of a quite different sort than what she sought. Cold stones that whispered of old battles, of ghostly wanderings, could not compare to the thrill of a dance with that special someone. She was sure she'd find poetry in a town.

As soon as she saw Peyton Clark at an assembly, his golden curls, his tall figure, the heated way he watched her, she was elated to find her heart's desire so quickly. And then they'd danced, and her heart soared. It had to be love!

But Uncle Charles did not approve. All true meant-to-be-together couples faced prejudice and misunderstandings that drove them apart, surely. It only gave them a chance for secret notes, hurried meetings in Sydney Gardens and behind pillars at the Pump Room. It felt so wonderful to feel *she* could decide something, for once! She could love who she chose, create her own future.

Now she was not so sure at all. When he had found her on the stairs, tried to kiss her—those flutterings she'd felt before when she imagined such a thing turned into panic. Could such a thing be part of true love? She thought of what Miss St Aubin said, that love was listening and understanding. Dear Miss St Aubin, Mary! The only one who seemed to understand how Adele felt, who didn't shriek and demand and say they knew better. Who listened. Uncle Charles was so lucky to have wooed such a lady.

But then, if Mary was engaged to Adele's uncle, was she not like all the rest? Sure they knew her heart better than Adele did herself?

'Adele! My bright flower, my angel, where are you?' Peyton called now on the wind, and Adele feared she hadn't hid so well, after all. She tucked her feet tighter under her.

But he peered over the side of the cart, smiling broadly. 'I have been looking everywhere for you. They are getting ready to go back to the house, and I needed to speak to you alone. To explain.'

She remembered what happened in the confusion of the hide-and-seek game, the way he kissed her, his open mouth devouring hers, frightening her. But now he smiled as if nothing happened at all. She was very confused, frightened.

'I just needed a breath of fresh air,' she said. 'All that claret…'

He gave her an indulgent smile. 'Fuzzy-muzzyheaded? My silly little mouse! I shall hold you steady.'

He laid his hand on her arm, and it didn't feel at all the way it once did. It felt icy, and she wanted to be by herself, to think quietly. 'I am quite well. I can make my own way back.'

'But I am in alt that we can be alone at last. This is all I could ever desire, to be near you.'

'My uncle says—'

'Your uncle! What does he know about true love, such an old stick in the mud? You and I are made for each other. You shall never find anyone more perfect together, no matter how many Seasons you have. It's why I couldn't help myself last night, I was overwhelmed by my love for you.'

'What are you saying?' she whispered.

He frowned, and it was as if his sunny smile had never been there in only an instant. 'I am saying, Adele, that I cannot wait for you to be my wife. To make you mine entirely. Come away with me to Gretna Green.'

Adele was shocked. She'd wanted romance, yes, but—was this too much? 'Gretna Green?'

'You are Scots, are you not? It will be like marrying at home for you.'

But Adele did not want to go home. She wanted to see more of the world, meet more people. And then she wanted to marry in a real kirk, not some grubby blacksmith's shop. 'I—I just don't know. This is very sudden. I cannot think…'

'No thinking, my love, just feeling. It's time for us to begin our lives together.' He stared deeply into her eyes, confusing her. 'Don't you love me, Adele, as I do you?'

She had thought she did. So very much. Then he grabbed her on the staircase during hide-and-seek, kissed her when she did not want it. 'I must think about it.'

A dark cloud seemed to slide over his golden features as he frowned at her. Something cold touched her deep inside, some fear. 'I thought I was sure of you, Adele, sure of our true love. That you were wise beyond your years, special.'

And she had been so flattered he called her wise, told her she was special, different from other ladies her age. 'Of course. I must just—'

He pushed himself to his feet in a whirl of anger, and she shrank back in sudden apprehension. 'We have until the ball. Arrangements are made.'

He departed, leaving her alone with all her doubts and fears, and she bent her head to her knees and cried with the loneliness of it all.

Chapter Thirteen

Mary thought she'd never known a more idyllic Christmas moment than this one. The guests were gathered around a giant carved fireplace that crackled with warmth against the cold wind howling at the windows, wrapping them in safety and cosiness. Goblets of spiced wine and platters of cinnamon biscuits and hothouse fruit passed around as Adele played carols at the pianoforte and everyone laughed together.

It felt just as a home should, Mary mused wistfully as she studied the scene. The Penningtons held hands, and Charles watched them, his gaze faraway…wistful, even. Did he think of his lost wife now? Mary felt such a sharp pang to consider it.

As Adele's song ended, she rose from the pianoforte and asked if anyone else would like to play. Mr Clark applauded her loudly from his seat at the back of the room, but she ignored him. Miss Tuckworth took her place, and she came to sit beside Mary and Charles, smoothing her pale blue muslin skirts around her.

'Uncle Charles,' she said, and he broke away from his thoughts to smile at her. 'Didn't you say when you were young, people would tell ghost stories for Christmas?'

He laughed. 'Aye, we did. I had many a nanny who could tell hair-raising stories, they kept me quite awake on Twelfth Night.'

'It's an old tradition,' Anthony said. 'To bring in the New Year and sweep the old out.'

'Well, I think we should try it now,' Adele said. 'That howling wind makes it seem just the thing. Shall you start, Uncle?'

Charles smiled and launched into a tale of a haunted castle harbouring a terrible beast in its dungeons, whose shrieks and cries brought curses onto the family living above him. He told of ghostly pipers wandering the hillsides as mournful music echoed in the distance. Sandrine added a story of a chateau in the French countryside, abandoned when its family perished under the guillotine, but now their pale shades drifted through the chambers, wailing. By the time Lord Pennington related the stories of Northland's own ghosts, grey ladies and fiery-eyed monks, everyone was quite on the edge of their chairs with tension.

In the last tale, a wailing white lady who warned of the death of someone near her, Mr Clark crept behind Lady Tuckworth's chair and shouted, 'Boo!' making everyone shriek. That was quite the end of the tales, and Lady Pennington quickly called for wine. But an unease still lingered in the air.

Mary felt very silly indeed, for she couldn't sleep at all. Every clang or clatter, every whistle of the wind beyond her bedroom draperies made her jump and shriek. She wrapped her arms around Miss Muffins under the bedclothes and held on tight.

As if the pup could keep spirits away. She shook as if just as afraid as Mary.

'Fool,' Mary whispered. She never should have listened to ghost stories! They'd made her have such horrors when she was a child, imaging faces at windows, footsteps on empty stairs, and it seemed nothing had changed.

When a branch skittered across the window pane, sounding like a skeletal touch, she'd had enough. She gave a little scream and leaped out of bed, grabbing up her dressing gown as she ran across the room. Miss Muffins was right at her heels.

She wasn't sure where she would go. The rest of

the house seemed silent, shadowy. All the doors were closed, and surely spirits walked free at that hour. As a child, Mary would run to Ella's room, but Ella wasn't there. So she turned to her other source of comfort, books.

She found a lantern on a table at the top of the stairs, a beacon for unwary wanderers, and tiptoed down. She passed niches where sculptures seemed positively phantom-like, curtains that trembled as if someone touched them. At last, she found herself safe in the library.

A fire still burned in the grate, light dancing on the rows of books that waited for her. She gave a sigh of relief and made her way towards its welcome, towards a stack of leather-bound volumes on the gilt table.

Only to find she was not alone in her sanctuary.

She shrieked as she came around a large brown velvet armchair and glimpsed an arm clad in dark blue brocade, a scarred, strong, sun-browned hand holding a glass of brandy.

Yet it was not a ghostly visitor. A head peered over the back of the chair, and Mary laughed in relief to see it was Charles, his hair tousled, his eyes wide as if she had startled him just as he did her.

She felt so very safe in only one instant—and

then not safe at all, for her emotions roiled and turned at being alone with him.

'I—I'm so sorry, I didn't know anyone was here,' she said. 'I couldn't sleep.'

'Neither could I.' He gestured to the chair beside his, smiling ruefully. 'The Northland spirits seemed rather restless.'

'I always was a beastly coward about ghosts,' Mary admitted. She sat down as Miss Muffins found a cushion near the hearth, and Mary was suddenly wrapped in cosiness with Charles. 'I hope you aren't reading *The Devil Monk*.' She nodded at the book in his hand.

He laughed, warm and rich. 'Not at all. John Donne. I often find comfort in his verses.'

'I love it, too. Would you read some to me?'

'Of course.' He put his glass down and reached for her hand as he lifted the book closer. His touch was steadying, warm, but it made her tremble all the same.

Mary remembered his words about his first marriage, how he'd had hope at first. Had he read poetry to her? Longed for her, as Mary longed for him right now?

'Is this how you spent evenings when you were married?' she dared to ask shyly.

He frowned down at the book. 'Never. Aileen did

not care much for books. She enjoyed excitement, romance, danger.'

Danger, like running off with someone else when she could have had Charles, and was the luckiest woman in the world to have him. 'Then she was very silly. Books have quite enough excitement for me. And danger will find us whether we look for it or not, so why create more of it?' She squeezed his hand. 'I wish life could always be just like this.'

'As do I. Such nights are made for seeking warmth and safety, a fine fire, a good book, a dog. A…' He studied her, unreadable in the firelight.

'A friend?' she whispered.

'A twin spirit, if we are lucky.'

'Such things are rare indeed,' she said. 'Like jewels.'

'Yes. More precious than rubies. They should be cared for, cherished.'

Mary had no words, nothing she could say about her own longings and dreams. She could only stare into his eyes, those beautiful eyes, and wonder if he could possibly feel the same. The whole world was narrowed to that one room, that one fireside, the two of them, and she yearned with every inch of her being to succumb to it all, possess it forever.

And yet—yet there was still such fear, always lingering in the background of her mind, her heart.

The fear of losing what she had, losing the work she'd come to rely on, losing the wondrous love she'd just found.

He seemed to sense her unease. 'Mary,' he said gently, and reached for her hand again. He eased back the lace ruffle of her sleeve, revealing the pulse that beat there, strong and fast with desire. He bent his head and pressed a soft, lingering kiss to her lifeblood.

She could not turn away from him, leaned towards him as if caught in his orbit. She reached up with her free hand and swept a tousled lock of hair from his brow, letting her touch drift over him. And at last he dipped his head and kissed her, a kiss full of all the longing and need she could find no words for, couldn't even understand. Her arms wound around his neck, holding him with her, leaning into his strength. He was all she should have fought against, this surrender to emotion, yet instead he felt like her only haven. She just couldn't stay away from him.

Their lips slid away from each other, from the desperation of that kiss. He leaned his forehead to hers, and they stood together there in sizzling silence, wrapped up in longing. Mary never wanted to let go again.

Chapter Fourteen

Mary sighed and sank down lower on the library settee the next morning as she tried to concentrate on the book she held, the morning light from the windows bright on the words. She'd thought she could hide there, press away thoughts of Charles and the temptations of his kiss, his touch. But probably the library, where they kissed, wasn't the best place for such forgetting. She looked at the chairs and remembered him reading Donne to her. Looked at the carpet and remembered their kiss.

She could hear laughter outside the room as everyone rushed about decorating. It seemed unlikely they would find her there, yet she wondered if being alone was really a mistake. Alone with her thoughts and daydreams and yearnings. She'd seen such obsessions and emotions from people at the agency before, but had never thought she would be their victim.

She snapped the book shut. When she was with Charles, it all felt so perfect. Fun and full of light. When he was gone, when she closed her eyes at night and was alone, she was beset with doubts and fears.

There was a quiet knock at the door. Happy for some distraction, she put aside the book and called, 'Come in!'

It was the butler. He held a folded note on a silver tray in one hand and a fur-lined cloak with the other. 'I beg your pardon for the interruption, Miss St Aubin, but I have an urgent message for you.'

'For me?' Mary said, alarmed. Was it her sister or one of the twins? She jumped up from the settee and reached for the note, quickly tearing it open. It was quite short, a dark, swift, spiky scrawl, and it seemed no one was ill or injured. Quite the opposite.

Meet me outside in ten minutes. A Christmas surprise. Charles.

Mary blinked, her heart racing as she read the message a second time. From Charles! He wanted to meet her!

The butler gave a discreet little cough and offered the cloak. 'I was told you would need these,

Miss St Aubin, as it looks like snow outside. And these.' He picked up gloves and a pair of sturdy boots. An outdoor surprise, then. Her mind whirled with imaginings, hopes, fears.

'Thank you.' In a confused, excited, hopeful haze, she quickly put on the warm clothes and hurried out of the library, avoiding the merriment in the drawing room to slip out the front doors.

Charles was indeed waiting there for her, holding the reins of his curricle at the foot of the stone stairs. She thought of their day snowbound at that inn, the heated intimacy of it all.

'Come out with me, Mary,' he called. 'It's a beautiful day!'

Mary laughed and drew her hood closer. 'If you enjoy freezing your nose off,' she said. She dashed down the steps towards him, and he caught her to lift her high onto the seat. He tucked a fur-lined robe around her and slid a hot brick under her now booted feet. 'It's a perfectly warm day. See?'

And so it was—with him. She couldn't remember ever being quite so warm, so sparkling with sunlight, before. He climbed up beside her and flicked the reins, setting them off on this unknown adventure.

'I do like surprises,' she said, leaning against him.

'Then you will especially like this one. Lady Pennington helped me set it up.'

Lady Pennington. Of course. She'd forgotten everyone thought them betrothed, and with so much romance wrapped around Christmas, they would want to help their engagement along. It made her feel terrible for deceiving them—and filled with fun laughter at the little secret.

The carriage flew along a narrow path just off the main drive. Frost sparkled on the bare tree branches like diamonds, and it was so quiet there, so magical, not another being in sight. She wound her arm through his and rested her head on his shoulder, wishing their mysterious journey might go on forever.

But it could not, of course. He guided the horse down a circular drive and drew up in front of the little summer house where they'd had luncheon. Up close, the tiny building looked even more as though it belonged in a fairy tale, with its columns and high windows, the winter ivy twining up its stone walls. A grey plume of smoke curled up from the chimney, a sign of real life.

'Does someone live here, then?' she asked, looking for faces at the windows.

'Yes. We do. At least for this afternoon.' Charles leaped down from the carriage and came around to help her. But instead of putting her down on the frosty ground, he swept her high in his arms, making her laugh, making her feel as light as a feather against his strength. He carried her through the little fence surrounding the summer house, through a tiny sleeping garden to the vine-covered front door, as if she were one of the agency's brides. Mary decided to forget all her doubts and fears today, to just linger in this perfect moment.

She giggled and held on tight to his neck as he swung her through the door and down a narrow little corridor, through a low portal and into a pocket-sized sitting room. She gasped in delight when she saw what waited there.

A bright fire burned in a little stone-fronted grate in the octagonal room, surely used for tea parties and liaisons in warmer months. Spread before its warmth was a picnic arranged on a silken quilt. Bread, cheese, Christmas cake with icing like white lace, hothouse strawberries and bottles of wine, with dried flower petals scattered over the polished parquet floor to cast the faint scent of summer in the air.

It was beautiful, like a romantic gesture she would recommend to agency patrons. Not like something she would imagine for herself.

'Oh, Charles,' she whispered. 'Is this the surprise?'

'Do you like it? I wasn't sure…' He glanced around doubtfully, and she kissed his cheek.

'I *love* it. It's the most perfect thing ever.'

'Such a delicious meal,' Mary sighed as she fell back onto the cloud-like softness of the quilt. She was so warm and content, the heat from the fire dancing over her, the wine drifting lazily through her veins making her feel she could float. How long had it been since all felt so very *right*?

Never. She'd never felt like that before, as if she was just exactly where she was meant to be. All due to Charles.

She rolled to her side and propped her head on her arm to study him. She'd never seen him look so very handsome, his hair tousled, cravat loosened to reveal the strong lines of his throat, smiling and content. In one hand he held a half-full goblet of wine while his other lazily stroked the folds of her skirt where it draped over his leg, binding them together.

'I do like your kind of surprise,' she murmured. She reached out and softly traced her fingertips over the sculpted, lean angles of his face. His cut-glass cheekbones, the rough dark bristles over his square jaw, his closed eyes, the satiny sweep of his dark brows. He lay there, very, very still, like a jungle panther about to pounce, eyes shut as he let her explore. She glimpsed the pink scar she'd seen at the inn and traced a healing touch over it.

Then she swept a gentle caress over his lips, and he suddenly snapped, catching the tip of her finger lightly between his teeth. She laughed in surprise, fading to a longing sigh as his tongue swept over her skin and he nibbled at her fingertip. A flash of fireworks went through her, crackling, sizzling. She pressed her palm to his cheek and wished they could be here like this forever, just the two of them.

He put down his glass and wound his arm around her waist, bringing her down next to him on the blanket. His palms planted to either side of her as he held himself over her on his powerfully muscled arms, bared by his rolled-up shirtsleeves. His green eyes were darkened, hooded and intense as he stared down at her, as if he could see into her very soul.

'Mary,' he said, universes in her name. 'Let me make all time like this for you. Let this engagement be real, I beg you.' He looked as surprised as she felt, but then he smiled and plunged on. 'Maybe I can't give you all you need, but let me try. We have such fun together!'

Mary was shocked. She stared up at him, frozen, tempted. Oh, so tempted. 'W-why?'

'Why? We like each other. We understand one another. We want the same things, I think.'

Like. Mary turned her head away. He said everything, except love. And she longed only for him to love her. 'Oh, Charles. It's not enough. I'm afraid.'

He turned her back to look at him, stark—was it fear on his face? 'Afraid of me? I would not hurt you for the world.'

'No, not of you! Of me. Of how I feel with you. So—so wild and free. As I once was. I couldn't bear losing myself, losing *you*. If you turned away from me, I could never...' She broke off, unable to explain even to herself. If he did not love her, only liked her, laughed with her, the future would be bleak for her. Would she become as unhappy as his first wife had been, as he had been in his marriage? Would she make him unhappy? She couldn't bear that.

She nearly blurted out that she needed him to love her as she did him, but she bit her lip to hold those most powerful words back. She let go of him and rolled over to cover her face with her hands. It was such a shocking but not surprising realisation. She *loved* him. More than she had ever imagined she could love anyone.

She'd seen such things at the agency, seen it with her sister and Fred, with the Penningtons and the Olivers. Love that transcended all else. When it was for other people, she could see it, control it. With herself, she felt like she was spinning away wildly and couldn't catch it. Couldn't get back her heart.

'Oh, Mary.' She felt his hands, those powerful scarred hands caress her shoulders. He drew her closer against his chest, his arms tight around her. She spun around to bury her face in his shoulder, and inhaled deeply of his lemon scent. Her only refuge and the only thing that could really hurt her.

He pressed a lingering kiss to the top of her head. 'I would never hurt you, my *cuisle*. Please believe me.'

'You would not, on purpose.'

He held her face between his palms as if she were the most delicate piece of porcelain, his thumbs caressing her cheekbones. She peeked up at him, everything blurry and bright through the sheen of her unshed tears, and she saw his tender wonder-filled smile.

His lips met hers, softly at first, gentle, questing.

'This is against the rules,' she whispered. She couldn't marry him if he did not love her; but she could take this moment and store it into her memories.

'Hang the rules,' he growled. 'We never paid mind to them, anyway.'

Very true. She closed her eyes and he pressed deeper, the tip of his tongue tracing the curve of her lower lip until she moaned with delight. His tongue slipped inside, twining over hers, tasting her deeply as if she was the sweetest wine. She felt his fingers in her loosened hair, tilting her head so he could kiss her even more deeply. More intimately.

How wondrous he tasted, of wine and strawberries, and that dark, swirling essence of himself that she always craved so much. She wrapped her arms around his shoulders and pressed herself even closer to him.

He groaned against her lips, and carried her down deep into the blankets. His kiss turned harder, wilder, and something inside of her answered his need with a burning passion of her own, a desire she'd fought against for too long.

She pushed his coat off, tossed aside his loosened cravat, and reached for the hem of his shirt to drag it up so she could at last touch him. He shifted, letting her fingertips explore the warm silk of his skin, running a caress over him as she felt his muscles grow tense. How she longed to feel all of him, see him, know him.

'Mary,' he whispered, his voice so hot and rough.

His lips slid from hers to kiss her cheek, the pulse beating at her temple, the edge of her ear. His teeth nipped lightly at her earlobe, brushed over a tiny, sensitive spot just below, his breath warm in her ear. He traced a ribbon of tiny kisses along her arched neck, the curve of her shoulder above her gown and, shockingly, the upper swell of her breast, making her whimper.

'Charles,' she sighed.

As if the sound of his name unleashed something inside of him, he tugged down her gown, her chemise, until she lay bare before him, and she did not even care. She felt wanton and free and delicious! She felt beautiful under his avid stare, his hungry touch. She'd never wanted anything more than this.

'Please,' she whispered. He nodded, and his head bent as his mouth closed hard over her bared nipple, his tongue swirling around its tip, his teeth lightly stinging then his kiss soothing again. She gasped and twisted her fingers in his hair to hold him against her. She followed her instincts and wrapped her legs around his hips as her skirts frothed to one side, pressing to the curve of his backside in tight woollen breeches, feeling the hard strength of him.

Her eyes closed tightly as she felt his mouth on her bare skin, felt his hand slide down over her side, feathering lightly along her body, closer and closer to that most aching part of her, then teasingly away.

'Please,' she whispered. 'Touch me. I need to know...'

He moaned and at last gave her what she craved. His fingers traced over that delicate spot between her legs, then one fingertip staggeringly, wonderfully, slid deep inside of her, and she knew that everything she had imagined, everything she had desired, was a hundred times better. It was perfect.

'Do you like that?' he said tightly, his lips against her neck.

'Yes. Oh, yes,' she sobbed as he thrust his touch deeper. Her legs fell away from him so she could plant her feet to the floor on either side of his lean hips to hold herself to the earth, sure she would soar away into the stars.

'Charles, please,' she moaned. He moved faster and faster, until she cried out, bursting into sparks of hot, wild joy.

Slowly, slowly, she drifted back to earth, still shivering, her skin tingling, until she found herself not among the stars, but beside the fire, with him. She held on to him tightly. She didn't want to let him go yet, didn't want to let the cold world outside encroach on this dream. It frightened her to realise how she forgot everything else here in his arms.

She felt him bury his face in her shoulder and press his lips to her damp, trembling skin. His arm looped close over her waist, holding her against him, as if he didn't want to let her go, either.

She sighed and glanced at the high windows. It was still light outside but turning pinkish-grey at the edges, the day waning. She gently stroked the damp strands of his tousled hair, felt the softness of his breath on her skin. She closed her eyes and wanted to cling to him and flee all at the same time. What had she done?

'We should go back,' she murmured.

His arms tightened. 'Stay. Just for a little while longer, please, Mary.'

Just a little while longer.

She wanted to stay forever just like that, wrapped in his arms. But she knew so much waited beyond those doors. If he did not love her, she could never stay. And she knew this moment was all they really had. 'I can't marry you, Charles. You know I cannot, not if it would make you unhappy later. We can continue until Adele is safe, of course, but—'

He sat up straight to stare into her eyes, his own narrowed, dark. 'But after what just happened…'

Mary reached up to gently touch his cheek, to let herself feel the ache of that moment, that longing and sadness and resolve. 'It wouldn't work, you know that. We would come to hate being together, resent our time, our responsibilities. This moment is perfect! Let it be just that. Please, Charles. I couldn't bear anything else.'

He stared at her as if he would argue, but then she saw the knowledge come into his eyes, the realisation that she would not budge. Could not move, for the sake of their hearts. He nodded and lay down beside her again. Mary wrapped her arms around him and held on for every ounce of her heart for as long as she could.

Chapter Fifteen

'This is intolerable!' Peyton Clark shouted. He
paced the clearing in the woods, kicking at the
drifts of snow, hitting a low-hanging branch. He'd
never known fury like that before, never been denied what should be his in such a brutal way.

Overbury watched from the edge of the circle,
his face red, his hands clutching at the edge of his
cloak. He glanced behind him uncertainly, a scared
rabbit who Clark realised would never have been a
reliable ally. 'I am sure matters cannot be so very
dire,' he bleated.

'Not so dire!' Clark clenched his fists as he
longed to grab the man by that ridiculous fur collar and shake him until his teeth rattled. But he
knew Overbury was not the enemy here. It was
Adele and her uncle. They were the ones who had
to pay. 'I shall soon be cut off without a shilling,
thanks to my uncle and Charles Campbell. How

dare they put me, *me*, in such danger! All because of that rabbity girl. That fickle minx.'

Overbury's eyes widened. 'I thought you loved her! As I love Miss St Aubin.'

'Love?' Clark laughed incredulously. 'How could I love someone like that? Simpering and spoiled. But I liked her well enough, when I thought her a true lady, and she seemed happy with what I offered.' And, most important, happy to offer her dowry. That was what he was due; that was what he needed so desperately. 'Do you not feel you are owed Miss St Aubin's affections, for all you have done for her?'

Overbury's mouth dropped open. The man really was quite like a trout. 'Not—not *owed*, I suppose. Just owed the chance to show her how very devoted I am, how much I love her, how I would strive to make her happy. If she would just see that!'

Clark shook his finger at the man. 'Exactly. We know what is best. And yet they stand in our way at every turn. They must be taught a lesson.'

He sat down on a fallen log, his thoughts racing, time running out around him. It felt like his world was melting into nothingness. 'I fear time is short for us, Overbury. We must act quickly.'

'Act?' Overbury squeaked. 'Have we not been...?'

'Indeed we have not. We have behaved like simpletons, waiting for them to see what they must do.

We have tried to show them what should be, what could be, and they refuse at every turn.' He tapped the toe of his boot against the snow. 'It is nearly Christmas. This party will soon be over; we must be bold.'

'Bold,' Overbury echoed.

'Once we bring the issue forward, make it a reality they cannot deny, they will have no choice. They will see it is all for the best.'

Overbury fell back a step. 'What—what exactly do you mean by that?'

Clark leaped up again, pacing, the excitement of a plan washing over him. That was the problem! He had not stood up for himself when he should have, had not been strong. That would change. 'Do you truly love Miss St Aubin, man?'

'Of course I do!'

'Then you must *show* her that. Catch her attention. Overpower her, as women long for men to do.' A plan finally started to take shape in his mind, one he was sure must work. 'First, we shall lure Adele out of the Christmas ball into the garden, and then...'

Everything was quite ready for the Christmas ball.

Mary stood by the window of her bedchamber,

watching the snow falling thicker outside as the day had promised earlier, closing them all inside like a winter painting. Daisy fluttered around behind her, putting the final touches to Mary's ball gown.

Mary tried to push down her sadness at what should be such a happy time, tried to smile and pretend. She'd been pacing her room all day, wondering if she had been too hasty to reject Charles's proposal that they marry for real. Surely she could have, *should* have, trusted in the connection they had built. She could help him move forward, as he had with her. She had to talk to him, to see if it was even possible!

Was she really, really, really ready to take a step into a new life? When Charles held her in his arms, vowed never to hurt her, she knew she could. Now, alone, she was afraid of the unknown.

'You should smile, Miss Mary!' Daisy cried as she held up Mary's new gown. 'It's Christmas. And just look at Mademoiselle Sandrine's new creation.'

Sandrine had indeed surpassed herself, Mary had to admit. As Daisy helped her into the gown and started to fasten up all the tiny pearl buttons along the back, she saw it was the most beautiful thing she'd seen, a creation of darkening shades of blue, satin and organdie, held up with silken bunches of lilies of the valley and edged with old lace. She felt like the fairy queen Charles called her. A fairy queen who could be brave and risk her heart.

As Daisy added the last-minute touch of a wreath of white silk roses and loops of pearls to Mary's upswept blond curls, she peeked out the window to find carriages arriving ahead of the snow, filled with ball guests to supplement the house party and fill the ballroom. Their occupants stepped down onto the green carpet that lined the gravel drive, wrapped in their furs and velvets, laughing with excitement.

There was no time to hesitate. She slipped on her mother's pearl earrings, borrowed from Ella for Christmas, and drew on her gloves.

'Are you ready, Miss Mary?' Daisy asked, and Miss Muffins gave a little bark from her cushions. Mary drew in a deep, steadying breath.

'Yes. I am ready.' And she knew she was. Ready for anything at all.

Even if what she really longed for was to hide under the bed. She, who'd always loved parties! But only if Charles would hide there with her. Instead, he waited for her in the ballroom.

Daisy handed her a lace fan, straightened her short pearl-edged train, and Mary held her head up high as she marched out of the chamber into the night.

The dining room was empty as she paused to examine it; everyone was still in the foyer or reception room. A buffet supper for midnight was being set up there, while she could hear the musicians tuning up in the ballroom. It all quite sparkled and dazzled as a Christmas party should, the rooms festooned with large wreaths and swags of greenery, gathered on their outings. Crimson hothouse roses, palm fronds twining in gilt vases, tables lined with round bunches of more roses, carnations, holly, all beautiful.

The warm air smelled of greenery and the spices of the Christmas punch, smoke from thousands of wax candles, the Yule logs in every fireplace.

Mary found Lady Pennington waiting on the staircase to greet her guests, empress-like in a golden silk gown. But there was no sign of Pen or Anthony, or of Adele, and luckily no Overbury.

And no Charles. What if he didn't appear that night? What if the summer house was a dream, and all her excitement and fear were for nothing?

At last, she glimpsed Charles strolling down the stairs, still smoothing his hair, straightening his cravat. He looked splendid, like her Scots warrior, powerful and tall, his hair gleaming, his smile warm and inviting even across the room.

His face lit up when she waved to him, brighter than the Yule log. 'Forgive my tardiness,' he said as he hurried to her side, taking her hand for a lingering kiss. 'I had an important gift to fetch.'

He handed her a small, ribbon-bound package. Eagerly, she opened the little box to find a brooch, an amethyst set in a silver thistle. It was delicate, elegant, beautiful. 'Charles,' she whispered.

'It was my grandmother's, from the Highlands where she was born. It was said she wore it at the ball where she met my grandfather, and it's blessed. That is her family crest etched on the back.'

'Oh, Charles,' Mary breathed. 'It is so pretty.' And so precious, so personal. What could it mean?

'If it is too plain…' he began doubtfully.

'It's the loveliest thing ever. But you should not give it away! It's too precious.' She held it out as if to return it, and he pressed it into her hands.

'It belongs with you,' he said simply. 'No matter what.'

She couldn't say anything else, for the ballroom doors opened, and a kaleidoscope of silks, satins, diamonds, pearls, feathers all flowed inside, set off by the stark black and dark blue of the gentlemen. The orchestra struck up the first dance.

'Shall we?' she said.

He grinned at her. 'Do you dare?'

'We can only try!'

She held tightly to his hand as they took their places on the dance floor, keeping her smile firmly in place even as she started to worry about what might happen next. If they might find themselves flat on their backsides in front of the whole party.

The music grew louder, a most lively tune. She squeezed his hand, and they stepped off—right, left, right, left, hop. Turn, spin. To her joy, the whirling movement went off perfectly, and they landed lightly together. They looked at each other, a thrill of accomplishment sparkling between them.

After that, the dance sped forward like magic. They spun and turned, clasped arms in allemande, twirled. It was a grand dance, perfect in every way, and she hated to see it ever end. She wanted the ball, Christmas, everything to stay just as it was so she would never have to part with him.

Yet it did end, of course, and they made one last slow turn together.

He bowed to her, and she dropped into a curtsy. She stared up at him, and they seemed to be the only two people in all the world. All the other guests, the grand sparkle of the room, faded away,

and she was sure this was where she was meant
to be.

Flustered, scared, exhilarated, she stepped back.
'I—excuse me, just for a moment.'

He nodded, and she felt him watch her as she hurried away towards the ladies' withdrawing room.
She needed to take a deep breath, think for a moment in the quiet chamber.

Yet once there, she found her fears seemed to
fade quietly away and left only the shine of the
dance. She couldn't help but smile at herself in the
mirror. She suddenly longed to giggle and twirl
around and around! She saw his smile in her memory, the glow of his eyes, and wondered if they really could find a way to be together. Surely it was
possible? Anything was possible at Christmas.

She patted her hair into place, and the candlelight
caught on her new silver brooch. He had given her
his grandmother's jewel. Surely that meant something? Surely that meant he wanted her, that he
could love her. All their scheming, their falsehoods,
had somehow come true.

She wanted to be by his side again. She hurried
out of the room and along the corridor. She could
hear music in the distance, beckoning her onward,
and she noticed a half-open door to the terrace that
ran along the back of the house, looking to the gar-

dens and the woods. Snow was falling, lacy, silvery, delicately against the glow of lights from the lanterns strung along the terrace. She went outside to take it all in for a moment, let the magic of Christmas wrap around her.

A flash of movement at the edge of the garden, just at the corner of the light thrown around by the lanterns, caught her attention. A pink streak, something pale and quick.

To her shock, she saw it was Adele. And Mr Clark held her by the arm, dragging her towards the darkness of the trees. Mary couldn't hear very much from that distance, but she saw Adele's mouth open in panic. This seemed no romantic elopement, but a kidnapping.

Her heart pounding, Mary opened her own mouth to scream and found that no sound came out except a terrified squeak. No one was nearby, the ballroom noisy with music and laughter, and she saw Clark and Adele were farther away at every second. Another figure emerged from the woods, and she knew there was no time to lose.

She ran down the steps of the terrace into the garden, her slippers sliding on the frosty ground, panic racing through her veins.

'Let her go!' she shouted.

Clark and Adele spun around. Adele managed to

wiggle free, but only for an instant before he caught her again, making her cry out. His handsome face was twisted with fury and frustration.

'Mary,' Adele sobbed, and to Mary's horror, she saw a dark bruise on the girl's cheek. 'No, no, go back! I'm not worth it!'

'This has nothing to do with you. You have interfered enough!' Clark snarled. 'She has agreed to be my wife. If you don't want anyone hurt...'

Someone suddenly grabbed Mary's arm from behind, and she screamed in panic. She whirled around and lashed out, trying to hit them—and saw it was Overbury. He looked as shocked as she felt, his face pale in the moonlight, but she had no sympathy for him.

'You are a part of this villainy?' she hissed at him. 'I should have known.'

'It isn't what it looks like,' he begged her, but his grasp didn't loosen on her arm. She knew she'd have bruises there soon. 'I swear it! I only wanted you to notice me, and he said—'

'Enough blabbery. We have to be gone,' Mr Clark said. 'Bring her or not. I don't care.'

He swung Adele up into his arms roughly, making her scream. Mary started to run after them, and Overbury reeled her back towards him, stronger than he looked. Mary had only an instant, and she loosened her new brooch with her free hand and let it drop to the ground so Charles would find it and know she'd been there.

Overbury moved to pick her up, and she fought with all her might, kicking and shrieking, desperate to get free. In mid-swing, a sharp pain flashed through her head, and she fell to her knees, dizzy and in agony. A warm wetness spread at the back of her neck, and she tumbled down and down, hearing Adele scream, a dog bark, all from a great distance.

Then she saw only blackness.

Chapter Sixteen

Charles was sure he'd never felt so nervous before, so filled with doubts and yet certainty, as he paced the floor waiting for Mary to return. Surely it would all come right now. He could dance! She wore his grandmother's brooch. He could persuade her this should be real, permanent. That he loved her. Truly loved her.

'Charles!' he heard Penelope call. He smiled and turned to her, only to freeze at the expression on her face. Her eyes were wide with panic, her cheeks pale. Penelope never looked like that; she was always calm and collected and serene. She held Miss Muffins under her arm, and even the dog seemed frozen silent. A footman trailed behind them, looking terribly confused.

Charles forgot the party, forgot everything. The world seemed to have stopped. Some sort of old battlefield instincts were roused within him, and he hurried to her. 'Pen? Is someone hurt, ill?'

She shook her head and gasped in a breath. 'No, no! But this footman—he saw something most strange, most alarming.' She waved the man forward, and he seemed nervous.

'What is it?' Charles demanded.

'I—I did see something odd, sir. From the music room window as I was collecting glasses. A lady was in the garden, arguing with two gentlemen just where the lanterns were strung in the trees, so I could see her pink dress. I thought that was strange, as it was starting to snow even harder out there.' He took a gulp of air. 'She pushed one of them and started to run away, but the other man grabbed her arm. I think—I think it was Miss Stewart, sir.'

'Adele,' Charles whispered, appalled, terrified, furious.

'It must be Mr Clark,' Penelope cried. 'I should have watched her better, I should have followed her every moment. And now surely he's taken her. This is my fault.'

Charles felt chilled to his very core. He knew he had to hold onto that coldness, had to use it to help him think straight and find her. 'What happened then?' he asked the footman.

'I started to run outside, and I saw another lady

appear. She—I think she wore a blue gown, but I can't be sure. There was a fight, and she fell down. By the time I got there, they had gone. There was this on the ground at the edge of the trees.' He held out a silver thistle brooch. The very one Charles had just given Mary. It must have been wrenched from her.

He took it, turning it over on his palm as fear and anger washed over him. 'It must be Mary.'

'I was in the dining room, and Miss Muffins came bursting in, running to me,' Penelope said, cradling the shaking dog. 'She must have known something terrible happened.'

Charles patted the dog's head. If something happened to Mary, Miss Muffins would never abandon her. 'Which way did they go?' he asked the footman.

The man shook his head. 'It was too dark by then. But there must be some footprints in that fresh snow.'

'Gather as many men as you can find and follow me on the search. Fetch lanterns, blankets. Have a doctor waiting. Pen, find our hostess and tell her what is happening, try not to let anyone else know yet. Ask Anthony to come with me. We don't need a panic to frighten Clark.'

He hurried out the front doors into the snowy

garden, knowing he had to stay calm. Stay frozen. He had to think only of finding them. They could not be hurt, they could not. He would find them soon. Mary needed him now.

He wouldn't let her down, as he had too many people in his life. And he could never bear to lose her.

Mary felt like she was sinking down into the dark waves of some warm ocean, falling deeper and deeper, more and more tired. She somehow knew she had to fight against it, pull herself up to the cold surface, but she only wanted to sleep.

Yet there was something she had to battle against, something most important she had to remember. If only she could think, think…

Then it came to her, a great flash of light. She'd gone after Adele, and they'd been kidnapped. She remembered screams, panic, a pain in her head, then darkness.

She could smell the faded remains of a fire, damp wool, could feel something under her cheek that was warm. She heard a ragged sob close by, felt arms holding her.

She sucked in a deep breath, nearly choking, and forced her eyes to open, that warm water rushing away from her. Pain shot through her head, sharp and frigid, and she thought she would be sick. She ground her teeth against it and took quick stock of her surroundings.

She saw a domed ceiling high overhead, and re-alised she was in the summer house. It was com-pletely transformed from her beautiful afternoon there with Charles. The firelight and blankets were gone, leaving only freezing stone walls and flag-stone floors.

It was Adele who held her close. Her strawberry-blond hair hung loose and tangled, the sleeve of her gown torn and a bruise on her cheek. Mary reached out for her, terrified she was hurt. Terrified she had not been able to protect her.

'Oh, Mary, thank heavens you're awake,' she sobbed. 'I was so, so afraid.'

Mary carefully touched the back of her head, and found a bandage wrapped there, a bit of or-ganza from Adele's gown. 'What happened?' she whispered. She wrapped her own arms around the girl, and they held on to each other against the cold and fear.

'They locked us in here and ran off when they heard someone and were afraid of being found.' Adele sniffed. 'They said they'd be back for us. Cowards. Probably they're in the next county by now. Everyone was absolutely right about what a scoundrel Peyton is. Too scared to face what they've done.'

'Let's hope they stay gone, then, until we can figure out how to get out of here,' Mary said, trying her hardest to think straight, make a plan.

'I was so stupid,' Adele cried. 'How could I be fooled by someone like that? He would have ruined me. He hurt you!'

'You were not stupid,' Mary said. 'You were deceived. How could it be otherwise? How could you have known?' She glanced around at the dark walls. 'There is no way out?'

'I couldn't find one,' Adele said. 'The windows are too high and small, and the door is firmly locked.'

Mary sat up slowly, her head swimming, and tried to remember something, anything, that could help. She searched the seemingly empty room until she found a bread knife left from her picnic there with Charles, dropped near the empty fireplace. It wasn't much, but it was something. She knelt down by the door and tried to pry it open, Adele hurrying to help her.

After what seemed like an eternity of futile digging at the stone, her hand throbbing, her head on fire, they saw the flash of light in the windows.

Adele grabbed her arm and whispered, 'Could it be…?'

'Mary! Adele! Are you there?' she heard Charles shout. Warm, wonderful relief washed over her, and she knew she'd never heard anything so sweet. For an instant, she wondered if she was still in a faint and this was a dream. But then his voice came again, louder, stronger, along with a pounding at the door. 'Mary! If you're there, please answer me.'

'I'm here! We're here!' She and Adele rushed to bang on the door together. 'Overbury and Clark have fled and locked us in here.'

'Are you hurt?'

Mary glanced at Adele, at her loose hair and bruised cheek, and wrapped her arm around her. 'I was hit over the head, and something is wrong with my shoulder. Adele has a bruise on her poor cheek, but other than that we are fine.'

'We'll have you both safely to Northland and with a doctor in only a trice, my love. Now stand back.'

Mary grasped Adele's hand and they hurried across the octagonal room as the blasts of the door being beaten down echoed around them. People came flooding in, footmen, Lord Pennington. But all Mary could see was Charles. He embraced Adele, held her close to make sure she was uninjured, before she broke away and ran to Pen, who stood tensely at the edge of the rescue party.

Mary almost burst into floods of tears as Charles gently gathered her into his arms and wrapped her in his heat. She clung to him and knew that she was truly no longer alone. That she was safe and always would be with him. She closed her eyes and held on to him, her rock in a storm. It was like the moments after they kissed and caressed here in this very place, all the worry and strife of life gone perfectly still and quiet.

'Let me help you stand, my love,' he said, his brogue strong with worry. 'I have you safe now.'

'I know you do. Always.' She took a deep breath and gathered every ounce of any courage she might possess. 'I love you, Charles.'

He stared at her, his eyes glowing. 'As I love you. You must know that. So very much. I never thought I could feel like this, not until I found you.' He pressed a gentle kiss to her brow. 'I won't ever let you leave me again, if you really do love me. I won't let anything hurt you ever again.' He lifted her high in his arms, carrying her out of the cold room into the snowy night, the stars blessedly sparkling above them.

'Beautiful,' she whispered, holding on to him,

staring up into their beckoning freedom high above her. Above them.

'It may not be the most auspicious moment,' he said as he carried her towards the waiting cart, where Miss Muffins barked anxiously from the seat. 'But, I beg you, say you will be my wife. Say we will never be apart. I can do anything if you're with me.'

And she knew she could do anything with *him*. He was truly the very best man she'd ever known, the bravest, the kindest, the strongest. The most handsome for certain. He would never hold back her dreams in life, no matter what they were; he would only add to them, make them even more glorious.

'Yes, Charles Campbell,' she said. 'I will marry you.'

He smiled down at her, the brightest light breaking through all the dark fear of the night. It was the most glorious moment she'd ever imagined.

As he placed her gently onto the seat beside Miss Muffins, who huddled close, Mary heard Penelope call to them. She peeked over the edge of the cart to see her friend rushing towards them, her pale cloak a beacon in the shadows. 'Oh, Mary, you're safe! They just found Clark fallen from his horse on the icy road, but Overbury is nowhere to be found yet. Such brutes!' She turned away to find Adele, still crying.

'It seems we are both found now,' Charles whispered to her. 'And it seems I owe Clark some thanks.'

'Thanks!' Mary cried.

'If not for almost losing you, almost losing what we had just found, I wouldn't have been able to say—I love you. Truly and with my whole heart. No fears should have stood in my way. You are the most perfect thing I have ever known, and I will never let you forget that again. Never let you doubt my feelings.'

Mary was sure her heart would burst with joy. This was all she could have dreamed of, all she could have wanted! 'If only our rescuers had waited a moment more for us to kiss,' she whispered back.

He laughed merrily. 'Well, we shall have all the time for all the kisses for the rest of our lives.'

Mary held her breath as she tiptoed away from the impromptu party that echoed with music and laughter in the grand gallery. The party meant for her and Charles, to celebrate his rescue of her, to celebrate their betrothal.

'Better late than never!' everyone had said with a laugh.

Little did they know her *real* betrothal hadn't begun until now.

She hurried down a narrow back staircase, trying not to laugh with giddy glee, with the feeling of delightful naughtiness that always came upon her when she was near Charles. She went farther and farther down a shadowed corridor, empty except for a few lanterns and wine barrels, her heart pounding. She almost ran around a corner, and shrieked when a voice suddenly called, 'Well, Miss St Aubin, there you are! Running away from our appointment?'

'Ack!' Mary sounded, though she certainly should have expected it. Wasn't the voice the one she was seeking? The one she ran towards? Yet she had been so wrapped up in hurrying to their rendezvous that she was startled, and she gasped as she lost her balance and almost slid down on the flagstone floor. 'Blast it, Charles!'

He caught her in his arms, holding her close to his heat in the gloom. Her heart pounded even harder. 'I'm sorry, my love, I thought you heard me here. Are you all right? I didn't mean to frighten you, not after all you have been through.'

'I am well, except my dignity,' she laughed. She clung to him, their bodies pressed so close not even a breath could come between them. Not now that they were safe together at last. 'What a terrible maiden of olden days I would make, falling down as I rush to meet my white knight. You might change your mind about our betrothal.'

'After I almost lost you because of my foolishness, because of my fear of love? Never,' he answered roughly.

'And my blindness,' she whispered. She feared she might start crying to think of it, to think of how close they came to living their lives apart. 'I can't believe we almost let this slip between our fingers!'

'We never will again.' He stepped back to hand her a cloak, and bowed low as he offered it to her. 'Will you accompany me, my lady, on the night of our betrothal celebration? We have time all to ourselves, Adele will make sure no one looks for us for a while.'

Mary studied his glossy hair in the flickering light, the long fingers of the hand he offered to her, and she nodded. She feared she could barely manage to speak. 'Of course. I would follow you anywhere.'

He swirled the cloak around her shoulders, enclosing her in its warmth and took her hand in his. As she held on to him, she felt the strong safety of him envelop her until all the ghosts of the past vanished and *they* were all that was in the world.

As he drew her closer to him, his other arm slipping around her shoulders, she felt that excitement expand and grow within her, tingling and irresistible, like life itself. Life with him.

She didn't want him to let go, ever. She didn't want to lose this glittering spell that wove around her when she was with him.

She smiled up at Charles and let him draw her down the corridor and out a side door into the night. The air was cold and icy sharp, catching at her upswept curls, and she laughed as they ran down a pathway through the moonlit garden. Behind them, the house was lit from every window, and she feared someone might see them, call out to stop them slipping away from their own party. But there was only the whine of the wind, their muffled laughter.

'Where are we going?' she asked, whispering even though no one could hear her.

'Can't you guess?' he said, leading her down another pathway, and suddenly she knew.

'The summer house!' she gasped. It rose up before them, shadowed against the stairs, a tiny flicker of amber light at its small window, its half-open door.

'Our place,' he said tenderly. 'I wanted it to be cleansed of any bad moments, any fear, and leave only happy memories here. I enlisted your maid to help me set it up, and crept down here after our first dance to make sure it was perfect for you.'

He suddenly swept her off her feet, making her laugh. She clung to his neck as he carried her through the door into their own little haven.

Just like it had been before when they were together there, a fire crackled in the grate, welcoming and warming. Spread before it was a nest of fluffy blankets and satin cushions, bottles of wine, plates of delicate pastries like wedding cakes. Mary's heart felt it would burst as she studied it all, studied what he had made to show her how special he thought she was. How special *they* were together.

'Magical,' she whispered. He slid her to her feet, and she smiled up at him. She wound her arms tightly about his neck so he could not fly away from her, so she could not lose this dream. His hair, so soft, like silk, curled against her bare fingers, and his body felt so solid and warm and delicious against hers. She yearned to stay right there, in his arms, all night—forever! To kiss him, *feel* him, and forget about kidnappings and agencies and Seasons and everything else.

'How very beautiful you are, Charles,' she whispered.

His emerald eyes widened in surprise, but before he could say anything, she went up on tiptoe to kiss him as she longed to do. She pressed one swift, bold caress to his lips, then another and another, teasing him until he moaned and pulled her even closer. He deepened the kiss, his tongue seeking hers, and she was utterly lost in him. Lost in her need to be just this close to him, always, to taste him, smell his summery scent, draw all he was into her soul until he was hers.

He was right. They had nearly missed out on this, but now their whole lives were before them.

He groaned against her, and their kiss slid into a humid hunger, filled with all the yearnings of their time together, their drive to be close and know this was real. This was forever.

Mary didn't question herself, didn't question her emotions for the first time in so long.

She shrugged off her cloak and reached for his coat, catching his arm in her frenzy to be ever closer to him, making them both laugh. It was always thus when they were together: fire and fun, all mixed up so perfectly. The coat fell away, and she unwound his cravat, tangling the muslin, making them laugh even more until they clung to each other.

She pressed her face to the curve of his neck,

bare to her now, and inhaled the salty, heady scent of him. This was what she had always sought.

'Mary,' he whispered, 'you are the other half of me.'

'And you of me.' She knew what she had to do. She had to let go of the past, of her emotional fears. She had to be bold. They were reborn there in that summer house, together.

She kissed him again, shaking with the force of her need, and he shuddered against her. She knew he felt as she did. This was their real betrothal, their real pledge. He lifted her to her feet, and she felt him carry her backwards, down into that nest of blankets, like falling into a heavenly cloud.

She opened her eyes and gazed up at him, the firelight a corona around the tousled waves of his dark hair, and was sure they were in a magical fairy circle, sparkling ribbons binding them together.

'Mary...' he began, his voice hoarse. 'We shouldn't— I didn't bring you here just to take advantage of you.'

'Shh.' She pressed her fingers to his lips, feeling their softness under her touch. She was finished with words, with worry and with thoughts. 'Just look at me.'

'I could do that forever.'

'Then know how much I want this with you. Forever and ever.'

He rose up over her to shed his shirt, revealing those old scars to her once again, never taking his gaze from her before he dove back to her, to a rain of kisses, caresses. Mary pressed up into him, kissing his cheek, his neck, as she felt his hands slide the bodice of her gown away from her shoulders, the touch of cold air and firelight and, *oh*, his lips on her bare skin.

Any words were beyond her now, lost in their kiss, open mouths, not to be denied any longer. She slid her palms over his back, feeling the damp silk of his skin, the heat of him. When she peeked up, she saw he was exquisite, more handsome than any classical sculpture for he was *alive*, glowing, vibrant with breath and desire and strength.

He caught her in his arms again, their heartbeats melding, nothing at all careful about this kiss. It was too urgent, too filled with need that couldn't be denied any longer. She felt free at last, and there was only this one moment with the man she loved.

She closed her eyes tightly, revelling in his caress, the press of his mouth on the bare curve of her breast as her bodice fell down. Her legs parted as she felt his weight lower between them, her skirts swept away. She knew what would happen; she had read things, and she had a married sister who was always honest with her. But the images mere pictures in books and whispered words conjured never hinted at how it all *felt*. Of that heady, dizzy sensation of falling and falling, lost in another person.

'I—I don't want to hurt you,' he gasped.

She smiled against his shoulder as she felt the press of the tip of his manhood against her. Her entire body ached for that final union with him, that moment when they were together entirely. 'You never could.'

She spread her legs wider, invitingly, and he slid inside her. It did hurt, how could it not? A sharp, burning pain, but it was nothing compared to the way it felt when he filled her, came to her at last. She arched her back against the pain, wrapping her arms and legs around him so tightly he could never escape her.

'You see? It doesn't hurt now,' she whispered. 'I feel completely perfect.'

He laughed tightly. 'Not half as perfect as I do right now. My beautiful, wonderful Mary.'

Slowly, ever so slowly, he moved again within her, drawing back, lunging forward, just a little deeper, a little more intimate every time. Mary squeezed her eyes closed, feeling that ache ebb away until there was only the pleasure. A tingling delight that grew and expanded, spreading through her arms and legs, her fingertips, out the top of her head like the flames from the fireplace. Pleasure unlike any she had ever known or even imagined. No wonder so many people came seeking matches at the agency! This type of love and passion was the most perfect thing in the world.

Mary cried out at the wonder of it all, at the bursts of light behind her closed eyes, blue and white and red like fireworks. The heat and pressure were too much, too much! How could she ever survive it without being burned up and consumed? But what a wondrous way to go.

Above her, around her, she felt Charles tense, his back arch. 'Mary!' he shouted out. And she exploded, consumed by those lights. She clung to him, and he to her, falling down into the flames.

After long moments—hours or days?—she slowly opened her eyes, sure she must have tumbled down into some bonfire or volcano. That she would find herself in a different world entirely. But it was the same room in the summer house, cleansed of fear, filled only with love. The stars outside, the fireplace, the blankets—transformed.

Beside her, collapsed on the pillows, his arms tight around her waist, was Charles. Her Scottish *laird*, her love. His eyes were tightly closed, his limbs sprawled out in exhaustion.

She smiled, feeling herself slowly float down to

earth again. She felt the blankets beneath her, the heat of the fire on her skin, the soreness of her limbs. It didn't matter, though. Nothing mattered, in this moment out of time. They would have to return to the party soon, pretend they had been engaged for many weeks, but they would know the truth of what had just happened. That here, in this summer house, they became their true selves together.

She snuggled closer to him, half drowsing, feeling as if she could float up and up into the stars. His arm was heavy over her waist, and she curled herself tighter into the haven of his body, feeling his breath on her bare shoulder, the strength of his muscles as she traced her fingertips over his forearm.

'Oh, Mary,' he whispered into her hair. 'I think I shall have to spend the rest of my life trying to discover everything about you. But I know one thing.'

She smiled. 'And what is that, my love?'

'That you are the most magnificent lass I have ever seen.'

She laughed and rolled over to face him. The moonlight and the orange flames outlined his beautiful face, casting sharp angles, mysterious shadows over his eyes, darkened now. She reached up and traced his features carefully, all those commonplace things like eyebrows, a nose, cheekbones, that made him up into what he was. The perfection of Charles. 'And you are unlike anyone else I have ever known or even imagined.'

He laid back in their nest, his arms stretched under his head as Mary sat up to gaze down at him, study him. 'Me, Mary? I am the simplest creature, easy to read as a book.'

She laughed. 'A book in Scots, maybe. I need translations.'

He caught her around the waist and drew her close again. 'You understood me well enough to-night.'

'Don't tease!' she giggled. 'But I suppose we have time to learn those mysteries now, don't we?'

'Oh, yes,' he whispered, just before he kissed her again. 'Every single little mystery is ours to discover now.'

Epilogue

'There now, Miss Mary,' Daisy said with a satisfied air as she straightened a wreath of white and pink silk roses on Mary's upswept golden curls. 'I think we've done a fine job here.'

Ella and Adele clapped in agreement, and Miss Muffins let out a long bark.

'Oh, Daisy. You have indeed!' Mary answered in glee, giving a joyful little twirl in front of the mirror. Her Mademoiselle Sandrine gown was a dream, palest blue silk with a froth of a white lace train. It looked like a summer's day, like a gown to hold dreams of warmth and sun and happy-ever-after. The future seemed bright, full of everything she could have longed for: a social season with the agency in Bath and the rest of the year spent in Scotland, with managers put in place to run the business in her absence. Work and family! Adele had even voiced ambitions to take over matchmaking herself one day, which filled Mary with such happiness, knowing she could pass on all she'd learned.

But today was only for wedding dreams.

Sandrine knelt to adjust a frill on the train. 'Just one more inch here—there, perfect. My finest creation.'

Miss Muffins barked again, and spun about until the bow around her neck came untied.

Mary spun in the glass again, taking in her mother's pearl necklace, the short lace veil attached to the wreath, the little silver thistle brooch attached to her bodice. It had been long weeks since she and Adele escaped their kidnappers, days of bad memories and bad dreams, but also days of wondrous healing. Wedding plans, a honeymoon trip to Scotland, Adele's new excitement for her Season as a chance to move forward, they had a great deal to anticipate.

Adele handed her a bouquet of hothouse roses, pink and white bound with looping ribbons. 'Are you ready… Aunt?' she whispered shyly, and Mary hugged her close.

'Much more than ready,' she answered, and they proceeded out of the chamber and down the stairs, Daisy holding the train high as they crossed the courtyard to the waiting Abbey amid streamers and confetti and beaming guests.

But Mary could only see the man who waited for her at the church door, her very own Christmas husband. The best match she had ever made.

He smiled wide, filled with joy, the shadows of the past forgotten. He hurried to her, as if he was unable to wait a moment longer, and took her gloved hand in his, raising it to his lips for a tender kiss. They were both exactly where they belonged, at long last, as the blessings of Christmas showered down on them.

* * * * *

While you're waiting for the next
book in Amanda McCabe's
Matchmakers of Bath miniseries,
why not check out her recent
Historical romances?

'A Convenient Winter Wedding' *in*
A Gilded Age Christmas
A Manhattan Heiress in Paris

Or fall in love with her Dollar Duchesses!

His Unlikely Duchess
Playing the Duke's Fiancée
Winning Back His Duchess

MILLS & BOON®

Coming next month

ONE WALTZ WITH THE VISCOUNT
Laura Martin

Sarah made the mistake of looking up and for a long moment she was lost in Lord Routledge's eyes. Of course she'd noticed them before—even in the semi-darkness it was impossible to ignore the man's good looks. His eyes were a wonderful deep brown, full of sadness and intrigue.

She swallowed, her pulse racing and heat rising through her body.

She knew she was passably attractive, and there had been offers from a couple of young men of her acquaintance to step out over the last couple of years. Never had she been tempted. But, right now, if Lord Routledge asked her to run away into the night with him, she would find it hard to refuse.

Silently she scoffed at the idea. As if the poised and eligible Lord Routledge would ask her that. No matter what he said, he probably had five or six elegant and well-bred young women waiting for him downstairs.

'You look sad,' he said, an expression of genuine curiosity on his face. 'The waltz isn't meant to be a melancholy experience. At least not if I'm doing it right.'

With a press of his fingers he spun her quickly, and somehow they ended up closer than they had begun, her body brushing against his. She inhaled sharply, and for a moment it felt as though time had stopped. Their eyes met. Ever so slowly, he raised a hand to her face, tucking a stray strand of hair behind her ear.

In that instant Sarah wanted to be kissed. She felt her lips part slightly, her breathing become shallow. She'd never been kissed before, but instinctively her body swayed towards Lord Routledge. Her heart thumped within her chest as he moved a fraction of an inch towards her, and then stopped.

Continue reading

ONE WALTZ WITH THE VISCOUNT
Laura Martin

Available next month
millsandboon.co.uk

COMING SOON!

We really hope you enjoyed reading this book.
If you're looking for more romance
be sure to head to the shops when
new books are available on

Thursday 19th December

To see which titles are coming soon, please visit
millsandboon.co.uk/nextmonth

MILLS & BOON

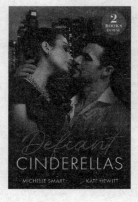

afterglow BOOKS

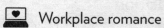

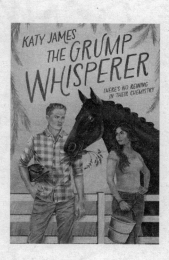

💻 Workplace romance

💻 Workplace romance

📶 Forced proximity

🏠 Small-town romance

🌶 Spicy

⛅ Grumpy/sunshine

OUT NOW

LET'S TALK

Romance

For exclusive extracts, competitions and special offers, find us online:

- **f** MillsandBoon
- **X** @MillsandBoon
- **⊙** @MillsandBoonUK
- **♪** @MillsandBoonUK

Get in touch on 01413 063 232